A Thousand Miles to Graceland

A
Thousand
Miles to
Graceland

KRISTEN MEI CHASE

FOREVER
New York Boston

Forever
Hachette Book Group
1290 Avenue of the Americas, New York, NY 10104
read-forever.com
twitter.com/readforeverpub

First Edition: January 2023

Forever is an imprint of Grand Central Publishing. The Forever name and logo are trademarks of Hachette Book Group, Inc.

The publisher is not responsible for websites (or their content) that are not owned by the publisher.

The Hachette Speakers Bureau provides a wide range of authors for speaking events. To find out more, go to www.hachettespeakersbureau.com or call (866) 376-6591.

Library of Congress Cataloging-in-Publication Data

Names: Chase, Kristen M., author.
Title: A thousand miles to Graceland / Kristen Mei Chase.
Description: First edition. | New York : Forever, 2023. | Summary: "Accountant Grace Johnson can't escape the feeling that her life is on autopilot-until her husband announces he's done with their marriage. Grace has a choice: wallow in humiliation...or grant her mother's seventieth birthday wish with a road trip Graceland. Buckle up, Elvis. We're on our way. Now outlandish mother and reluctant daughter are hightailing it from El Paso to Memphis, leaving a trail of sequins, false eyelashes, and painful memories in their wake. Between spontaneous roadside stops to psychics, wig mishaps, and familiar passive-aggressive zingers, Grace is starting to better understand her Elvis-obsessed mama and their own fragile connection. Apparently the King really does work in mysterious ways. But after all these years, will it ever be possible for them to heal the hurts of the past?"—Provided by publisher.
Identifiers: LCCN 2022037056 | ISBN 9781538710463 (trade paperback) | ISBN 9781538710180 (ebook)
Subjects: LCGFT: Domestic fiction. | Humorous fiction. | Novels.
Classification: LCC PS3603.H3793645 T48 2023 | DDC 813/.6—dc23/eng/20220805
LC record available at https://lccn.loc.gov/2022037056

ISBNs: 9781538710463 (trade paperback), 9781538710180 (ebook)

Printed in the United States of America

LSC-C

Printing 1, 2022

To my mom, Audrey
You may not know this, but you are
always on my mind

A Thousand Miles to Graceland

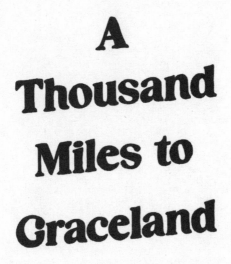

Chapter 1

How do you get your eyeliner to stay on like that?" Jane Choi, our summer accounting intern from Syracuse, peeked through the door that I thought I had closed all the way. She waved her hand over her eyelids. "Mine always looks like *shit*." She whispered "shit" as if I were her mother, which did exactly what I'm pretty sure she intended: it made me feel like it. "That part, you know, in here. How do you…" She gestured to the inner corner of her eye.

"Epicanthic fold." I cut her off, then went back to typing. Jane was notorious for asking questions about what conditioner I used or where I got *that* sweater, all of which would devolve rather quickly into some sort of gossipy conversation about so-and-so doing you-know-what. My new tack was looking busy.

"Oh my god, it has, like, an official name? You do

know everything, Grace!" She gave me a shrug and a wide smile before scurrying off to her cubicle.

I examined my client's quarterly calculations on my laptop screen, surrounded by framed degrees and a photo of me with Mama from my high school graduation more than two decades ago, which made me feel oddly self-conscious. It was the only picture I had of Mama and me where she looked semi-normal; none of the cheap wigs or bejeweled bell bottoms and platforms that made every other photo look like I was taking a picture with a Vegas showgirl. I had begged her to dress like all the other moms, so she went with "Priscilla Presley in mourning," which involved black from head to toe. I didn't care if she had to pretend she was at a funeral instead of my graduation; it was the most subtle outfit I had ever seen her in. Between our rigid poses and the wall-to-wall Elvis collectibles behind us, we looked like a page out of Awkward Family Photos. She knew exactly when she got each and every one of the ceramic figurines, which she organized chronologically by Elvis's career. And anytime anyone made the mistake of asking about one of them, she'd tell its entire backstory: where she was, who sold it to her, and how much she paid.

It had been so long since I'd done more than glance at the photo that I'd forgotten our faces, me grinning as if someone had put a gun to my head and told me to smile. And her face, like someone about to say goodbye to her best friend.

The end of September at an accounting firm is like April all over again, except with an extra sense of urgency because there's no extending extensions. Most of the employees at Whit, Warner, and Hodges, PC, lined up out the doors at the end of April, not to return until fall. They'd leave their offices with tax forms still piled high on desks or covering the floors, as if the firm were under attack and everyone had made an exit through their escape pods, except me and a few other idiots who fed their avoidance of the outside world by working all summer long under the guise of "getting ahead."

I chose accounting because it was at the top of the list of college majors, alphabetically speaking, and I felt terribly embarrassed when Mama would brag about how her daughter was going to be a CPA, knowing full well that I just picked it because it was the first thing I saw. Anything to get me out of my house.

At first, all the numbers made me think I should have gone down the list a little bit farther, to anthropology or archaeology, just something where math problems weren't the center of my universe. But I grew to love the predictability, and by my junior year, I couldn't imagine doing anything else.

Mama described accounting like it was some exotic job that no one had ever heard of: "And she takes these forms, you see, and does all these calculations, and *TADA!*" She'd sing "TADA" like she was on stage doing a musical number at the annual Fort Bliss Talent Show.

"Mama, it's really not that exciting," I'd interrupt. She'd smile and wave me off, rolling her eyes about me to whoever stuck around long enough to endure her performance.

The secret I never told anyone was that you didn't need to be a star mathematician to do accounting. It's rigidity and solitude that you need to find satisfying.

But even the mundane had become mundane. Or at least now, I was just noticing it more. I was starting to get the Sunday scaries—this feeling of doom that the weekend was ending and I'd have to return to the office—every single weeknight, right before bed, like clockwork, which was doing wonders for my sleep. I could usually rally myself with the incentive of a Starbucks latte on my way to work, and on extra difficult days, on the way home too.

But my downward spiral of boredom required more than just a fancy coffee. Instead of seeing numbers, I found myself calculating the sums of my clients' exciting lives—airfare, hotels, "office furniture"— which was code for "I just bought a killer porch couch to go on my new beach house deck"—whereas pressing send on emails had become the sum of mine. The contrast between their lives and my own was stark, and I found myself spending more time trying to figure out where I had gone wrong, which is a recipe for depression, especially with a job like mine.

My phone buzzed. *"See you at therapy later!!!—Jeff"* He always signed off his texts like I wouldn't know who was three-exclamation-points excited about marriage counseling.

Even though I'd been seeing my own therapist for years, the whole couples therapy thing was completely new to me, and not my idea whatsoever. But the distance between us had become so vast, even for Jeff and his cockeyed optimism, so he suggested we see someone, and I obliged, even though I had a sinking feeling deep down that there was no fixing something that had always been a little broken.

The first time I met Jeff, he was working at the Chili's near my office. My friend and I just wanted a cheap, unpretentious night of drinking after a late night of tax season cramming, free from pathetic pickup lines delivered by greasy, suited men with their top buttons undone and loosened ties around their necks. We kept getting drinks we didn't remember ordering delivered to our table, which our server finally told us were compliments of the manager. She pointed to a cute guy probably in his late twenties, hovering by the hostess stand, with super slicked-back dark hair and a slightly overgrown five o'clock shadow. He was wearing crisply ironed khakis and a polo shirt that was a bit too small for his dad bod, with chest hair peeking up above the buttons, which didn't look purposeful, though I remember thinking that if his chest was so hairy, what might the rest of him look like? But his extremely toothy grin distracted me, as did the huge ice cream sundae he walked over to us and placed in front of me.

"Thanks, but...I'm allergic to dairy," I told him, grinning sheepishly. His face sank.

"I am so sorry for your loss," he replied, as if he were walking through a receiving line at a funeral, which made me giggle. He hurried off into the kitchen and brought me every other dessert item on the menu that didn't have dairy, then stopped back at our table just enough to seem friendly and not weird, asking what I did for a living and why the hell I was drinking gin and tonics at a Chili's, in between greeting and seating customers with gestures far too grand for a college campus chain restaurant. He acted like the manager at a Michelin-starred establishment, and he made everyone who came in feel like they were eating at one too, which I found to be quite charming.

So when he asked for my number, I decided why the hell not. That's also what I decided when he asked me out.

On our first date, he took me to this little hole-in-the-wall Italian place in the middle of a strip mall, which had me a little concerned for my poor, already sensitive bowels. He assured me that they had the best pasta in Boston, and he wasn't lying. The entire staff greeted him, and then me, with hugs and double-cheek kisses, followed by a tsunami of the most amazing food and then sorbet, which he asked them to bring in just for me. I felt special in a way I hadn't experienced, which I suppose wasn't too hard considering every date with my last boyfriend conveniently ended up at a bar with a group of his friends, all gathered watching whatever sports game was on the big screen above us.

But he sealed the deal when we got back to his car and found a hefty dent in the fender, to which he just said, "Damn Boston drivers!" and shrugged his shoulders. No yelling. Not even gritted-teeth grumbling, which made me feel relaxed and comfortable. What he lacked in soap opera star good looks and a svelte physique, he made up for with his thoughtfulness and even temper, which felt lovely and stable at first.

But as time went on, the thoughtfulness became obligatory, like it was his job, and his constantly cheerful mood made me think I was doing something wrong by having feelings. I'd bring up a tough part of my day, like the terrible meal at a super important new business luncheon I had personally planned, and he'd give me some sort of "could be worse" scenario. Let's just say, nothing can compete with "the starving children," which he actually said to me, like he was my mama trying to get me to eat one of her terrible concoctions she called "dinner." All I wanted to do was bitch about the undercooked chicken and wiry long hair in my boss's salad for a couple of minutes and not get the sunny side of the street shoved down my throat.

For the last few years, we'd felt more like room-mates than lovers, or even really friends, two ships passing during the after-work hours, him to the gym, and me to the bedroom, where I'd binge-watch several seasons of some television show in rapid succession, popping out to grab food and feed the cat. Any effort for a date night had to come from me, after I made one complaint about his choice of activity (axe throwing, really?), so we usually ended up having dinner and drinks, that was until he started amping up his workout regimen and weigh-ing all of his food. Then we'd just sit on the couch, watching some obscure indie movie or foreign film that the millennial servers he worked with at the restaurant had recommended, his hand rubbing my leg in a robotic motion as if it were programmed to do so. We slept in the same queen-size bed, but it felt like we were miles apart, the late-night brushing of our arms or legs no longer the start of romance, but rather a reminder that one of us had encroached on the other's space.

I started texting him back but then decided on the most unenthusiastic reply—a thumbs-up on his message—then turned my phone off to try to get some actual work done. But instead of finishing up the extensions, all I could do was stare at Mama's face in the framed photo on my desk.

Chapter 2

Grace? Grace. If you're there, pick up..." There was complete silence, which amplified sounds of the passing traffic and the lull of my car engine. Mama still didn't understand the difference between an answering machine and voice mail.

"Well, okay then. I just wanted to talk to you about something. I know you're always very busy..." I suddenly felt bad for always feeding her that line, but it was the nicest way I could put her off and not feel engulfed in guilt.

"But if you could please give me a call back, that would be great. Thanks." She paused again, and in a different, less friendly tone added, "Oh, it's your *mama*." She emphasized the m's, which was her way of expressing her disappointment that we hadn't spoken in a while. At least, that's what it felt like to me. I called her out on it a few times, and she shrugged it off, saying I was just hearing things. "You were always so sensitive, Grace!" as if that were a bad thing. And she wondered why we were on a strict once-a-month call schedule. I needed the full twenty-nine or so days to gear up.

I tried to convince her that she would hear from me more often if she'd just text, but she refused to upgrade her flip phone, which made texting harder for her than solving a quadratic equation.

"When you come visit, you can take me to the store and get me a new phone that texts you. All my friends have those little smiley faces. I want little smiley faces."

"Emojis, Mama. They're called 'emojis.'" The fact that they had a name blew her mind. Then every time she remembered to use the word she felt so smug.

I pulled up to a stoplight. "Siri, call Mama." It was rare to get a call from her outside of our scheduled monthly check-in, so I figured I might regret not using the twenty minutes I was about to spend in traffic talking to her.

"Hello?!" Her twangy voice squeaked upward, as if she were surprised that she was getting a phone call from me. I preferred to believe it was because she was still unsure how to use her phone and skeptical that anyone would actually be on the other end when she picked up.

"Mama. It's Grace. I got your message. You do realize that no one else can hear you, right? It's voice mail."

"Grace, you know I'm just not good at these *thangs*." Mama's accent still gave me a jolt, even though I'd heard it my entire life. After years living up North, the sound of it felt like the electric shock I'd get from rubbing my feet on the carpet and touching a metal door handle.

I'd spent my entire college career trying to ditch my southern accent, thanks to a vocal coach who traded me lessons for tax preparation services. When Mama came up to Boston for graduation, people looked at her, then me, then back at her, and me again, like they were watching a tennis match whenever she spoke. I suppose you don't often hear a Chinese woman speak with a southern accent, let alone one who looks like she's been dragged off the stage at the Grand Ole Opry.

"Okay, it's just that I tell you this all the time. But whatever. What's up? Is everything all right?"

"Oh, never better, darlin', but you know, my birthday is coming up, and I wanted to make a big splash this year. The big seven-oh!"

I knew what was coming, so I tried to head it off to lessen the sting. "I know, Mama, and I know I promised that I would come down, but the client extensions this year…" My voice trailed off, which was the tell that I was completely full of shit. I had plenty of time between now and mid-October to get them done.

"Oh, hush, I don't want a visit. I'm turning SE-VEN-TY. I want something bigger, Grace."

I couldn't quite imagine what would be bigger than a visit from me, not because I think I'm so special and important, but because Mama hadn't done anything but the same thing for years. No amount of Xanax could get her on a plane, and the cataract taking over her left eye made it hard for her to do anything outside of daytime hours.

"I'm taking a road trip...to Graceland!" Her statement was followed by a single white-girl "woo-hoo!" And then silence, as if she were reading from a script and giving me the space for my next line.

I suddenly wished that I had just waited to call her back until I was sitting on my couch with a glass of wine in my hand.

"Wasn't one trip to Graceland enough?" I could have sworn she had taken a bus trip with her retirement village buddies a few years back. Even then I was surprised that it had taken her that long, but her fear of anything with wings—birds *and* planes— forced her into a bus or car, and Mama could barely drive herself to the grocery store on a cloudy day, let alone a thousand miles to Memphis.

"Didn't I ever tell you that we never made it on that bus trip? Sally Rogers passed away right before we were going to leave, and then I just couldn't ever bring myself to go."

That was right. "Bad juju," I recalled. I felt slightly relieved that I wasn't going completely nuts.

"Very bad juju."

I guess Mama had talked so much about the trip

that it felt like she had gone. It didn't help that when I'm on the phone with her, I'm thinking about all the things I have to do, and her rambling just becomes background noise to my thoughts. I suddenly started to question other things I thought she had done. Or hadn't done. But with the therapist's office right around the corner, I wisely stopped myself before diving headfirst into that swirling cesspool of memories and guilt.

"But still, Mama. You driving alone all that way is just not an option. Listen, I'm about to pull up to my meeting…" Liar. She interrupted me.

"I'm not going alone…"

I did a quick scan of all the people she knew who could possibly drive her, and I ended up playing a game of "dead or senile" with the first few names that came to mind.

"…I want you to take me! Think about how fun it will be. Just the two of us ladies, hair blowing in the wind, sun beating down on our faces."

It sounded like she was describing a movie she had just seen.

"…Like Thelma and Louise."

And there it was. "Mama, Thelma and Louise become criminals who kill themselves."

"Oh god, you are so dramatic, Grace. That's not at all what I meant."

Mama always accused me of being dramatic when my truth-telling harshed the buzz of her rich fantasy life, like the time she was convinced she could somehow get an invite to Lisa Marie and Michael Jackson's wedding.

How exactly did she think this would work? "Mama, I'd love to if I could." Liar, liar. "But this stupid job. And Jeff. And..."

"Gracie! I've got the whole thing planned out. All you have to do is drive. And take some vacation days. I'm sure Jeff would understand."

He'd probably be glad to have some space. But I wasn't about to tell her that.

I pulled into a parking spot right in front of the office. Apparently it was my lucky night. "Some? Mama, okay, now I really have to go. I promise I'll think about it."

That wasn't a lie. I *would* think about it, along with all the times we'd spent longer than a few hours in the same room together, let alone crammed in a car for days on end, and then I would come up with some excuse to get out of it. Whenever we'd get together, it was like a master class in guilt trips, and she was the guest teacher, which would end with me feeling like I was rationalizing all my life choices to someone who wasn't really known for making good ones. To be fair, I never believed that her intention was to make me feel like a failure, but that doesn't quite matter when you're being judged by your own mother.

So avoidance had become second nature to me. And while I couldn't keep skirting around the large, probably neon and bedazzled, elephant in the room,

I'm pretty sure that this was not the time to call it out.

"Well, just think about it, Grace. It'll be *amaaaaaazing*."

I hung up, then turned my car off, slumping heavily back in my seat, like someone had pushed me, still a few minutes early for my session. I could feel the faint pounding of a headache about to make its full presence known, so I shut my eyes, hoping that might fend it off before I had to reach for some ibuprofen.

"Grace! Hey, Grace!" It was Jeff, standing in front of my car on the sidewalk outside our therapist's building, as if we were about to go get a massage or see our favorite band play. He was always cheerful and smiling, even in the most uncomfortable situations, which made him super easy to be around—something I was definitely not used to when I met him. And it came in handy, like the time he ended up getting me my new Subaru Outback at the friends-and-family price. No one ever gets a deal on a Subaru.

"You ready?!" He gestured toward the therapist's office building, and I reluctantly nodded back, pushing my door open and climbing from the car.

"I guess," I whispered to myself, slamming the door.

"Everything okay?"

"Fine." I pushed a smile out through my lips and grabbed his outstretched hand. It was cold and sweaty, but I didn't think twice.

———————

The receptionist du jour called Jeff's name, and he popped up out of his seat like a jack-in-the-box. I followed him through the door, down the long hallway lined with diplomas and certificates that I had never really paid much attention to before this very second.

I took the spot at the far end of the couch, but instead of sitting closer to me, in the middle of the fancy leather sofa that practically swallowed us when we sat, Jeff sat clear on the other end, then started gushing over Dr. Wakefield's pretty basic blue tie, which turned into a rather bizarre but not surprising conversation about tie storage options. I started to braid the tassels on the pillow, when Dr. Wakefield abruptly interrupted Jeff's snore-fest about the restaurant customer who once offered to pay him for the tie he was wearing.

"Jeff, I don't want to interrupt you…"

Even though his face totally said, "Please stop now or I'm going to need therapy."

"…but didn't you have something you wanted to talk to Grace about this evening?"

Jeff smiled, of course, then puttered like an old, dying car about to run out of gas. "Um, well, yeah, so, uh, yep…"

I turned toward him, hoping it would ease all our pain.

"I…I…met someone." He mumbled the last words

under his breath. "And we're in love," he added. Knife inserted, then twisted.

"What the hell?!" My eyes instantly filled with tears, and it felt like I was looking at the room through a fishbowl. I reached my hand out toward Dr. Wakefield, and waved it around, which I think is the universal sign for "hand me the damn tissue box," though I would have taken a pair of boxing gloves had he offered.

"Grace, I understand you're upset. Jeff felt that it would be best to tell you about his relationship in a safe, neutral environment. It was important for him to be respectful to you." He stumbled over the word "respectful," and I wondered if even he thought this whole thing would have been better done behind our own closed doors.

"Best?" The heat of my anger was burning my throat, making my voice sound pressured and gruff. "Telling me in our own house, where I can use my own goddamn tissues, would have been the *actual* best, asshole." I wiped my eyes, then my nose, which was now embarrassingly stuffy, while Jeff just sat there, looking down at the floor, biting his nubs of nails. *Respectful, my ass.*

"Being respectful means considering how the other person might feel, not doing what you think is right because you saw it on *Intervention* or some bullshit show. Did you think about that in your grand scheme?" I turned to Dr. Wakefield, who looked as comfortable as someone getting a blood test with a drill bit. "Aren't you supposed to be *our* therapist?"

"Well, I'm technically your marriage's therapist…" he replied hesitantly, as if changing "our" to "your" would somehow quell my anger. The regret in his response was almost palpable, so I did my best to toss it right back at him, hoping it would take form and land on his head like seagull crap at the beach.

"My husband just tells me he's cheating on me and you're going to be technical? I'm pretty sure you know exactly what I'm trying to say." Dr. Wakefield wiped his brow, and I imagined the beads of sweat like stinky bird shit.

I scowled at Jeff. "So, wait, all this time we're essentially paying enough in marriage counseling fees to send *his* kid to college, you're rendering it completely pointless with your dick?"

I thought that might get a rise out of him, but instead, he just sat, staring at the wall past Dr. Wakefield.

"I just didn't know how else to tell you, Grace." His eyes remained fixed, his voice calm, like always.

"Well, you were certainly able to ask me to marry you all by yourself. How do you throw away something so easily that you wanted so badly?"

Jeff's glare remained unmoved, but I could see tears slowly sliding down his cheeks. The therapist handed him a tissue box, but he refused, choosing to use his fingertips instead.

"Or maybe you never really wanted it in the first place."

His head whipped around at me so fast I thought it might keep going and fly off his neck. I'd never seen him show an actual negative emotion like this in the entire time we had been together. He leaned in, and I could hear his breath getting heavier as he pushed out the words through his gritted teeth and tight jaw. "Maybe you should be asking yourself that question."

Jeff wasn't completely wrong, but I didn't want to get into it now. Not like this.

He stood and took a step toward the door, but I jumped up.

"You can stay. I'll go." I walked right past him and grabbed the doorknob.

"Grace, *I* feel really uncomfortable letting you leave like this," Dr. Wakefield interjected.

I turned around. "What about me? Did either of you think about how I feel?"

Only Dr. Wakefield responded as Jeff sat, head in his hands. "You're right, Grace. How you're feeling is important."

"You mean you're actually feeling something, Grace? So this is what it takes?" Jeff looked like he startled himself with the outburst.

"Maybe you should be asking yourself that question, Jeff." My pettiness felt justified, shooting his own words back at him as I stormed out, the door slamming behind me. It was the dramatic exit

I instantly regretted. And yes, much to my own surprise, I did finally feel something—shock that he had had the gumption to pull something like this and relief that I didn't have to be part of the charade any longer.

Chapter 3

Jeff and I rarely fought about anything, and if we did, he would usually just apologize within minutes of our disagreement, so I knew this was serious when he didn't come home that night, or the next one after that. This was the longest we had gone without speaking to each other, but I had no intention of being the first one to reach out.

I felt like I should have been sadder about losing my husband to someone else, or angrier that he decided to end things this way. But mostly, I was replaying ten years of memories on loop, trying to understand where exactly things had gotten off track with us.

Even though Jeff wasn't physically in the house when I got back, his presence was pervasive, from the leftover and carefully portioned chicken breasts and broccoli in the fridge, which I could simply toss and forget, to his garish paint color choices that were not so easily erased.

I saw a few missing shirts from the color-coded row in our closet, his side always pristine like a rack at Bloomie's, mine like someone had set off a pipe bomb. In recent months, he had abandoned his identical pairs of black loafers and pleated khaki pants he insisted would come back in style for trendy sneakers and jeans. Truthfully, I had suspected something was going on with him for a while, starting with the late-night restaurant closing times that he had been promoted out of years before. The infinity sign tattoo on his ankle threw me off, and I wondered if it was less an affair, more a midlife crisis. Apparently it was both, neither of which prompted any sort of action out of me. So who was the broken one?

Through the stack of my mismatched shoes and donation piles that sat like termite mounds on my side of the closet, I found exactly what I was looking for: my neglected black suitcase, still sporting the airline bag tags from our last trip to Texas, which I'd been too lazy to rip off.

I tossed it up onto my bed, when my phone started buzzing. The front door slammed downstairs, and then a muffled voice called out to me, but I could only make out my name. I figured no murderer would try to get my attention before killing me. I rushed over to the top of the steps.

"Grace! You there? I don't want to scare the shit out of you."

"Too late." It was Asha, the only friend I'd kept in close touch with after college, even after she turned into super mom and pushed out a gaggle of kids, while I stayed firmly planted in the DINK camp.

Asha stomped up the steps. "You can't just text me to come over and then not answer your phone." She sounded mad. I used to always think I had done something wrong until she asked me why I kept apologizing all the time. "I just always sound like a bitch," she wrote to me on my freshman seminar notes. It was our first class together, basically just a way for the administration to keep tabs on the baby students to make sure we weren't flunking out or soiling their good retention numbers.

"Sorry. I got distracted by Dexter's closet."

She peeked in and then laughed. "Dexterrr? Even after all these years in Boston? I've failed." Asha was Indian but also a native Bostonian, who took it upon herself to orient me to the New England ways, like making fun of how I emphasized my r's.

I rolled my eyes at her, then nearly lost my left contact lens in the process.

Asha giggled at my failed comeback. "Not your problem anymore, I guess."

"He needs to get all of this out of here before I'm back, or I'm going to donate it."

"Don't insult Goodwill with this crap." Asha tossed a loafer at me.

"Good point."

"I promise to take good care of Puddles, so that's

one thing you don't have to worry about while you're gone," Asha said. "Though Loralynn might like him as a travel companion. You sure she doesn't own a cat-sized wig?"

"You know her scarily well," I said. Even though Asha hadn't officially met Mama until graduation, she was already quite familiar with Mama's antics, but not close enough to them to be annoyed like I was.

"Yeah, but in a famous-movie-mom kind of way." Asha paused. "Hey, at least she never tried to marry you off to a family friend's son any chance she got."

I wish that was the only annoying thing my mom did. "Are you sure you're okay taking him? On second thought, I'll probably never get that cat back."

"I might also rename him while I'm at it."

I couldn't disagree with her: Puddles was quite possibly the lamest name ever. That was all Jeff, and his goofiness, giving our pets monikers based on silly words we liked saying.

"So who's going to keep him when you guys, you know…"

"It's okay. You can say it. Divorce?" But then even I had trouble saying it out loud. With no kids and equal incomes, we could split things pretty easily, but we weren't about to Solomon the cat. I was never really a cat person. To be fair, I am not really a dog person either.

I picked Puddles up, scratching his head as he purred in my arms. The poor cat didn't know what he was getting into, but considering how much I was gone, he'd probably be thrilled for the company. The days and nights were pretty lonely for him, left to be entertained by Animal Planet in the company of a robotic feeder, water dispenser, and litter box. Now I was sending him off to fend for himself with a bunch of kids.

"Thanks for being here. And for taking the old boy." I had lost count of Puddles' lives after nine.

"So have you informed your mama of your grand gesture or are you just going to show up on her doorstep with a suitcase full of…?" She pointed at the mound of clothes I was now sifting through.

"No, I have not. I'm waiting until the decision fully sinks in."

"So you don't talk yourself out of it while you're telling her?"

"Something like that."

"Well, if there's anything else I can do, just let me know. I'll be here when you get back."

I scratched Puddles' head, then dumped a few pairs of shoes into the open suitcase next to me.

"So what's your plan?" Asha asked, folding clothes from the now dwindling pile.

"Enjoy my time away? Get some time to think? Try not to lose my mind in the process?"

"Such high expectations for your first vacation in years. Are we calling this a vacation?"

"More like familial deployment? Is that a thing?"

Asha knew just as well as I did that Mama and

I hadn't spent this long together since I graduated from college. We'd call each other the last Sunday of the month, and then Jeff and I would visit every other Christmas and Thanksgiving, mostly to get a break from the cold Boston winters. Then, after listening to embarrassing stories interspersed with random Elvis facts and songs, I'd declare to him that this would be the last year of doing this.

"I understand why you're doing it. You're a good daughter."

Asha always knew how to say the exact right thing at the right time, turning my guilt into heroism in just a few words.

"I'm not sure if it makes me good. Just a daughter, I guess."

"Well, not everyone would do it. So just remember that after you've listened to the Elvis playlist for the four hundredth time."

"I don't think anything will save me from that."

I grabbed my wineglass and plopped down on the bed, trying not to look as overwhelmed as I felt. Asha slid in next to me.

"Drink up, sister. You've got this."

"I've got something, all right." I slugged back the wine, then hopped back up and walked over to my dresser, victoriously slamming my glass down on it. "Okay, I've got to finish packing. And this bottle of wine isn't going to drink itself."

Asha kissed the top of my head and picked up Puddles.

She hummed the chorus to "Always on My Mind," walking toward the steps.

"What have I done?"

She turned. "A very good thing."

God, I hope so.

The phone rang so many times I was rehearsing my voice mail script in my head. Just when I had mentally prepared to hear Mama's high-pitched vocal rendering of "Are You Lonesome Tonight?" she picked up.

"GRACE?!" She was completely out of breath. "Is it our Sunday already? Is everything okay?"

I hated that we had come to a place where out-of-schedule phone calls meant some sort of emergency. "I'm fine, Mama. It's fine. Are you okay? You sound like you were just running a marathon or something."

"Oh god, no. You know the only reason I'd run by choice is if I was being chased by a bear. I'm doing this new thing where I'm leaving my phone plugged in so I don't get addicted. It's a thing, Grace. They say these phones are like *drugs*." She whispered "drugs" like she was sitting in an NA meeting.

"Mama, you felt the same way about debit cards. And now look at you. Ordering your wigs online like a regular millennial." I realized after I said it that Mama would have no idea what a millennial was, and I'd have to spend the next fifteen minutes explaining it, so I kept talking. "So about your birthday. That's really why I'm calling."

"Oh, yes. Seven-oh, SEV-EN-TY. Can you believe it? Jane Pardue said I don't look a day over sixty, which, well, they've never seen an elderly Asian woman. We don't raisin!" She chuckled. Lord only knows where she heard that. "All that tan skin of theirs just wrinkles away. That's why I always stayed out of the sun." Mama's voice trailed on about skin care and umbrellas, which used to always embarrass me, but add it to the list, right under warm lemon water, of things I now completely understand and totally do myself. I have become the person in the sun carrying an umbrella.

"So this trip. Graceland. You still want to go?"

"Well, of course. I've been planning it for years now. I've got the whole thing mapped out. Ronnie Albertson said she would drive with me if her husband would let her go, but Lord knows I could not put up with that woman in a car for two weeks, even for Elvis."

"Do you still want me to take you?"

The phone went silent.

"I'd love it," she said robotically, as if someone were forcing her to read off a piece of paper.

I'd never heard her say anything so succinctly, and it caught me off guard.

"All right, um, well, let's do it? I'll…fly down to El Paso, and we'll hit the road."

The phone went silent again.

"Mama? Mama?"

"WOOOO-HOOOO!" Mama shrieked. I pulled the phone away from my ear. She kept squawking, gleefully rattling off a to-do list. "See, I told you Jeff would be glad for you to go!"

"Mama. He..." I debated whether I should tell her about the separation right then, but I didn't want to harsh her buzz. "Yes. You were totally right."

"Oh, darlin', this is just magical! Finally! I might make you an Elvis fan yet."

"Don't push things, Mama. Think of me like your Uber driver."

"Uber what?"

"Forget it. Just go pack. I'll send you all my flight info when I get it."

"I will, I will! I just can't believe it. I never thought you'd ever say 'yes.' Sometimes things do just work out, don't they, Grace?"

Or in my case fall apart.

"Indeed, Mama. Indeed they do."

———————

When I was a kid, Mama insisted on soaking any cuts or scrapes in large amounts of hydrogen peroxide, at which point I'd scream directly into whichever earhole of hers was closest, as if that would somehow salve the stinging pain that always seemed to hurt worse than whatever the hell I had done to myself in the first place. I couldn't really tell if the soaking helped heal things more quickly, but it distracted me from whatever had happened, because I could never really remember how I got hurt after she gave me her treatment.

So when I decided to take Mama on her epic road trip of a lifetime, I figured it would hurt at first, but then I'd come back to a fresh start. And maybe I could distract myself from replaying all the decisions I'd made that led me to this point.

I didn't expect to hear from Jeff, especially after so much radio silence, so I was surprised that he texted me and asked to meet up. I toyed with the idea of asking whether we needed to have a therapist in the room to communicate, but that seemed unnecessarily mean and unproductive. As annoyed as I was— mostly at him but also at myself—I didn't want to leave things the way they were.

I obliged his request, then remembered I'd actually have to face him, and I wished that I had just grown a pair and made first contact. I would have much preferred to just text things out and be done with him until mediation. Can you ghost yourself out of your own marriage?

He suggested our local coffee shop, a choice clearly made to ensure his own personal safety, and mostly intact eardrums. I had never been one for public outbursts, save the time he accidentally let Puddles out, and I stood in the middle of the street alternating between shaming him and screaming for my decidedly indoor cat to come back. But to be safe, I asked him to meet me at a spot one town over, not because I was worried that I'd start tossing sugar packets at him, but rather I didn't need the peanut gallery of work colleagues busting in on our private conversation. The last thing I needed was Jane Choi to get wind of my impending divorce and blow up the water cooler with my personal business.

When I arrived, he was already seated near the back of the almost completely empty shop, his hand wrapped around an awkwardly large coffee mug, the steam from his drink wafting up and fogging his glasses. He was dressed for work, in one of his many gray suits and colored shirts I had just stared at in our closet, and for once, he actually looked how he was feeling. In fact, his lack of cheerfulness was reassuring. Maybe he wasn't a robot after all.

I grabbed the seat across from him and jumped in before he could say anything. "I'm surprised we're not meeting in the therapist's office. Now you're comfortable talking to me without a third party involved?" Saying it out loud gave me much more satisfaction than texting it ever would. The sight of him made me angrier than I had expected.

He started to bring his hand up to his mouth to bite his nails, but quickly put it back on the table, perhaps remembering how gross I always thought that was. I should have known that gnawing at your fingers until they were bloody wasn't just a bad habit. I was naïve to think that he was just always happy; his stress came out in different ways, like the nail biting, for one.

"Can you at least tell me what went wrong?" He sounded legitimately confused.

I made a face. *Really?*

"I mean, uh, you know what I mean." He stumbled, realizing the ridiculousness of what he just said.

"Maybe *you* should tell me?" I countered.

"I honestly don't know. We never fought..." His voice trailed off, perhaps trying to remember the last time we had.

"Yeah, but we never laughed either."

"You used to think I was funny."

I still did, though I could see why he didn't know it. His witty banter gave our relationship energy at first, but it wasn't enough to sustain us through the stressful days at work or the emotionally draining stuff with my mama. He met them all with the same thing—goofy puns and dad jokes—and I was tired of stuffing my feelings down. I still remember the day I got passed over for a huge promotion, and as I stood there, crying in the kitchen, Jeff did an awkward comedy routine to try to cheer me up, like I was a kid who had had a bad day at school or something.

All I wanted was for him to tell me he understood why I was sad, but he was so uncomfortable with any negative emotions that I started feeling like I did growing up: that I wasn't allowed to have them. And if I couldn't be myself around him, then what was our marriage built on?

"Not everything requires a laugh, Jeff. People aren't always happy, you know? It's called 'being a human.'"

"So you're mad at me because I'm a positive person? *That* makes sense," he said sarcastically, taking a sip from his mug, which I felt the urge to knock right out of his hands. Yes, he was positive, to the point of being toxic. No one can have that sort of Pollyanna attitude all the time without it being forced.

"It just feels fake. Don't you ever get annoyed or sad or frustrated? Oh, wait, I guess you do." I was tired of the whole grin-and-bear-it crap.

"Look. I didn't come here to fight with you." I wasn't even sure if he knew how to fight. But I didn't really want to start now. "I actually wanted to tell you that...I didn't plan on this happening."

I'm pretty sure that's what most people say when they have affairs. "Do you think that makes what you did any better? The road to hell is lined with people saying they didn't mean it."

"No, no, that's not what I mean. I just want you to know that I tried."

I wanted to call bullshit on him, on all the times I felt alone in our marriage, sitting with feelings he couldn't handle, wishing that he could hold them, and me, without jokes and judgment. To him, *trying* was doing the dishes and making dinner, being the equivalent of a housekeeper, when all I wanted was to be seen and heard. But then I wondered if he sincerely believed that he *was* trying, and that was the best he could do.

"Jeff. It's fine. Really." That was a total lie. My tears welling up in my eyes were a dead giveaway, but I couldn't deal with him and all of this right now, so I did what had always worked for me before and just sucked it up. I liked to think I was so highly actualized that I could see the other person's side, then carry on like nothing had happened, a "remarkable attribute," my boss once told me. I never stayed mad or upset for very long, replacing the typical moping and self-loathing with empathy and action.

He looked at me as I blinked the tears away, and for a second, I thought he might acknowledge them, but instead, he changed the subject, like always.

"I'm going to grab a few things from the place, and then we can…"

"Sure, whatever." I stood up, breathing the tears back into my face, and walked away. I may not have been able to speak my truth, but I couldn't sit there and keep pretending anymore.

Chapter 4

I never quite know how to describe El Paso when people ask me about growing up there. Most people don't know I'm technically a Texan since my accent has mostly faded, save the "heys," and the "y'alls" that could never be replaced with "you guys," even though I've lived in Boston since college. Put me around a few Texans and it's a different story; my drawl takes over like a spring morning sunrise spreading across the sky, and it's like I never left.

Using a factual descriptor, like "border town," doesn't really do El Paso justice, even though that's exactly what it is. But going on and on about its "small town vibe" and "quaint downtown area" feels like you're overcomplimenting someone with a new haircut, when all you really want to say is, "Wow, it's so...short!"

El Paso sounded so alluring to my college friends in

Boston, but to other Texans, especially anyone from Dallas or Houston, I was just green and backward, which isn't that far off. I had never actually seen a skyscraper in person until I left home for school. My first taxi ride wasn't until I was in my early twenties, visiting a friend in New York City after graduation.

Maybe I would have had a different opinion about El Paso if I had lived off the military base, or if Mama hadn't made every bit of my existence a spectacle. Being a part of such a tiny army community in a small rural town was a double whammy.

But growing up in El Paso became synonymous with growing up with Mama, which meant I probably never gave it the credit it deserved.

The drive from the airport wouldn't give anyone a great first impression, the blunted tans and grays and lack of greenery tricking your brain into thinking you're suddenly stuck in a sepia filter. It's a stucco-and-pavement oasis in a bleak desert, surrounded by mountains. The Franklin Mountains, to be exact, though I prefer their original name—La Sierra de los Mansos—which seems more fitting. Either way, no one knows what the hell I'm talking about when I mention them.

Mama had long since moved off the army base that brought her to this town from Alabama, her family making the trek south from Washington, D.C., to find warmer climes for their dry cleaning business. She landed in a quiet retirement community that had now been her home for years. The adjustment was tough; most people spoke good Spanish and poor English, and the assumption that she only spoke Chinese meant she spent most of her time telling her story to people who only half understood her. But her pale white skin juxtaposed with bouffant wigs and sparkly jumpsuits superseded the language barrier, and she became a celebrity of sorts.

The SunRidge at Palisades sounded much fancier than it was. What one might imagine as rows of mountain-lined homes, with big majestic bay windows overlooking a golf course, was actually an armory of brick-faced apartments that looked more like college dorms. The lone security guard at the gateless entrance waved me through, and I wondered what his actual function was if only to give the residents and guests the facade of their safety.

Mama's building was the farthest back in the development, which as an original owner gave her more open space, but kept her a bit isolated from much of the community. I still remember how excited she was to have her own place, and it really wasn't until I got mine that I understood why it was so important to her. She'd married Daddy at nineteen and moved right from her parents' house to a tiny two-bedroom home on the base. And even though they eventually moved into larger quarters with each of Daddy's promotions, giving her more room for her growing Elvis collection, she never truly had a space that was just hers.

I tipped the cabdriver, then punched in the code for

the outer doors and made my way up an extremely slow elevator. The hall smelled like a bar bathroom—smoky, with a hint of urine—as I walked briskly to the very end unit. The bright green door, bedecked with a fake flower wreath, was surprisingly subtle for Mama. Below it, the sign read: "An Elvis fan lives here!" The door swung open before my finger pressed the doorbell.

"Grace!"

I jumped. "Mama! Were you standing by the door for the last hour?"

"Don't flatter yourself, darling. I was just about to go check the mail."

"In that?" I joked.

"What exactly is wrong..." She started to defend her outfit choice, then gathered from my face that I was kidding around. Her leopard-print bike shorts were just a different enough pattern from her leopard-print halter top that they looked even more ridiculous than an actual matching set. Somehow she decided the whole thing needed a large hot pink belt, and of course, her signature beehive wig that added the few extra inches to her height that her wooden platforms couldn't deliver without her falling over with each step.

"I can't believe you're actually here!" Mama said, sounding completely sincere, a tonal rarity given her penchant for slathering on the guilt.

"Of course I'm here. Where else would I be?" I picked up a small Jailhouse Rock Elvis figurine from the full shelf of them and examined it closely, running my fingers over the cracks and glue remnants. I always loved Jailhouse Rock Elvis much more than Las Vegas Elvis. The cape thing never made sense to me.

This must have been one of the many that my dad had smashed in his frequent fits of booze-filled rage. He mostly left Mama alone about her collection, but the combination of a bad day at work, plus his almost nightly bottle or three of wine, and he'd grab whichever of Mama's prized figurines was closest and toss it. He'd tell her how stupid she was, bitch about the money she spent, then pass out in his chair. Mama would scurry like a cockroach in the dark to pick up all the pieces, spending the rest of the night and on into the next day gluing it back together, seemingly unfazed by his judgment and anger.

Mama grabbed the Elvis out of my hand and placed it back where it was, carefully turning it to the exact angle.

"Are you packed?"

Who was I kidding? Mama had probably been packed since I had told her we were going on the trip two weeks ago.

She rolled her eyes at me, then wrapped her arms around my waist, squeezing me so tight a little drop of pee leaked out of my forty-something bladder. Her head nestled into my chest. At nearly six feet tall, I towered over her. We always looked like a mother embracing her child, and not the other way around, but in a Benjamin Button kind of way. We would get a kick out of people looking at her, then looking at me, and trying to figure out exactly what had happened. In rural Texas, an Asian girl was a head turner. A tall Asian girl was sideshow material.

"The only good thing your father gave you," she would say, which wasn't completely wrong. I loved being tall. It did make finding pants terribly difficult, at least as a teenager. No one sold "long" or "tall" pants until the early 2000s, because apparently no women over five foot eight needed pants back then? I got used to most things looking like pedal pushers, which wasn't that bad when they were actually in style for that embarrassing six-month period most of us would love to forget. But being oversized in the height department meant that for the most part, no one really messed with me. If only I had been tall in middle school; instead, I shot up at the ripe old age of sixteen, with a solid five years of bullying well behind me.

"There are no dumb questions, Grace. Except that one." She pointed to a giant vintage suitcase in her foyer. Of course she was packed.

"I just need to finish my makeup and we can go." She waved a pile of papers in the air at me. "I've got the whole trip right here, maps and everything."

I was tempted to make a comment about paper maps, but I was too eager to hit the road to get into it with her. I followed her toward the bathroom, and the silver clasps of her luggage caught the light. I looked more closely at her old green suitcase, trying to remember why it looked so familiar and why I suddenly felt a wave of discomfort rush up into my face like I'd just seen a ghost.

Getting out the door with Mama was always a process in which time stood still for her and no one else. It didn't matter where she was going—grocery store or gala—she spent an awful lot of time in the bathroom, starting with heavy layers of creamy too-light foundation, and finishing with deep, dramatic eye makeup, all of which covered up the best parts of her Asian-ness: the coveted skin tone and her beautifully shaped eyes.

Mama got all sorts of attention because of her Kardashian-level makeup and garish outfits, and that attention only egged her on.

"We're going to be sitting in a car, Mama. Is that amount of mascara really necessary?" I peeked into the bathroom.

She smiled, then went back to making her mascara-application face, the one where you contort your mouth and entire side of your face just to apply the slightest bit of black liquid to your eyelashes. Or in Mama's case, all the black liquid.

"Falsies too? Jesus! Who are you trying to impress? You do know Elvis is dead, right?"

Mama made a fake gasp and kept on applying. She

stopped to check out her handiwork in the mirror, and at reaching the satisfactory level of eyelash volume, she tossed the applicator into a large open makeup case sitting on the closed toilet seat next to her. If you didn't know better, you would have thought Mama was a makeup artist. For drag queens.

"Almost done, darling. Just need to pick a lipstick and we can be on our way."

I knew from experience that "just need to pick a lipstick" was an intensely complicated process that involved many swatches on her wrist before a final candidate was worthy, that being the official shade du jour. Surprisingly, she just grabbed a hot pink one from the top, then flipped the top of the case shut, pulling the handle, but forgetting to fasten it closed. I saw it all unfold too slowly to stop her. Instead, I was a bystander to all of her makeup crashing down onto the bathroom floor.

"SUGAR SNAPS!" she screamed, dropping to the floor as if the faster she picked everything up, the less damage would occur. But as she dove, her wig went flying in the other direction. Her bald head reflected the light like a giant moon.

"Mama. Your hair. It hasn't grown back? I thought…"

"It would grow back? That's what they said, but they said a lot of things that never happened either, Grace. Bad things! So if the chemo took my hair for good, well, it can have it."

Mama's chemo had been done for a year, or at least

that's what she told me. She had lung cancer, which was extra cruel for someone who never smoked a day in her life. But "it's oddly common for Chinese women," the doctor told me, followed by possible causes like "cooking oils at high heat." It was easy to judge Mama by her looks, especially for a South Texas doctor who had probably only ever seen Asian women in the kitchen or in porn. The joke about Mama was that Chinese food was not worth the trouble. "My wok is used to keep the robbers away, Doctor."

They had caught the cancer early, which only reinforced Mama's late-in-life hypochondria, and after a grueling regimen of treatments, she was deemed cancer free, which I had taken her word on, since tax season stopped for nothing. She assured me that she would be fine going to her follow-up appointments alone, reminding me she had done all but the first of her treatments alone. She made it perfectly clear that she was capable of getting chemo without a babysitter, and so I let her, making her promise that she'd let me know how each treatment went. Her doctors were impressed with how well she powered through the sessions, and how active she remained when each was over. But her last chemo treatment was more than a year ago, so seeing her wispy salt-and-pepper hair like paintbrush strokes on her pale head surprised me.

"Well, I guess if there's anyone who can deal with hair loss…" I held up her wig, which she grabbed and tried to wriggle back onto her head. "How many of these did you pack?" She shot me a side-eye without even turning her head.

"How long are we going away again?" She shimmied her hair into position, then finished styling the front of it around her face. When I was growing up, Mama had been a special-occasion wig wearer, her black hair damaged and thinning from overdyeing to cover the gray hair that started taking over her head when I was in high school. But now her hobby had turned into a full-time obsession, all fueled by her desire to outdo Priscilla Presley.

Mama hated Priscilla like a bad rash, and would take any opportunity she could to rattle off her offenses, from changing her hair color to having an affair. They were emblazoned in my brain like the Apostle's Creed for a good Catholic. My recitation of the blessed list was robotic, thanks to years of programming. "That greedy bimbo," she would tell me as she flipped through her *Life* magazine. "She didn't know how good she had it."

I took great pride in naming Mama's wigs, a skill my friends and I used to laugh about. There was Too-Young-to-Be-Dating Priscilla, I-Can't-Believe-She-Married-Him Priscilla, and Sad-Excuse-for-a-Mommy Priscilla. No one ever wore wigs in our town, or really, anything like the clothes Mama had in her closet, so it just added to her infamy.

"Now are you ready?" I looked down at my imaginary watch.

"It's a vacation, for Lordy's sake, Grace. Why such a rush?"

"Elvis waits for no one, Mama. Isn't that the saying?"

"He's been waiting seventy years. I believe he can stand another week."

"Are you talking about him or you?"

"Go, I'll be right there."

I walked out of the bathroom, but the squeak of the medicine cabinet caught my ear, which also seemed to catch Mama off guard too, as I turned around and watched her shove a bunch of pill bottles into her makeup case, as if someone might catch her. Someone like me.

"What's with all the drugs, Mama? Social Security not covering your wig habit anymore?"

She laughed nervously. "I'm an old lady, Grace. It's a miracle I'm even standing up."

"All those pills and I'm pretty sure you'll be doing more falling down."

"Okay, Doctor Nosy, I'll take your advice into consideration. Now can we get the heck out of here already?"

Mama zipped up her case, then brushed by me toward her suitcase. I made a mental note to play detective later, because as good as Mama was at covering up her eyes and skin, she was terrible at hiding the truth.

I grabbed my phone, hoping Asha would give me the pep talk I suddenly needed.

GRACE: Remind me why I agreed to do this again?

ASHA: It's that bad already? Have you actually left yet?

GRACE: No. And I'm exaggerating. Mostly.

ASHA: Is it better than watching Jeff move his stuff out of your house?

GRACE: Good point.

ASHA: How's the great Loralynn?

GRACE: Very excited. So, basically, the same. Although it's weird. Her hair hasn't grown back.

ASHA: All those wigs can't help, right? I'm not up on wig culture or anything, but I feel like that has something to do with it.

GRACE: Yeah, I guess. Something's a little weird, but I can't tell if it's a normal weird, because I haven't seen her for so long, or an actual weird.

ASHA: That is a tough call, my friend. I guess you'll just have to keep an eye on her.

GRACE: Welp, considering I'm going to be sitting in a car and sleeping in a bed with her for the next week, that should not be a problem.

ASHA: Keep me posted!

GRACE: Oh, you know I will. 🛡️

Chapter 5

Mama insisted on handling every single part of this trip, which made my inner control freak silently scream. She had probably been planning it for forty-five years or so and promised to take care of all the details, as if that would have been the deciding factor for me to go with her. But as the planner of all the things in every aspect of my life, it was best for my own mental health, which was decidedly fragile as of late, to just let her do it. If Mama could keep her figurines on a military-grade cleaning schedule, she had to be able to plan a simple road trip. Straight shot east. Then north. Easy.

The only issue: Mama rarely drove anymore. On a perfect weather day, she was fine. Just your typical almost-seventy-year-old woman in an old hybrid going a solid five or ten miles per hour under the speed limit. But in any sort of weather, or darkness, she was rendered incapacitated.

And so when she told me she had made the rental car reservation, quite possibly the most important part of a road trip, I just said, "Great." Mama insisted on driving me there. Thankfully, it was a perfect weather day.

"It's like I drove the first leg!" she said, pulling out of the Palisades drive and onto the main road at a snail's pace. I'm pretty sure I walk faster than she was driving. She could barely see over the steering wheel, and the wig that she had so carefully styled around her face was nearly over her eyes.

"Mama. The lines on the road are there for a reason."

"Oh, hush yourself." She turned her head toward me, then remembered, thanks to my waving and pointing, that she was in a moving car and not at a dinner table.

"Drive. I will do my best not to make any jokes about your stellar car handling skills until the car is in park."

She smiled the smile of parental victory, then kept her eyes focused on the road ahead of her, hands on ten and two o'clock like a teenage driver taking a road test. The blinker went on, and she slowed to almost a full stop to turn into the parking lot of the rental car place. She parked in the only open spot, then told me to wait for her to return, which happened much more quickly than I had expected.

"Loooook, Grace. Look!" Mama was jingling keys at my open window, and when she had caught my attention, she backed up to reveal a gigantic antique purple convertible that was parked only a few cars down.

"We're driving in that?"

"It's PURrrrrrPLE!" she sang. "Can you believe it? The man said some lady requested it for a wedding, but then the bride changed her mind...so we got it!"

I almost laughed, but then I remembered that she would be enjoying her windblown "guaranteed real hair" in her eyes, while I attempted to mask myself in a hat and sunglasses. No normal human likes that much wind in their face. Clients would try to sell me on the value and function of their convertibles, and I would just shake my head, debating whether I should bring up how dangerous they are. Why do people insist on driving so fast in a car with no roof?

"There is no way in hell we are driving across Texas in this. Also, this must have cost a fortune." The car was Barney with four wheels.

She looked shocked that I'd have any objection to driving in the car. "This is the most beautiful thing I have ever seen. Well, except for..."

"Yeah, yeah, we know. Elvis. But really, Mama. This?"

"Oh, come here and take a look!" She ran over to the car and hopped into the driver's seat, starting it up and revving the engine. My exit from her car was not as enthusiastic.

"It even has my station!" Mama still didn't fully comprehend that she had pretty much every Elvis song ever recorded saved right on her phone, the Spotify playlists I had so lovingly created for her collecting digital cobwebs. She also didn't understand how Alexa knew so many things. I picked my tech battles.

She turned up the dial, blasting some old song I'd never heard, and started dancing in the seat.

"Mama, you really need to slow your roll. We have a whole lot of driving."

"Oh, Grace, this is exactly how I imagined it would be!" She leaned back, her head resting on the seat, arms stretched out on either side. "You're not going to be a fuddy-duddy about everything on this trip, are you?"

Ah, yes, good old Grace, the prude. That was me. What was so wrong about being a strict rule follower? Oh, right, I never did anything fun.

"Did you just call me a 'fuddy-duddy'? Them's fightin' words!" I used my best, deepest southern accent.

"Well, we haven't even left El Paso and you're probably worried about getting decapitated in a car accident."

Sadly, she wasn't that far off. I had already run several catastrophic convertible scenarios in my head that, happily, was still attached to my body. "Okay, FINE."

"Fine, you'll actually try new things and not be

a big old chicken?" She laughed as if that would ease my feelings about the fact my own mother was calling me a chicken.

"I'm not even glorifying that with a response." Then I made a chicken sound, and she giggled. If you can't beat them, join them in making fun of you, I guess. "Just out of curiosity, how are you paying for this?"

"Well, it is my birthday! If a girl's not going to splurge then, then when can she?"

This was a huge splurge for Mama, who had been living off Daddy's military retirement and Social Security for years now. I should know. I did her freaking taxes. She didn't go without, but she was definitely on a fixed budget that didn't include antique convertible cars. But it wasn't my money. Or my road trip. So I didn't argue with her. Or even give her a hard time. That's what a two-hour time difference does to you when you're over forty. Makes you tired. And nice.

"All right, birthday girl. Give me the keys to Old Faithful here, and I'll follow you home."

She rummaged through her bag, then tossed her janitor's wad of keys out the window.

"Try to keep up!" she yelled at me as I walked back to her car.

I crawled into the front seat, my knees bent uncomfortably under the steering wheel until I was able to find the lever to slide it back so I didn't look like I was strapped into a set of stirrups at the gynecologist.

She beeped the horn, and much to her delight, it played a five-note tune as she hit the gas and sped back onto the main road. I scrambled to back out to catch up with her, doing my best to enjoy the last few peaceful moments I was bound to have in the next week, and trying to quell the accountant in me who was still confused as to how she had paid for that thing.

All that revving of the engine was clearly for show. Mama barely made it above ten miles per hour. I spent most of the ride back to her house looking at the teased bump of her wig peeking up over the seat and wondering at what point she got so old. In my mind, she's still just about to celebrate her fiftieth birthday. Since her voice hasn't seemed to age much, I'm not reminded until I see her that she's a well-established senior citizen.

Mama rolled into the Palisades to show off the car to the guard, who peeked into the driver's-side window, then waved her on in as if he was somehow in charge of giving her permission to enter. She yelled to a few residents taking a walk, but I gave her a little beep to nudge her back home. Half the day was already gone, and I wanted to get on the road before dark, which made me sound like a well-established senior citizen myself. She pulled into her parking spot while I headed to a corner that would be out of the way from old people recklessly swinging doors open. Mama hopped out of the car and raced into the house like there was a fire inside and she needed to grab her one important item, so I walked over to the car to take a closer look. No USB. No phone stand. Could I even get this car over sixty miles per hour on the highway? I poked around the convertible roof. This should be a blast trying to raise.

Mama pushed out of the door, rolling my suitcase in one hand and dragging hers along the ground in the other.

"Mama, just wait a second. Let me help you." But it was too late. Her suitcase busted open, and everything was dumped out onto the sidewalk. She fell to the ground, shoving wigs, clothing, and shoes back into the one side that was completely empty.

I ran over to help her, but she batted my hand away. "I've got it, Grace. I'VE GOT IT." Her voice rose a couple of octaves as she scooped up all her belongings. I backed away slowly and watched as she frantically stuffed all her items back as best she could, then closed the latches on either side.

"Mama, see here. They're not closed all the way." I opened them up again, hooking the parts carefully, then locking them with a click.

She sighed, then used my shoulder to push herself up, using the momentum to pull her suitcase up toward the trunk.

"You're so smart, Gracie. I could never get those darn latches to work myself. Now, you wait here, I'm going to do one last check before we leave!" Mama practically floated back through the door.

I stood back up, dusting my hands off on my pant legs before pulling the trunk closed. My eye caught those latches again, and then I remembered the last time I had seen that suitcase: clutched in her arms as she ran into the house, then stumbled up the stairs, not even taking a breath to greet me, holding the suitcase tightly, like she was protecting a briefcase full of money.

I don't think I had turned sixteen yet, because if I had, I would have been home as little as possible and missed the entire scene, her dresser drawers clacking, followed by her frantic footsteps, which shook the ceiling like an earthquake. The buzzing of the bathroom fan did nothing to mask the bathroom cabinet slams. The two hundred hair spray bottles clanged like church bells. And then silence.

I tried to ignore it, hoping she'd come running down the stairs to relieve me of my curiosity. But instead, all I heard was a loud, deep thud, which was enough for me to get off my ass and run upstairs, skipping every other step in large leaps. I reached the top of the stairs and swung myself around the corner into her room, nearly missing the turn, and nicking my shin. I hobbled a bit farther, but my path was blocked by the green suitcase lying open, with clothes pouring out of each end, right in the middle of the floor. The room looked like it had been ransacked by a careless, determined thief. Every dresser drawer and closet door had been opened—some with clothes still hanging out of them. Shoes were scattered around the room like hail after a bad storm. And I could still see the indentation on the bed, where the case had been, and next to it sat my mother, in a heap of beadery and fringe, hunched over with her head in her hands, sobbing.

She didn't say a word, but she didn't have to. "You wouldn't!" I screamed at her. "Actually, you probably would. Who am I kidding?"

She didn't look up. She couldn't even move, which was how most of our fights went: me screaming while she sat, practically catatonic, her lack of emotion fueling my temper. I'd end up yelling some version of how terrible a mother she was, or how much I hated her, then slam my bedroom door and blast music to cover my sobs.

I had witnessed my parents' fights and heard the stinging words my father spewed at her. But for me, he saved the belts, chasing after me until he could find an open swath of skin, an archaic and abusive punishment method for the most arbitrary of offenses. I never quite knew what would piss him off; when he was drinking, it was anyone's best guess. But even in his sobriety, he'd use the belts to keep me in line. When I hit my teen years, I wasn't as scared of his wrath. And while I'd still take a hand on the upside of my head every now and then, I'd look him straight in the eyes while he did it, which turned out to be quite an effective deterrent. So did the ability to drive away in my own car.

But what stung more than the leather on my skin was that my mother never said a word. She never even tried to stop him. For most of my childhood, I was so busy trying to defend myself that I didn't even notice Mama was nowhere to be found. She could easily disappear into one of the bedrooms while Daddy gave me a piece of his mind and, eventually, a welt on my back. Then one night, he swatted at me while we were sitting at the dinner table, and she just kept shoveling food in her mouth like we were on a television screen in front of her. But even then, I'd like to think she might have at least yelled at the screen.

"*I'm* going to be the one to leave, Mama. And trust me when I say this: I will never come back."

I waited for her to say something—anything— hoping that she would share the same enthusiasm for begging me to stay that she did for packing her bag to leave. But she didn't even bat one false eyelash. Part of me wanted to make sure she was breathing before storming back to my bedroom.

"Get out!" she screeched, which was definitely a sign of life, but not the one I had expected. It startled me, and I ran as fast as I could—out of her room and into my bedroom, the door slamming behind me so hard that I still remember the *Saved by the Bell* poster I had on the back of my door flapping onto the ground. I kicked it a few times, then threw myself down on my bed, the pillow pulled over my head to block out Mama's sobs.

The next morning, I hung the poster back up on the back of my door, doing my best to smooth out the dents my foot had made, then walked down to see if maybe I had just dreamed the whole thing. There was no sign of the storm that had hit her room. I hadn't seen the suitcase since that night. And I had no idea that seeing it again now would feel like such a shock to my system.

I slammed the trunk, batting back the tears that had welled up in the corners of my eyes and trying to make sure Mama didn't see me wipe them away. I dabbed them off with my sleeve, then blinked through the rest of them and forced a smile, a technique I'd learned from my beauty queen friend in college.

I walked briskly back into Mama's building, grateful that the outer door hadn't quite closed all the way, so I could use the bathroom before the long drive and reapply makeup to cover any remnants of what I had just remembered.

The paper map and printed out step-by-step directions à la Mapquest felt very 2001. Mama insisted that we would be on this road for a "bazillionty" miles. And even though I told her we would, at some point, need to stop and get a car charger so I could get an actual number of miles from a reliable source like Google Maps, I decided I would save my phone battery and trust her and the small forest now folded in my lap. I had a decent sense of direction and figured for the first bunch of hours, we would need to head straight east, which did not require the assistance of my trusty app.

Mama got me caught up on all the Palisades news, which was better than me catching her up on mine, so I didn't interrupt or even try to change the subject. The more she talked about herself, the less I would have to say about what was going on with me, so I did my best to keep up with great interest and attention. Keeping up with her friends was like a telenovela plot line. To be fair, I was happy to hear that Mama was so enthralled with her community, because it made me feel a little less guilty for being the infrequent holiday visitor.

My carefully curated Elvis playlists looped in the background from my phone speaker. They were the soundtrack of my youth, my own memories so attached to specific Elvis tunes, whether I liked it or not. Growing up, it was mostly *not*, but after years of not hearing "Jailhouse Rock" or "Blue Suede Shoes," I didn't mind them so much. I might have a different opinion after a few days of it, though.

She chattered on, and my attention waned, distracted by the vast emptiness—no homes, no people, not even any animals—once we left El Paso and entered the Texas "outback." Living in Boston for so long made this part of Texas look like a completely different country to me. And to be fair, it almost was, as the road followed the borderline to Mexico for a stretch of miles, with a border control checkpoint in the middle of the highway. The twenty-something agent looked as if he was going to ask us a question, but I can only guess that with the way Mama was dressed, and her over-the-top "howdy" as we pulled up to the stop in a freaking purple convertible, he didn't need to hear us speak to get the answer he was after. He waved us through without a peep.

Even my cell phone didn't recognize where we were, sending me a "Welcome to Mexico!" text, complete with international calling rates.

This all felt how I had imagined it would, the wind blowing through my hair and rushing up against my sunglasses. Straining to hear Mama's stories but not hard enough to ask her to repeat the things that I missed. The sun beating down enough to keep our shoulders warm, as the air cooled us. I could do this. I can do this.

Then Mama started yelling.

"Grace, Grace, turn in here. TURN!"

We had just happened upon a small oasis of civilization. At Mama's command, I whipped the car off the highway, which had transformed into a small town road for the last mile and a half, and pulled abruptly into a parking lot of what looked to be an abandoned diner, except for the glowing "OPEN" sign over the door. Mama jumped out of the car as I moved the gear to park.

"Mama. You told me our first stop isn't for a while now." Then I saw it.

"ELVIS SHOW. INQUIRE INSIDE." The big plastic sign was hung under the specials outside the front of the diner, half of it flapping in the wind.

"MAMA! Really?"

She put her hands up like she had just been told to drop her gun. "I had no idea this was here, Officer, I swear! Plus, this girl's gotta use the little girl's room. And based on what time it is, you do too."

"My bladder takes offense at that statement."

"Menopause. I get it, dear."

"I'm barely over forty. I am not..." An elderly couple wearing full-length woolen winter coats walked out of the door and down the steps, and I briefly pondered how our bodies can become so temperature challenged. It was easily eighty-two degrees out.

Mama adjusted her wig and hopped out of the car, swaying to and fro like a baby giraffe just out of the womb. I had to hustle to keep up with her as though I was corralling a toddler.

The diner was almost completely empty, except for a man sitting at the counter, shoveling grits into his mouth like a machine, barely taking time to swallow or breathe. I stepped up in front of the "Please wait to be seated" sign next to the empty hostess station, clearing my throat as I scanned the restaurant to see if anyone actually worked here or if I had just walked onto a movie set. Mama was already there, brushing the wrinkles out of her outfit, as if her hands could magically release what a couple of hours crammed in a car had done.

"Oh, honey, there is NO ONE HERE!" she said, walking right into the dining room and plopping her purse down in a booth near the back. "Order me a sweet tea if she beats me back. I'm sure you're starving." Then she raced off to find the restroom. I followed her to the table, still hesitantly, even though every spot in the entire place was open. I could never break the rules, which was good for her when I would roll in at my curfew, or a few minutes before, but terrible for my friends and me. Shackled by the need to do everything by the book, I weighed all my decisions by cost and benefit, and even though all signs pointed toward "SIT THE HELL DOWN," I still felt bad about not waiting for someone to seat us.

I slid into the seat across from her purse, flipped open a menu, and scanned the hundreds of offerings, none of which looked remotely appetizing. I'd spent my years after college acquiring a taste for healthier food, like green vegetables that had a crunch, not ones that were nearly brown, swimming in lard, and soft enough to eat with a spoon. After I'd practically memorized the menu's contents, a waitress finally sauntered over to our table, as if we were an inconvenient interruption to her quiet afternoon. Mama returned just in time to order, sliding into the seat across from me.

"I would love your finest sweet tea!" Mama

announced. The waitress looked as though she would roll her eyes if she actually had the energy to. Instead, she just wrote it down on her pad, then stood there staring at me as I flipped the menu back and forth, hoping something would jump out at me.

"We got an early dinner special that's pimento cheese on white bread with fried pickles and a sweet tea for $4.99…" she drawled, then started to continue but I cut her off for fear I'd be spending the whole afternoon listening to her read off the list of specials.

"That's fine! Great!" I slapped the menu closed and handed it to her. My mother gave her an awkward, apologetic smile as if to explain her Yankee daughter's rudeness.

"I'll have the same, thank you." She reached out and put her hand on top of mine as the waitress walked away. "Gosh dang, do we all talk that slow, Grace?" she whispered, then snorted as I started laughing myself, and kept laughing until the waitress came back, plunking our sweet teas down on the table in front of each of us, then storming off. I leaped up to use the restroom myself, and when I returned, our sandwiches were being brought to the table.

"Anything else I can get you girls?"

"We would like to inquire about the Elvis show," I said. I sounded so…snooty. Who says "inquire about"?

The waitress looked confused.

"The one from the sign. Out front." I pointed toward our car.

"Oh, right. Five o'clock. Over there." She gestured toward the back of the diner, to a curtained door under a "SHOW" sign.

"Tickets at the desk." The waitress rushed back to the kitchen.

"I think we have to do this." Mama's grin looked devious.

"Of course we have to do this." I'd be the worst daughter ever to leave before an Elvis show on a road trip that was all about Elvis.

"Then it's a date!" Mama took a huge bite out of her sandwich, and pretty much the entire slathering of cheese oozed out of the side and dropped to her plate, turning her sandwich into pimento cheese with a side of bread. She laughed and grabbed her spoon, piling it back onto whatever was left in her hand, which might have made it seem unappetizing to anyone watching, but I was so damn hungry, I didn't care. I did, however, learn from her mistake and took smaller bites. It wasn't until halfway in that I realized that my lactose intolerance would probably be a little angry at my choice of food. I'd never taken those enzyme pills after the fact, but it was worth a try. No one deserves to be stuck in a car with a woman who shouldn't really eat dairy after she downed a sandwich full of soft cheese.

Even my slow approach to the sandwich had me finishing well before Mama, who was savoring every last awkward bit. I decided to grab tickets while I could and settle our tab, so I ran up to the cashier.

"Doors open at four forty-five, Mama!" I yelled back to her after paying. We had five minutes to go. "I'm pretty sure we'll be able to get good seats. We can just wait at our table."

But no sooner had I said, "We can just wait at the table" than a group of thirty or so people filed into the front door, chatting and laughing. It was a veritable AARP club. They were dressed like Mama—where you ask yourself, "Is it a costume? Or is it clothing?"—all waving tickets while lining up behind the curtained door.

Mama didn't even wait for me to get back to the table, rushing over to grab the first spot in line, beating the crowd of blue-hairs. I went back to leave a tip, then walked much more comfortably over to meet her.

"You don't even know what you're rushing in line for, Mama." But she wasn't listening to me. Instead, she had already busted through the curtains, which seemed to separate us from an entirely different era.

A few men were setting up tables and chairs lining the outer rim of the room, which looked and smelled like an old church basement: musty, with a hint of superiority. Instead of coffee and tea, a woman was standing behind a bar selling beer and wine to an already steady line of people to our left. In front of us, a dance floor opened up to a small stage with a gold glitter fringe backdrop that flapped haphazardly courtesy of a small fan positioned directly at the microphone. A man wearing shiny gold pants was fiddling with a speaker and greeting the guests by their first names as they strolled to get in line for a drink. The overhead fluorescent lights had been switched off and replaced by dance club lights, the flashing reds, blues, and whites making it look like a Fourth of July celebration. As people continued to file in, the musty air was replaced with the overpowering blend of flowers and mothballs, swirling around like a bad fart.

"Good to see you, Ted! How's it going, Hazel? Love that skirt!" The man pointed and clicked out the side of his mouth, then leaned down to kiss the woman on her cheek. He finally got the microphone into the position he wanted, then ran off behind the stage.

Mama was in her glory, sucking everything in like a thirsty child with a juice box. She grabbed the seats closest to the side of the stage, then pulled her mirror out of her bag to check her makeup, reapplying her "Hot Pink #828" lipstick with a flourish.

"Want some?" She held it up, waving it in front of my face like I was a puppy being tempted with a treat, but I was too busy watching the crowds of people file into what was about to be a standing-room-only show. I'd waited in shorter lines to see Gaga at Madison Square Garden. The sequins and beads adorning the ladies reflected off the lights for the least aesthetically pleasing bokeh. And the overstarched shirts on their male counterparts were practically criminal, at least by good laundry standards.

"Good evening!" The microphone screeched, and

everyone looked toward the stage at a tiny woman wearing a pink Frenchie-in-*Grease* wig so big that if she leaned too far in one direction, she might fall over from the weight of it. "Hellooooo. Hello?" *Tap, tap.* She banged on the microphone. Someone ran up and started adjusting some knobs on the small speaker, and it squawked a few times. "Welcome to tonight's show! You are in for quite a treat. I'm your hostess, Tanya Dawn!" Only in the South is "Dawn" a two-syllable word. Her voice was high and squeaky, as if a tiny mouse had suddenly been given the ability to speak.

She gave various announcements that had nothing to do with us out-of-towners, like Johno's weekend lawn mower sale and Miss Caroline's missing tabby cat, plus a few drink specials and rules. Apparently jumping on the stage was unacceptable and would result in being escorted out of the ballroom, which seemed like a generous description of where we were. It also seemed unlikely that any one of these folks would be doing any sort of jumping.

The crowd clapped. A few people cheered. A man sitting in the back corner alone at a table whistled. Then her voice kicked up a few octaves. "I'm here to present the one, the only...ELVIS PRESLEY!" She squeaked and squealed as she positioned the microphone back into the stand, then ran off one side of the stage as Elvis entered from the other.

Mama stood and shrieked, clapping her hands over her head to the beat of the music that was blasting out of that same small speaker. Most of the crowd had already jumped to their feet and were paired up in the middle of the dance floor.

"Well, it's..." he sang, and the crowd screamed at the small, slight man we had seen earlier setting up, now with a gold jacket to match his pants. He was head-to-toe Elvis, from the bad black wig to his shiny gold-tasseled loafers. No one would ever mistake his rough, husky tones or really his entire appearance for Elvis, but also, no one seemed to care. His moves, however, were pretty impressive for a guy who I had to guess was at least sixty. He did the pole dance (made famous in the "Jailhouse Rock" video) and hip slides like the real deal, just with about a quarter of the BMI of the real Elvis Presley.

Mama elbowed me. I wasn't sure if it was one of her dance moves gone rogue or if she was trying to get my attention. Jab. Jab jab.

"What?!" I yelped, turning around to discover that it was actually a combination of both. Mama was on the outskirts of some sort of organized line dance, popping her elbow into my side every time she side-stepped by me.

At first, I scooted away from her to avoid yet another poke from her frail, bony elbow. But then I bumped into another sideline dancer, and I began to feel like I was watching a 3-D movie, the people around me popping out right in front of me, the blood in my head rushing to everywhere in my body except where I needed it most right now. I reached out to brace myself, wondering if I needed to pound some sugar, then raced over to the bar to grab a soda, which didn't do anything but make me burp. My hand started to shake, and I realized the ginger ale wasn't what I needed.

Breathe in for four, hold for seven, out for eight. Everything was still jumping out at me as I hobbled over to my seat to get my bearings. *Stay in the moment.* But the moment was so loud and crowded. *Find five things in the room, four things you can smell...* The lights, the dancers—everything was moving too quickly. *Let it go. Give in to it. Holding back makes it worse.*

I ran out the way we came in—through the diner and out the front door, my heart racing as the warmth slowly returned to my face. "I'm sorry. I'm so sorry," I wailed to myself, walking briskly over to the car while trying to remember where I had put the Xanax my doctor had prescribed for me when these first started happening.

I'd been having panic attacks like this for a few years now, though looking back, I probably had them as a kid too. I'd feel a combination of desperate and helpless, none of which I could actually verbalize. Mama would say, "Gracie's doing her dramatics again," as if I had control over what I was feeling.

The panic attack that finally got me diagnosed as an official anxious person was when I was visiting Chicago with Jeff in an attempt at a romantic getaway. I'd learned the hard way that the Magnificent Mile was not so magnificent on an empty stomach with a person whom I didn't feel very romantic about. I had long sustained myself on a coffee-only breakfast, so at the time, I figured I was just hungry, but the repeated shots of orange juice from the bartender at the restaurant Jeff and I ducked into weren't doing anything for my sudden-onset shakiness. In fact, I started to feel worse. Turned out too much caffeine, not enough food, and a whole lot of emotional discomfort is the recipe for my panic.

I raced out of that Chicago restaurant and circled the block repeatedly until I eventually started crying, and the feeling of imminent danger subsided. Jeff found me crouched over on the sidewalk, rocking back and forth, unable to stop apologizing, for what I had no idea. He didn't know what to do, so he just stood there in moral support, but his presence was enough to stave off the panic.

Even though I learned quickly that one panic attack meant I was susceptible to having more within a short period of time—sort of like earthquake aftershocks that happen one or even two weeks past the main event—they still took me by surprise, like I was sitting at that bar in Chicago again, believing that I just needed a little blood sugar boost.

Apparently this was my brain trying to protect me from what it was already doing to protect me, my therapist had told me. "Your defenses have defenses," she would say, and we'd laugh about it together.

I'd started seeing her after I got back from Chicago to try to figure out what was causing the sudden onset of panic attacks. It was harder to pinpoint than I thought it would be. I guess the lack of food and caffeine turned off my body's protective shield, giving light to pent-up feelings that had built up over the years. "It's your body's way of trying to get everything out," she'd tell me.

I learned and practiced a bunch of different techniques that could work at the initial onset, but the only thing I could do once the fire alarm in my head had been pulled to signal I was safe, other than reach for my stash of pills, was to cry and apologize. The challenge was getting myself there.

I could never quite place exactly who I was apologizing to, and *what* I was so sorry about. Sorry that I was stuck in an incredibly unsatisfying job? Sorry that I could never express my feelings to Mama? Sorry that I had said yes to Jeff, even though my gut wanted to tell him no? And now, sorry that I didn't like being stuck in a crowded room with a group of senior citizens wearing way too much polyester? I hope it wasn't *sorry that I decided to take this trip*, because if that was the case, it was going to be a terribly long seven days.

I popped the trunk and found the pills in my backpack, still unsure as to why I had taken them out of my purse. If anything, I should have had them stashed in my bra. Even the sight of the bottle calmed me down, so much so that I was starting to believe I could just carry aspirin around in the bottle and it would have the same effect. Just knowing they were there with me had become enough to stave off my anxiety.

I'd been nervous about taking Xanax at first, believing that even the lowest dose possible would send me on some sort of acid trip. That's also why I was never a drinker or drug user in college. The idea of forgetting where I was or what I was doing scared me so much that I'd never have more than a glass of something; puffs and sniffs were completely off limits.

But the fear of losing control of emotions scared me more than being Lucy in the Sky with Diamonds, so I decided the Xanax was worth a try, and it worked, at least at staving off the tinge of a potential panic tornado brewing. I never actually knew if the meds helped during a full-blown attack, but tonight I was about to find out.

The pharmaceutical magic worked almost instantaneously, leaving me alone in the diner parking lot, waiting to see what came first: Mama realizing I was gone or the clean-up crew kicking her out.

———————————

ASHA: So did you figure out what level of weird you're dealing with?

GRACE: Enough weird to trigger a monster panic attack.

ASHA: Oh babe. That sucks. What happened?

GRACE: Just imagine a room with about 75 clones of

Mama, dancing to live music being performed by
a man dressed like Elvis.

ASHA: You just described my own personal hell.

GRACE: Exactly.

ASHA: Ugh.

GRACE: That combined with all the remembering. So
many memories.

ASHA: Are you okay now? You have your meds?

GRACE: Yes, just sitting in the car, waiting for Mama
to figure out I left.

ASHA: So basically, you might be sleeping in the car.

GRACE: She'll come out once it's over. I can use the
quiet, anyway. Oops, there she is now. So much
for that.

ASHA: All right, well, if I can do anything, let me know.

GRACE: You've already done it. Thanks, A.

ASHA: 😘

To my surprise, Mama came flying out of the front
door just a few minutes after I made my hurried
exit. She knocked on my window, then opened the
door, seeing as it would take me forever to manually
roll the window down, neither of which was really
necessary considering I was sitting in a convertible.

"Grace! Grace, are you okay? I went to slow dance
with you and you were gone. Poof!"

"I felt sick. My stomach still can't take that pimento
cheese, I guess." I didn't want to get into it, though

I'm pretty sure the stupid cheese didn't help. And the heat. And all the people. I stopped at the cheese.

"Oh, of course not. You always had a very sensitive stomach. All those calls home from school. I remember. Some things never change."

If by "things" she meant holding everything in to the point where it would hurt my stomach, then she wasn't wrong. But I didn't want to get into it now. Or maybe ever.

"Do you want to go back in?" I asked her. "I'm fine sitting out here for a while. The air is actually bearable...at five fifteen p.m."

"Nah. I'm good to leave. It was a little much, even for me. All that yippin' and yelpin'. And heavy breathin'." She shook her body like a dog covered in rain, then walked around to her side and hopped in. "And some of those outfits were just..." She rolled her eyes.

I flipped down the visor on her side to reveal a mirror. "Have you seen yourself, Mama?"

She closed it back into place. "Honey, they are nowhere near my league."

"Yes, you are definitely in a league of your own." I breathed heavily, finally feeling the effects of the medicine setting in. She batted my arm, her long nails tapping on the side of my shoulder.

"I will take that as a compliment, Grace."

"As you always do, Mama."

Chapter 6

Texas is a long state. It's not particularly pretty, and I can't think of a reason why anyone wouldn't just fly to their destination to avoid driving through it. After miles of nothingness, each little town surprised me like a picture pop-up book. If I blinked, there was a good chance I'd miss it completely.

The repetitive scenery made it easy to replay all the times I chose resentment over the discomfort of having an adult conversation with Jeff. I tried to remind myself that we were both culpable for the state of our relationship. But I couldn't spend the whole trip as my own punching bag, so I decided to try to focus on the hilarious road signs, like the one that said, "Hitchhikers might be escaping inmates." That distracted me for a solid ten miles of the hundreds we still had to go to get to Dallas.

I'd just as soon drive right through, but Mama insisted we spend a night in Odessa.

"What the heck is in Odessa, Mama?" I sifted through random Elvis facts in the deep recesses of my brain, and it didn't sound familiar. A pungent, fishy smell that I couldn't quite place wafted through the car, which I figured was just the price you pay for driving a convertible, but that still didn't make it any more bearable.

"This here is oil country, my dear. You'll get used to it." My face disagreed. "And...I have my reasons."

"Care to share?"

"There are very few surprises left in life, Grace."

"Good surprises or bad surprises?"

"That will be for you to decide. Stop trying to figure it out. Not everything is a math problem."

If only. There were formulas for most of those, which meant a high probability of getting them right. And if not, I could just move a few figures around and try again. But this whole trip felt like someone was just shaking a bunch of numbers around in a giant bowl and then dumping them on my head.

"Just go with the flow, Grace. For once."

She patted me on the leg, then leaned her head against the door. Her almost instantaneous ability to fall asleep was enviable. She must have been worn out from all the fangirling.

"I'm trying," I whispered, partly to her but mostly to myself. My grip on the wheel loosened, and I did my best to relax my shoulders from their usual position up near my earlobes. With each mile, it got a little easier to swallow the fact that I wasn't in charge, which was actually a rather delightful realization, until I pulled up close to the Odessa address on the map. My attempt to slowly and inconspicuously roll into the only open spot on the street was foiled by my heavy foot and the car's spandex-tight brakes. It was going to take me a lot longer than these few hours to get used to them. Mama jerked awake.

"STOP!" she screamed, which only made me slam the brakes harder. We both flopped forward, then slapped back into our seats. Not again. For someone who had so carefully and thoughtfully planned this trip out, there was no reason for all these surprises. Or the yelling.

"What the hell, Mama? There is literally no one to stop for, so stop trying to drive for me..." She wasn't listening. Instead, she had opened the car door and was walking toward a row of homes, or little boxes with doors, a few surrounded by concrete fences, if you could actually call them that. The lawns were immaculately manicured, until I looked more closely and realized most of them were Astroturf and not sod. There were no trees at all, which also meant no respite from the heat, ever.

"Mama!" I screamed back at her, now slowly driving beside her as she walked, one hand on her head to keep her wig from flying off, the other pumping at her side, propelling her forward.

"Where are you going?" Her head was turned

away from me, looking at the houses as we passed, and I could hear her mumble to herself. She stopped briefly in front of a simple tan home with pots of fake flowers lining the walkway up to the door, which she walked right up to without even stopping to smell the plastic roses. I didn't know whether to duck down or hop out of the car and go with her.

"Come back over here," I whispered loudly, but clearly she didn't hear me. Or more accurately, she was choosing not to. Then she knocked. I jumped out of the car and ran up to her.

I couldn't make it to her before someone opened the door a tiny crack, just the one eye showing. "I'm so sorr—" I started, but before I could finish, the door had swung open, and Mama was screeching.

"DOTTIE LIPPINCOTT, YOU LITTLE DEVIL, YOU!"

A tiny woman emerged, barely five feet tall, gray curls carefully lining her head. She shuffled up to Mama and wrapped her wrinkled arms around her waist and squeezed.

"I've been standing by this door all day, Loralynn! My back is about to give out." She ushered Mama through the doorway, then looked up at me, gesturing to follow. "Aw, Grace doesn't remember me now, does she? Because you're a terrible mother, ain't you?"

I stepped up, and the woman grabbed my hand. Hers was soft, nails painted with an illegal color of pink.

She was wrong about me, though, because I

remembered everything about her. It would be hard to forget the only other Asian woman in Fort Bliss. Dorothy, or Dottie, as everyone called her, was Japanese, but in Texas, no one bothered to differentiate. Almond-shaped eyes and black hair just meant you were a misfit, no other label needed.

The house smelled like her old one back on the base, a mix of sesame oil and soy sauce. Since Mama only made TV dinners and hot dogs, I spent most of my meals over at Dottie's house, where she insisted on cooking as much Japanese food as she could find the ingredients for in our small town.

It looked like her old house too. The wood paneling. The red carpet. The slight scent of mold. The music squawking from an actual record player. Even the photos on the wall lining her foyer looked familiar.

My eyes were drawn to one in particular, and as I inched closer, I realized it was a wedding photo, with faces I knew quite well. There was a much younger, still full-faced woman, presumably Dottie, standing next to a beautiful bride. *Mama.*

I gasped, then realized I had done it out loud. I clapped my hand over my mouth, falling backward. I caught my balance and knocked right into... a man.

"Oh, shit. I mean, shoot, I'm sorry!" I scrambled for words and my balance as I turned around and looked up. He was tall. Very tall. As in, *I'm tall and I'm still staring at his Adam's apple* kind of tall.

"They look happy there, don't they?" He nodded toward the same photo I was looking at.

Was it? Could it be?

"I meant your mama. And mine." He reached out his hand to me, and I grabbed it robotically, still not exactly sure what to think or say.

It *was* Wyatt.

"Oh. Yes! I knew what you meant." I struggled to string words together in a coherent sentence, trying to mask whatever it was I was feeling, which surely was coming across as uncomfortably awkward.

"It's been so long I wasn't sure if you'd—"

A screech came from the kitchen, and we both instinctively ran to see what had happened, him first then me following blindly, only to discover two old ladies sitting at the table, poring over a box of old photos. They didn't even stop to acknowledge us or our concern.

"Can you believe I ever wore such a thing?" Mama said to Dottie, who was laughing so hard she wasn't making a sound.

"Mama," Wyatt said. I stood staring at him, finally able to take in exactly who I'd just accidentally backed into moments before.

The last time I'd seen Wyatt was, well, the last time Mama saw Dottie, which was over two decades ago. We had spent our days after elementary school rearranging and hiding Elvis figurines, though he would always stop me before I did anything too terrible, delighting only in the planning and plotting, which mostly involved us locked up in my room with milk and an entire box of Oreo cookies, and not much on the actual execution.

During high school, he was sweet and kind to me, even with my constant joshing, which could be relentless at times. But he just laughed all my snarky comments off, never giving it back to me at all. Considering I was the quintessential nerd, he had a ton of ammunition. Mama told me that he put up with all my crap because he liked me, but that was a complete impossibility. And hell if I'd take any sort of relationship advice from her. Wyatt had plenty of more attractive girls vying for his attention, all of whom had parents who weren't half in the bag most of the time or obsessively cleaning their Elvis figurine collection. Besides, I was too busy trying to ace my SATs and get the hell out of Texas.

The more I looked at him, the more the memories of what had made us such instant friends came flooding back, like the time he'd answered the dreaded "What are you?" question from a nosy classmate. "I am a robot," he'd said in a monotonic voice, moving his arms like they were made of metal. Everyone started laughing, even the kid. He had always looked more Asian than I did, which meant he got that question a lot. He schooled me in the art of witty clapbacks, which would usually shut them up.

His face was long, and thin, like his mother's, but now more chiseled and lightly bearded, the grays peeking through the dark brown on his chin and head. His smile was full and inviting, so much so that I wondered if my hormones had failed me as a teenager, though they were certainly catching up now as I looked into his deep, nearly black eyes, hoping what felt like my cheeks flushing was only my imagination.

"My mother likes it balmy in here."

Wyatt nodded to the hallway we had just walked through, and we snuck out of the kitchen, not that anything could have disturbed our mamas at this point.

"Well, I'm sensing we are not wanted," he said, walking over to the couch and sitting down. "So let's try that again. Grace, hi. Wyatt." He extended his hand toward me. I grabbed it tightly, shaking it firmly once, then regretting not having wiped off the sweat before doing so.

"Of course I know who you are." I searched for more words, my tongue suddenly caught by the Maneki-Neko (aka Japanese lucky cat) collection on the shelf behind him. It paled in comparison to Mama's Elvises, which wasn't necessarily a bad thing.

I noticed his computer open next to him, and a huge stack of books and papers on the other side.

"What are you working on?" I asked, grabbing a spot beside the couch on the velvet armchair that was covered in plastic, of course. It made a weird farting noise as I sat down, and I felt my face flush even more.

"That chair has embarrassed many a guest. I'm pretty sure that's why Mama leaves the cover on it."

He laughed. "I'm writing a book," he continued. "I come out here as much as I can to check on Mama and let her do the Asian mom thing."

I looked at him curiously.

"Make me feel bad about being single and childless at the ripe old age of forty-six? And tell me I'm too skinny."

Ah, yes. Mama did her own version of that, except I was married and childless, which might be even worse, like asking me how the baby-making was coming in the grocery store checkout line when I'd visit. And she wondered why my trips to Texas were so infrequent. "Those hips were made for childbearing. What a waste!" she'd say, with a little shimmy shake of her own and a conspicuous wink to the cashier. And she couldn't wait to gossip and voice her disappointment about all the divorced children of her friends, like their lives were her own personal soap opera, and she was somehow Mama Superior. I'm surprised I still have a tongue in my mouth after biting it so hard.

"Little did she know you used to eat full packages of hot dogs right out of the fridge." He was like Bugs Bunny eating a carrot.

He laughed. "Only slightly worse than watching you eat tiny folded-up squares of Kraft cheese slices."

"Hey, those are freaking delicious." I tried to say it with a straight face but failed miserably.

"Remember when your mom caught us sitting in

your closet surrounded by soda cans and candy wrappers? She acted like we had been doing drugs."

"Sweet Baby Elvis!" I exclaimed, in my best impression of Loralynn's drawl. "Okay, but seriously, how are you? It's been forever." That wasn't an exaggeration. I felt old.

"Well, honestly, besides the book? Feels like I'm just barely scraping by. You?"

"Sadly, I know the feeling. Except the writing-the-book part. That would be life's way of torturing me."

"What? With all those stories you have to tell?"

I forgot how much he knew about me.

"I try not to remember those."

"What? No way! I still crack up thinking about Loralynn getting her wig stuck in the toilet. Or when she was dancing in the kitchen and she didn't realize her entire outfit was on backward? That was classic."

I laughed, feeling relieved those were the stories he remembered, because there were plenty of others I'd sooner forget. The problem with the funny stories is that there are four or five not-so-funny stories that piggyback in my memory. He was there when my dad just decided not to pick us up from our church youth group, both of us standing in the dark on the side of the road—no cell phones back then—waiting for someone to get us. Eventually Dottie showed up and drove us home, the whole car completely silent for the entire twenty-minute ride. And he was there when my dad tore up our mail and started throwing it at us, for no apparent reason beyond being drunk and angry. Through it all, Wyatt was there, never once making a joke, which would have been easy to do given the circumstances. Instead, he'd tell me that it wasn't my fault and that they didn't deserve to have me as a kid.

"Dinnertime, kids!" Dottie bellowed as if we were still ten, playing hide 'n' seek in their basement.

I jumped up, shaken out of my memories. I was surprisingly hungry for someone who had just had dinner a few hours ago, but then half a pimento cheese sandwich was hardly a meal.

"Saved by the yell!" Wyatt smirked, jumping up.

I burst out laughing, suddenly remembering how much Wyatt loved puns. He snickered, and between the two of us, we couldn't stop until Dottie came in to check on us.

"I hate to break up *Laugh-In* over here, but if you don't get here soon, these noodles will taste like your mama made them, which is fine if you don't actually like to chew them."

We both giggled, mostly at Dottie's *Laugh-In* reference. I could tell she was trying to be cool, but it was pretty much the exact opposite. But also about Mama and her penchant for completely overcooking noodles or letting them sit too long in the broth so that they'd basically disintegrate upon contact with a utensil or a mouth. Gross.

"Hey, I heard that!" Mama yelled from the kitchen.

We popped up out of our seats, Dottie shooing

us out of the room with a dish towel, and for a second, it felt like how I had always imagined it might be coming home. Except my house never felt that way.

The table was neatly set, with four large matching bowls full of steaming noodles in a light broth, waiting to be dressed with various ingredients, from shredded beef to green onions.

"Eat, eat!" Dottie invited. We eagerly grabbed our chopsticks, and the slurping began. I learned how to eat ramen from Dottie, and I felt proud of my ability to shove them into my mouth with audible gusto.

"So, Wyatt, what have you been up to all these years? Your mama tells me you're writing a book."

Dottie jumped in. "No wife. No children. I thought by now we'd be grandmothers, Loralynn. These kids of ours!" I started to eat faster, anticipating the questioning that would soon be directed toward me. A full mouth would surely keep me out of the hot seat.

"But I'm happy!" Wyatt replied. "And I know that's what matters most to you, Mama." He grinned at me.

"We never worried about happiness, did we, Loralynn?"

Mama smiled with her mouth full, then gestured toward me. I took that as a cue to answer for her, but she jumped in and replied before I could say anything.

"That's true. There was no happiness in our house!"

Okay, maybe I should have answered for her.

Dottie looked confused.

Wyatt smiled and jumped in. "So tell me about this road trip, Loralynn. How did you get Grace to agree to drive you?"

"To be honest with you, I have no earthly idea. That's probably a better question for Grace." She looked over at me. I was running out of noodles.

"Well, it's hard to resist Mama's begging. Plus, it's her big seven-oh!"

"And I *still* had to convince her. Surely you would just say yes to your mama's birthday wish, Wyatt, no questions asked?"

I just kept my head down, shoving the last few noodles into my mouth and chewing slowly. Mama hated when people spoke with food in their mouth.

"Not exactly," he replied. I looked up and he closed-mouth smiled at me, as if to remind me that our mothers were harmless, even in their passive-aggressiveness. Though it certainly didn't feel that way. "Grace is like me—a thinker—which is an important quality to have."

I jumped in, already regretting it before sound came out of my mouth. "I did agree, eventually," I stumbled. "I mean, what kind of daughter would I be if I had refused?"

Mama didn't miss a beat. "*My* daughter, for one." I was waiting for her laugh, but she looked completely serious. The silence at the table was awkward. "She won't say it, but I'm pretty sure her husband convinced her to go," she whispered, as if she were telling them some big secret and didn't want me to hear.

Wyatt jumped in. "Lucky guy!"

I gave him a pithy thank-you smile, grateful to him for saving me from what might have been the start of a dinner-long guilt trip.

But Mama did not get the hint. "You only turn seventy once. Some of us are lucky to get to seventy at all."

I breathed out loudly, like I had been holding my breath for the last five minutes. Even Dottie noticed.

"Are you okay, Gracie dear? You need more noodles!"

"Actually, I think I'm good. Mind if I lie down for a bit?" I quickly excused myself, pushing in my chair.

"And miss my homemade mochi?" She looked visibly disappointed. I had always been a healthy eater, and clearly she remembered me as such.

"I'll do my best to keep these two in line," Wyatt interjected at the perfect time. I saw him smile at me out of the corner of my eye, but all I cared about was getting some space from Mama, only one full day into our trip.

———

I hadn't thought about Wyatt Lippincott for nearly three decades, and now he was the only thing I could think about. The way he tried to take the heat off me during dinner. The way his eyes could be so dark, yet so bright. The way his lips danced as he spoke.

My breath started to quicken as I felt a yearning that I instantly tried to shake off. *Desperate much, Grace?* This was Wyatt, after all. The guy who dressed up like the back half of a cow with me for Halloween, and who took pride in his covert whoopie cushion placement.

I tried to think back to how he was in high school, his eyes and mouth surely not that unchanged since then, but my memories were of us getting yelled at for silly shenanigans by our parents or planning our great escape from deep in the heart of Texas. Surely his were too, not that our mamas didn't try to match-make the heck out of us any chance they could. Maybe that was why we'd never dated—an act of protest against our mothers, who were already naming our children. Mostly, I'd been too preoccupied with school and steering clear of my dad's wrath and my mom's weirdness to even comprehend the idea of being romantically involved with Wyatt. Now I had to wonder if I had just been protecting my heart from getting broken by the one person I knew truly cared about me.

Lying down for a few minutes turned into my early bedtime, which meant I was wide awake at my actual bedtime. I rolled over and turned away from Mama, who must have snuck in while I was incapacitated, now sawing large tree stumps next to me, both of us squished together in a double bed in Dottie's guest bedroom.

I tried desperately to put Wyatt out of my mind and fall back asleep, but that seemed unlikely, especially with the rhythm of Mama's snoring. I started anticipating each purr, half thankful to hear them, half annoyed that more sleep was nowhere in my foreseeable future.

"I need to get some air," I mumbled, pawing around the night table for my glasses. I stepped out of the room, slowly and carefully closing the door behind me, then crept past the kitchen toward the entryway, where my shoes were neatly lined up by the door.

"Leaving without a goodbye? And your mama?"

I backed up to see where Wyatt's voice was coming from. He was sitting in the dark, the light of his laptop glowing on his face, as he sipped from an old mayonnaise jar at the kitchen counter.

"We like to keep it classy here." He chuckled.

"Well, clearly I am the epitome of class." I gestured to my own clothing, which was exactly what I had been wearing when I arrived.

"It's like the walk of shame…"

I could tell he was searching for a joke, so I started it for him. "Except instead of a drunk hookup, you just fell asleep in your clothes because you're old."

"I would have gone with adorable, but…I guess old works too." He winked, and I smiled.

Wyatt was still as funny as I remembered him. We'd spent so much of our time together laughing, which was way better than the alternative, given how shitty things were in my house. At any moment, my dad could fly off the handle, leaving me scared and tearful at first, then as I got older, angry and indifferent. Wyatt was always good for a silly prank or, on many occasions, putting himself in an awkward situation as a form of entertainment, whether it was making arm farts in the dairy aisle at the grocery store or breaking into some sort of terrible dance in the middle of the street. Back then I thought he didn't care what anyone thought—anything for a laugh—but now I was wondering if I had completely missed his intent, which now felt protective of me. He wasn't trying to pretend things weren't weird or avoid the awfulness of my situation. His jokes acknowledged that things were shitty, and that maybe a little lightness could ease my pain.

"Thanks for babysitting the granny-wannabes."

"Oh, they went so deep into a pile of old photos after dinner, I didn't even see them. You doing okay? Two Asian mothers at one dinner table...there's a joke there somewhere."

"Yeah, clearly I had not properly prepared myself for the onslaught."

I plopped down next to Wyatt and peeked over at his computer. The screen was blank. "Getting a lot done, huh?" I chuckled, and he smiled, closing his laptop and popping up to switch on a light. It flickered above, both of us squinting at the bright glow.

"I suddenly feel like I'm about to be interrogated," I said, and he laughed.

"Maybe..."

"I will brave the search for another cup. Or, um, jar."

From the looks of it, Dottie accumulated kitchen wares like my mom collected Elvises, no rhyme or reason to where things went in the cupboards, though I imagined she knew exactly where everything was. I rooted through the various colanders and salad bowls to find a glass measuring cup, which I figured would be the best I could do, at least before the sun came up and I could ask where exactly she hid her drinking glasses.

"So what have you been up to all these years?" he asked.

I held out my measuring cup for him to fill up, swigged a big sip, then sat down again, leaning over the table with my hand holding up my head. "Hell if I know."

He sat there, pensive stare, his eyes beckoning for more than my pat answer.

"Boston University, marriage—as you heard today at dinner—and...recently separated." I guess wine was my truth serum.

"The separation definitely gets you sad points, but I think I might be more upset by BU, Yankee."

I picked up a balled-up paper off the table and tossed it at him. "Yeah, well, what about you? Make me cry."

"Oh I will...out of boredom. Loyola, marriage,

divorce, and writing the next great American novel for the last four years. I went nerdy with my midlife crisis."

"You weren't kidding."

"I'm so sorry about your marriage." He paused. "I feel like I should be able to wordsmith something more poetic than that, but it's all I've got."

"It's okay. Really. No fancy words necessary. Sorry's plenty."

He grinned. "If it helps at all, I told my mama about my divorce *after* Jennie and I had signed the papers. It was just easier for all of us that way. Even Mama, though she might beg to differ."

"Is there a point where you stop feeling like a massive disappointment?" I asked.

"If I knew the answer to that, well…I'd probably write a book about it."

"What are you waiting for?" I pointed to his computer, then got up, my head finally clear enough to try to sleep again.

"Good night, Grace."

"Night, Wyatt." I turned back toward my room to walk away, then stopped and slowly turned over my shoulder, watching him pretend like he was writing.

Neither Mama nor I remembered to close the curtains before we crashed out, a lesson we learned the hard way as the sun shone into the windows at six a.m.

Mama flipped her head over and instantly fell back to sleep. I was not as fortunate, the light bouncing off the white walls making the room brighter than the actual lamps.

I slipped my glasses on and snuck out of the room, hoping to find some coffee and quiet before Hurricane Loralynn hit land.

"Good morning. Fancy seeing you here." Wyatt looked up from the table pretty much exactly where I had left him the night before.

"You did..."

"Sleep? Oh god, yes. Or whatever it is you call lying down on a bed that's way too small for you and closing your eyes for a few hours." At his height, his feet must have been completely hanging off the bed or uncomfortably curled up the entire night in some awkward position.

I plopped down next to him. "It must be so hard for you," I said solemnly. "Being so tall."

He laughed. "Shorties!" I was hoping he would remember. Back in high school, there was this group of girls we used to call the "shorties," who would always say the dumbest things to us about our height, thinking that they were so mean, when really their jealousy was unintentionally hilarious. They never quite understood when we would both burst out laughing, an unexpected response from two losers getting bullied by a gaggle of short white girls. We'd stand our ground; they'd stomp off like a bunch of angry preschoolers.

He rustled around for a clean mug, then delivered the steaming cup of hot black coffee right in front of me on the table.

"What, no measuring cup?" I asked, wondering if he had purposely allowed me to drink from one just for kicks.

"No, sorry. I do actually have standards. Now how about we do something other than drink coffee together today? There's no way in hell my mama is going to let yours leave just yet, and I'd be a terrible host if I just let you sit here and watch me write. Besides, I never ever get to go out when I'm here, and it would be nice to actually do something other than write or listen to Mama talk on the phone."

I slugged a hot sip of the coffee that went down more like slime than liquid. "Ugh." I shook my head, and he laughed.

"Don't judge me based on how I like my coffee."

"Too late. But, lucky for you, I don't hold that against people. I would love to go out with you and break you out of 1967."

"It's a date!"

I knew he was just being sweet and polite, but to my own surprise, I kind of liked the way it sounded.

If there actually is a best time to be in Texas, it's fall. I found plenty of reasons to leave this damn state, but if there was one reason to stick around, it would be October. The change of season from hot to somewhat bearable meant people could finally leave their homes during daylight hours and spend longer than the few seconds it took going from house to car to school or office outdoors. People would emerge, especially on weekends, like they had been held captive for a few months, hanging out on their sidewalks or making pilgrimages to the local parks to sit on benches without sweating and watching other people do the same. It felt dystopian—but with southern accents and children playing on jungle gyms, not fighting each other to the death.

"So where are we headed?" The door slammed behind me, and I walked down the pathway to the sidewalk, where Wyatt was standing quite confidently, like a man who had been planning this for much longer than a few hours. It was refreshing, and to be honest, a little intimidating. I suddenly wished I had taken the extra few seconds to peek into the mirror before heading out the door. And my teeth? I moved my tongue across them to make sure I hadn't accidentally missed part of breakfast.

"How about we take a little walk toward town and try to find some food that actually has some flavor."

"Hey now! We have spices in Boston!"

"Mmm-hmmm," he replied, and I knew exactly what he was thinking. There's nothing quite like Texas queso and barbeque brisket, and as much as I wanted to believe I didn't miss it, having become quite a seafood connoisseur, it was pretty damn tasty.

"Okay, fine! But we do know our lobster."

"*Our* lobster? Traitor!" He smiled at me, his joking never going far enough to piss me off; just enough where I wanted to zing him back just a little bit more. I was competitive that way. "So what's your plan?"

"You know, I don't actually have one, which feels foreign and a little bit frightening."

"Just a little bit?" he asked.

I liked how he listened to the details of my words.

"Well, this will be a good distraction."

"Yes, Loralynn's distracting, all right." We both laughed. "Good for you for doing this for her."

"It's actually been a while since I've seen Mama. It feels more obligatory than noble."

"Whatever," he said. "You can downplay it all you want. But it's a big deal."

"You don't know how awful I've been."

He stopped walking. "By awful do you mean getting the hell out of your house to save your ass from the crazy?" His tone was serious and empathetic. "You don't think we all knew what was going on with your dad and mama?"

I thought my family had hid it well, but apparently the open windows were like megaphones.

"I still remember him screaming at her one night when y'all were over for the Fourth of July barbeque. You could hear him from under the water in the pool.

My mama had to call the police. Do you remember that?"

"I guess I do. It all runs together now." I started walking.

That was a lie. I remembered the entire event like it had happened earlier that morning. Daddy got drunk and, as usual, was embarrassing himself. When Mama tried to get him to go home, he started yelling at her, how his drinking was her fault, how everything was her fault. And by everything, he meant my baby brother's death. It was a recurring pattern, a predictable storyline—but never in public before. Rather, he'd wake up my mother and me in the wee hours of the morning, sit us down on the couch, and yell at us.

It was always the same exact thing. "Your mama should have taken him to a specialist. Not that crackpot doctor. When we finally took him to a real pediatrician, they sent him to the hospital. Whose fault is that, Loralynn?"

We'd grown so accustomed to his near weekly rants that we didn't let his words penetrate us. I knew that Mama had done what she could, her feverish nine-month-old wailing for hours on end. No one knew he had meningitis. How could they know? By the time he'd been admitted to the hospital, it was too late to save him. They took him off life support a few days later, the day *after* my birthday, a last-ditch effort to save me from a lifelong cloud of sadness. But day before, day after, it's all the same; my baby brother died at the same time I was celebrating my fourth year of life. Or trying to, anyway.

The pool water sloshed up against my face and ears, muffling Daddy's rants as the police took him away. I peeked over the side and watched Dottie comfort my embarrassed mama, while Wyatt's dad took him inside. I could hear Wyatt yelling something—not at me, but at his mom or maybe his dad—but I just sat in the pool, trying to hide. The other guests rounded up their children as well, all of whom had witnessed his rampage from around the yard.

It didn't take long for the whispers to become audible chatter about our family, and I ducked down to avoid any sympathy from the clueless but well-meaning parents. We had already suffered enough judgment, some of which we couldn't control—the white army guy and his Asian "concubine," as I heard someone describe Mama one time, in front of me, as if I wouldn't be able to look that word up in a dictionary. But some of it, courtesy of Mama and her flamboyant style choices, we could.

I sank down under the water relieved, then worried, knowing he'd be back once he sobered up, and the cycle would just repeat itself all over again, most likely with more vindictiveness than before.

"Hey, you in there!" I blinked and saw present-day Wyatt waving his hand within inches of my face. "I lost you there for a minute."

"Just remembering," I said.

"Oh god, don't do that!"

"Look, I don't feel awesome about all of this. In fact, I probably feel terrible. I left her alone with that asshole, to collect Elvis figurines and wigs."

"Or you took care of yourself when no one else could."

"Who are you, my therapist?"

"If I was, you'd owe me more than lunch. Take it easy on yourself. Do you really think your mama is holding that against you?"

"I honestly don't know. But from her comment yesterday, it sure sounds like it." We'd never actually talked about it. I just left for college and started limiting my visits to holidays. We never had a sit-down about why I was getting the hell out of there.

"So where's this spicy food you're talking so much about?" I needed to change the subject.

"I deeply appreciate that your first thought goes to eating."

"At least some of us have our priorities straight. And a drink wouldn't hurt either," I suggested.

"I'm down for some day drinking. I know the perfect spot."

"I see this is a regular occurrence."

"Have you met our mamas?" he asked.

"Good point."

His smile was permission to take a break from thinking, at least for now, and do something I hadn't done in forever: enjoy myself.

———————

I forced my heavy eyes open, shook my left arm, then felt the side of my face where it had left an indentation.

The clock on the wall said "3:37 p.m.," which couldn't be right. I had just eaten lunch with Wyatt, and now it's three hours later? So much for that twenty-minute refresher. I'd spent years trying to turn myself into a catnapper, but apparently I had yet to master that art, even with an alarm on my phone. Without fail, I'd wake up three hours later, or worse, the next morning, usually with a splitting headache.

It didn't help that we had had drinks over lunch. Or rather, lunch over drinks. I grabbed my phone.

> **GRACE:**   Hey, we made it to Odessa.
>
> **ASHA:**   That's good! (Is that good?)
>
> **GRACE:**   We're staying with old friends.
>
> **ASHA:**   Oh, well, that does sound good.
>
> **GRACE:**   It's this guy I was friends with as a kid.
>
> **ASHA:**   This sounds very good. I will require many details. 😁
>
> **GRACE:**   Well, I just woke up from a day drinking nap.
>
> **ASHA:**   😲 Wait, you're a day drinker now? Where the hell has day drinking Grace been? So unfair.
>
> **GRACE:**   Hanging out with a guy she was friends with in high school, I guess. In Odessa.
>
> **ASHA:**   Friends with. Uh-huh.
>
> **GRACE:**   Yes. Just friends. Though he is pretty cute.
>
> **ASHA:**   OMG I need all the details.

GRACE: There are none! I mean, he's sweet and nice and funny and…

ASHA: You totally like him.

GRACE: Uh, he's an old friend, Ash. That I haven't seen in ages.

ASHA: Who YOU LIKE. Okay, make sure this Grace does not stay in Odessa.

GRACE: Based on this headache, she might.

ASHA: That is why they make Advil. Does this boy have a name?

GRACE: Good point. Off to find some. 🖤 And yes, it's Wyatt.

ASHA: I like him already. 🖤🖤🖤

I was about to toss my phone on the bed when it started buzzing, probably just Asha wanting to give me an extra hard time about day drinking. But before I answered, I looked at the name. It was Jeff busting in, like he somehow knew I had just awakened from a slightly tipsy nap after lunch with an old friend I'd suddenly found attractive. For a second, I thought about picking up, just in case he was in some sort of trouble, but I declined his call instead. I did care about him, but now was not the time to feel the guilt and shame that had kept me in a state of inaction for so long. I finally felt like I was moving forward, or at least just moving, and I didn't want his voice to remind me of what I was leaving behind.

I peeked into the small, oval mirror that was ill-matched for the large dresser below it. I hadn't taken off my makeup, and I was wearing all my clothes, save my shoes, which I knew I had to leave by the front door. It was clear I had only intended to take a catnap, and not the toddler one I actually got.

There was no point in touching anything up, other than a quick brush of my hair, which was slightly matted on the same side as the pillow lines on my face.

I carefully cracked open the door, then set my sights on the kitchen, which was only a few steps away in this tiny house, but full of booby traps in the form of creaky floorboards.

"You must have been exhausted." Clearly I wasn't expecting to see anyone, especially not Wyatt.

I turned around to wipe my mouth and straighten my shirt, then spun back with a smile that I'm pretty sure revealed I had just done all of that.

"I don't think I've taken a nap in years. I also don't think I've had day drinks in that long either."

"Yeah, when I saw your cheeks start to get flushed, I knew it was time to head back."

I had never known Asian Flush was a thing until college, when my Korean friend Sunny pointed out my bright red face at a party freshman year. "Trust me, you're going to want to cut yourself off right now," she said.

"What are you, psychic or something?" I said, laughing. She was so serious.

"Your face. It's bright red. It's an Asian thing. You'll feel sick after the next one, and it's not pretty."

I never drank more than a glass or two of wine, or anything, after that. If my flushed cheeks weren't a tell, the taste of my drink, whatever it was, would turn sour and unswallowable in my mouth. Most of the time, anyway.

"I just wanted to put my feet up for a minute, and the next thing I know...well, the day is gone."

"Oh, Grace. The night is still very young here in Odessa. I'm sure there's a church social or choir practice we could crash."

"As tempting as that sounds...where are the girls?" I looked around for Mama, but there was no sign of her or Dottie.

"Out for a walk. They wanted to let you sleep."

"Get any work done?" I gestured toward his open computer on the table.

"Nah. Honestly, I've been sitting here feeling terrible that I brought up your dad. I'm sorry. You seemed anxious for that Bloody Mary, or three, at lunch."

"Oh, those were more 'I'm on a road trip with my mama' drinks than 'my daddy was mean' drinks."

Besides, it wasn't my mean father that I wanted to drink away. It was the last time I saw him before he died that I wanted to forget.

I hadn't really told anyone—and neither had Mama, that I knew of—and for now, I planned on keeping it that way. I had tried so hard to make things right with Daddy, even after he'd taken off without telling anyone during my freshman year of college, then returned out of the blue a month later with a mouth full of cancer, his tongue, to be exact. I should have been indifferent by then, but with my flame of hopefulness, I raced home after finals to see him, believing that this was finally our chance to make things right. I sat by his bedside after the surgery to remove his tongue, the irony of his empty mouth and inability to speak, or yell, not lost on me. I drove him home from the hospital, telling him what I had been up to the past year, while he sat motionless in the passenger seat drooling over a bucket. But then I watched him order Mama around using a white board, spewing his hatred for her and me again.

That last night, Mama had gone out with friends for a much-needed break, and he had called Mama a "bitch." The woman who had taken care of him all those years, and now, as he sat dying on our couch, the woman who was changing his IV, cleaning his mouth, and emptying his bucket of saliva.

"I don't think she's the one acting like a bitch," I said.

He scratched something out on his board.

"You're ungrateful, just like your mother," he wrote.

I grabbed the board and wiped away his words.

"You deserve every bit of this."

I handed him back the board and got up to leave.

And then it happened, a series of events that still swirl around in my head whenever anyone mentions my father. He tossed the board at me, nearly hitting me in the head. It fell to the floor next to me, and as I looked up at him, I could see the rage in his eyes. I ran toward our kitchen to grab the phone, to call...the police? Mama? I wasn't even sure, my fingers not even really capable of dialing anything. But it didn't matter anyway, because he had gotten up from the couch, unhooked his IV, and chased me into the kitchen. He grabbed the phone out of my hand and slapped me across the face.

"Is this how you want to die?" I screamed. "Is this how you want to leave things? Because this will be the last time you ever see me."

He nodded. And I raced out of the door, and straight to the airport to go back to Boston, the expensive plane fare worth every penny. I never saw him again.

Mama called me the next day, and when she heard what had happened, she begged me to forgive him.

"What will it take, Grace? What if he apologizes?"

But my decision was final: "No more, Mama. No more." And so it was.

When I retell the story in my head, it feels like I'm making it all up. And the further I get from it actually happening, the more it reads like a work of fiction than my actual life, except I don't feel like I'm the one writing it.

I shivered a bit and rubbed my arms with my hands trying to warm myself up. Wyatt plunked a huge cup of coffee in front of me.

"This will definitely do the trick."

"If it's like what you made this morning, I'll be awake until next Tuesday. Can you please hand me some cream and sugar?"

"Blasphemy! Look what living up north has done to you!" he cried, sliding the sugar bowl my way before grabbing the half-and-half out of the fridge for me.

"A whole lot of good," I said. And by the look on his face, he knew exactly what I meant.

Mama was determined to stay on schedule, which meant we had to be packed and on the road before dusk. Usually a fast, efficient packer, I felt reluctance like it was holding my hand and pulling me back into the house. I'd forgotten what it felt like to be around him, and I didn't want it to end. My stomach dropped as Wyatt walked into my room.

"I can sit on that if you need me to," he offered. "I'm handy like that."

He assumed that I couldn't close the suitcase because it was too full. I was just avoiding having to leave.

"Do I look like an overpacker to you?" I pressed the top down with my hand and finished zipping it in one sweeping motion.

"You say that like it's a bad thing. You mean I'm not supposed to pack a pair of shoes for every outfit?"

I laughed, then struggled to get my suitcase off the bed, sliding it clumsily, so it crashed onto the floor. Clearly I needed more time at the gym and less time watching any reality dating series I could get my hands on. They were a much-needed palate cleanser.

"So what's the plan?" Wyatt asked, rolling my suitcase to the door.

"I actually have no idea. I'm just the chauffeur."

"Don't hate me for saying this, but it kind of sounds...fun."

"Well, so far, it has been..." I paused. It had been fun because of him, and I struggled with whether he should know that, and whether he should know how sorry I was that we hadn't stayed in touch. We'd been such an important part of each other's lives and suddenly, not at all. I breathed in deeply so I wouldn't cry. "...but we've only been gone a day," I choked out. "This next leg will be the true test."

We stood in the doorway, waiting for Mama to finish packing up, and I decided I was tired of keeping things in, and that needed to change, starting now. "I'm so sorry, Wyatt."

Wyatt looked confused. I suppose it had come a bit out of nowhere.

"Thinking again?" he asked.

"You, your family, you did so much for me." I blinked back tears. "I should have written, or called..."

He stopped me. "I could have too. We were kids. You were a kid." A few droplets slipped down my cheeks.

"It seems so simple now."

"Of course it does. We're old. And brilliant."

I started laughing, then scanning the room for tissues to wipe my face.

Wyatt walked out of the room for a few seconds, then returned with some tissues. His face softened. "I'm sorry too, Grace. I want you to know that. I mean it."

He gently squeezed my arm as I dabbed the tears from my eyes.

"And now" —he grabbed his smartphone out of his back pocket and waved it in the air—"there's Facebook."

I appreciated the laugh that gave me. "And texting," I added.

"So you could say, we were just waiting for technology to catch up to us."

"Exactly. Thank Zuckerberg," I joked.

"Never!"

I smiled, and in that moment, it felt like we were teenagers again, except I was more keyed in to certain parts of him that I had missed before. The way his deep brown hair could never keep a part for very long. The way his neck curved into his shoulders like someone had painted it.

Mama barreled in with her suitcase and dropped it on the ground. I jumped.

"Looks like it's time for you two to hit the road," Dottie said. Her eyes were red and welling up.

"There's nothing like a Texas sunset," Mama agreed.

"Which I've seen a thousand times, Mama. You do know where I grew up, right?"

"And I haven't driven in a car at night in years. You know it's the only pleasant time of day in this godforsaken state." She did have a point there.

"Well, thank you so much, Dottie. I'm so sorry it's been so long. Too long." I got up to hug her. She grabbed me tight around my waist and dug the side of her head into my chest. She sniffled, which actually felt comforting to me. The sound of her emotion gave way for the humanity that I'd tried to squash for so long.

Mama hugged Wyatt, which looked like a *Toddlers & Tiaras* contestant hugging Asian Paul Bunyan. "You're as sweet as I remember you, Jeff."

"That's Wyatt, Mama." Wyatt gave me a confused grin as he hugged her.

"Of course it's Wyatt. That's what I said." She looked annoyed that I had corrected her, which was very Mama. But forgetting names was not. I couldn't tell if this was a product of *SEV-EN-TY* or if something else was going on, but the anomalies were starting to add up. To what, I couldn't be completely sure, but I decided to file it away with the others and take some time on the open road to do some calculations to see if they all pieced together into anything that might make sense.

She started to drag the bags out to the car, but could only get to about a shuffling pace before she plopped them down on the ground.

"Let me get them, Loralynn," Wyatt said. "I'll bring them right out to you in a minute." He cocked his head in my direction, and Mama did what she does best: awkward.

"Come now, Dottie," she said in a loud, robotic tone. "Let's go have our goodbyes at the car." She grabbed Dottie's hand, and they walked away like two schoolgirls.

"She's not great with names, but she can sure catch a hint." Wyatt was restless.

"When you throw it at her like a grenade," I finished. We both laughed, trying to figure out what exactly was supposed to happen next.

"It was great to see you, Grace."

"Same." I reached up to hug him, even though I was never a hugger. It just felt right. He kissed my cheek, which sent an unexpected jolt through me, then wrapped his arms around my waist, squeezing me in a way where I felt like I could let go and he'd hold me perfectly upright without any effort on my part. "Let's not wait another twenty-five years," he whispered into my hair.

I nodded into his shoulder, feeling the swell of tears moving from my throat up into my cheeks. I stepped back and noticed that he too was looking down, then away, as if perhaps he was feeling the same.

I gathered myself, walking toward the door, our

mamas hugging and chattering. "All right, ladies, the Texas sunset waits for no one!"

Wyatt walked behind me with the suitcases, lugging them around to the back of the car and putting them into the trunk with white-glove treatment, closing it ever so carefully.

Mama had made her way into the passenger seat and was eyeballing her directions through bedazzled reading glasses.

I stepped up to the open car door, and as I was sliding in, Wyatt stuffed a folded paper in my hand.

"For later." He stepped back on the sidewalk next to Dottie.

I smiled, flush with an energy I hadn't felt in years. Even though I had no idea what was written on that paper, I was filled with a girlish hope. Perhaps as I had been scanning the intricacies of his facial features into my brain, he had been doing the same, both of us feeling like the connection between us was more than just a couple of old friends reunited. Whatever our relationship had been in the past, something had been ignited.

The engine roared with the quick twist of the keys. I stuffed the paper into my pants pocket, then pressed my foot slowly on the gas. Mama screeched and grabbed her scarf-covered head, reaching quickly to fix it under her chin. As I peeked into the side mirror, I saw Wyatt, waving, then watching as we grew smaller in the distance.

Wyatt's friendship and Dottie's loving care had

been lost in the rubble of my father's tyranny and my mother's complacency, whole relationships built up and torn down, in what felt like a lifetime. But here we were, picking up right where we left off, not as if nothing had happened, but rather, acknowledging that everything had, and we were better for it.

Chapter 7

The blue sky turned orange, then pink, like a mood ring on a hot finger. Mama was right. There is nothing like a Texas sunset, and even though I had seen thousands in my lifetime, it had been many years since I'd seen one in more than just my memory.

Mama drifted off as the last bit of pink evaporated into the darkness. Even with distant lights glowing, the sky was the darkest I'd ever seen, lit only with stars, planets, and orbiting satellites, a fact I'd learned in a summer astronomy course I took to fulfill my one college science requirement. The idea of dissecting anything was mortifying enough to force me into one of the hardest courses. As it turned out, we spent half of the class doing equations and the other half on the ground, staring up at the sky, combining two things that Jeff always said I was extremely good at:

math and lying down. And he wasn't wrong; even though I wasn't a napper, I would do as much as I could with my feet up and my back supported by a billion pillows, like someone recovering from surgery. Movies, dinner, homework—it didn't matter. I always thought I was being lazy, but maybe that's just how I was around Jeff: feeling immobile, and trying to make the best of it.

Jeff never raised his voice, not at me or at anyone, for that matter. I'd visit him at the restaurant and eat at the bar while he worked, and I'd watch as customers would call him over and rudely complain about their food. He'd just smile and nod, speaking to them calmly and taking their plate, while doing everything he could to appease them. At home, he was pretty much the same, doing everything he could to make me happy and never expecting much from me in return, so I figured after all the fraught years of me doing everything to make everyone else happy, I was finally thinking about myself. I deserved to have someone else work hard for me for once. That might be the least romantic way to describe a relationship, but it worked for the most part, until he wanted kids.

He'd go off on these tangents about family and children, and all I could think about was my parents, and how as much as people try to not be their parents, they are always their parents.

Jeff would talk about "our legacy" and tell me how adorable our baby would be, but I knew that in reality, parenting would be really freaking hard, especially given my less than stellar role models.

So I did what I had perfected with many years of practice: I pushed my real feelings out of the way and pretended to share his dream, telling myself I was somehow protecting him from the pain my mothering would cause him and our unborn child. It's no wonder I spent my days feeling awful, at least deep down.

I figured at some point, he'd give up or I'd come around. But that never happened. And now I was wondering whether it was never me all along. It was more that Jeff wasn't the right person. *My person.*

The comfortable breeze that had been a welcome respite from the humidity had turned into a cold wind, which brought me back into the present moment. Mama had reached to pull her jacket around her shoulders in her sleep. And my hat and hoodie combo wasn't going to cut it for the rest of our drive to the Best Western in Dallas that Mama had booked for the night. Before she drifted off to sleep, she assured me, "I'll tell you when we get there, darling. You just worry about the driving." Which I had, except for the part of driving a convertible where we both freeze our asses off. I needed coffee and warmth, which is what I hoped the Allsup's Convenience Store could offer.

Mama didn't budge as I parked, even though I was tempted to wake her just to get an extra hand with the convertible top, which was not nearly as simple to attach as the directions in the manual might make you think. I gathered pretty quickly that the car was really meant to be driven with the top down, and it seemed to be resisting this transformation. With Mama snoozing, I ran into the store to grab a coffee, for warmth and willpower, then realized I had left my wallet in the car. I scrounged around in my pockets for a couple of bucks, but instead pulled out the crumpled note Wyatt had given me. With all the hubbub of leaving, I had forgotten about it, which was probably a good thing with Mama privy to my every movement.

I WOULD HAVE ASKED FOR YOUR NUMBER, BUT I THOUGHT THAT MIGHT COME OFF AS A LITTLE OPPORTUNISTIC. SO HERE'S MINE. I'D LOVE TO HEAR FROM YOU.—WYATT

His handwriting was clean and symmetrical, which didn't surprise me. Every letter in caps, but not like he was yelling. More like he had taken the time and effort to write those words just for me, as if they had been carved into a piece of wood. Seeing it felt so personal, like he had sent me off sharing just a little more about himself than he had before. And I was relieved that I hadn't just been imagining the flushes and flutters.

"Just take the coffee."

I startled. The guy behind the counter was audibly annoyed, and with two actual paying customers waiting to put cash on their pump, I could understand why. I stuffed the note back into my pocket.

"Oh, um, thanks!" I grabbed it, then walked quickly back to the car, trying to think of what to text Wyatt. Mama had woken up and was trying to fix her wig in the car mirror.

"There's no hope for that, Mama." I leaned into the open window, but she ignored me, sliding it back and forth on her head, then picking at it with a comb. "Just take it off. It's only the two of us."

I slid back into the front seat, coffee in one hand, my phone in the other, deciding whether I should text Wyatt.

Hey… I deleted it. *Hi!* I erased it again. *Yo.* Terrible. I shook my phone to cancel the writing.

I felt certain Mama would ask what I was doing, but instead, she slid the wig off her head, then flipped the mirror closed, her hand running back and forth on her bare scalp.

"I miss my hair." The words hung in the still, humid air between us.

It surprised me, hearing that, because for as long as I could remember, Mama seemed to love covering her hair up. At just about shoulder length, it had been a wall around her neck, swinging back and forth in unison. As much as she tried to make me love my waves, I coveted the straightness and unity of hers, except for the year she tried a perm and it looked like a Ronald McDonald wig on her head, which she immediately covered up. Most days, she'd twist her hair into a bun and shove it under a wig cap, hiding its glory with a flip or bouffant that made her look more like a caricature than an actual person. But when she'd wear it natural—which happened less as I got older—I felt like I got a glimpse of someone else, a mystery Mama I longed to know.

"I'd miss it too," I replied, unsure as to whether she was actually looking for a response.

"Oh, I'd definitely miss my hair if I had yours, darling. Those waves are delicious." She ran her fingers through it. "You got your father's hair, thank goodness. Mine was so uncooperative."

"I didn't think so. I always thought yours was so smooth, and when you moved, it was like watching ripples on water."

"I tried everything to make it hold a curl—hot rollers, sponge rollers. I even used tin cans. In Texas, that dark, straight hair only meant you were different. Less than."

She stopped. I knew exactly what it meant.

"You couldn't imagine how mean people can be."

Actually, I could. The apples didn't fall far from their racist trees. My classmates had plenty to say about Mama, calling her all kinds of Asian epithets and pulling the outside corners of their eyes back toward their heads. They made fun of me too.

Then when they saw Mama sashay into the principal's office in one of her favorite jumpsuits, topped with one of her particularly over-the-top wigs, to pick me up, it escalated to a whole new level, with frequent visits to the school nurse for unexplained stomachaches that would subside in the quiet of the infirmary. But then when I'd go back to my classroom with a couple of Tums in my belly, the pain would come back, sometimes so bad Mama would have to pick me up, which started the whole cycle all over again.

The worst part was that Mama never seemed to care. She'd just remind me to stop drinking the chocolate milk at school. And no matter how much I begged her to stop and dress like everyone else's mama, she would tell me to be proud of who I was. "You're a beautiful tall girl, Grace. Oh, how I wish I could be you. I'm just a stumpy little thing." What she never really understood was that I *was* proud of me. *She* was why I was so embarrassed, which, as a kid, was easier than being sad.

"It'll grow back, Mama. It's just going to take some time."

"If only we had endless amounts of it," Mama mumbled. "Maybe I wouldn't even need these silly things."

"You never needed those silly things."

"Well, that's easy for you to say."

"I guess." It didn't feel easy.

"Just look at you, Grace. You could have been a model!"

"But I didn't want to be one. I hated all the attention."

"For being beautiful? Such luck, wasted." She sighed.

"I didn't feel beautiful. I felt…different."

She shrugged, then shook the wig out, shimmying it onto her head. Nothing was ever easy to say to Mama, but this conversation was a start.

I hopped out of the car, struggling to release the convertible top. With a few forced tugs, it opened up and was snapped in place much more easily than I had anticipated, though it was definitely more of a two-person job. Mama looked too distracted to be of any help, and I didn't want her to break a nail. I'd never hear the end of it.

I slid back into my seat and started the car with a twist of my wrist. I reached for my phone to check directions and saw a text from Jeff.

Hey. Tried to call. Hope you're okay.

He texted as if nothing had happened between us and everything was somehow copacetic, which was so very Jeff of him. There were never any bad feelings with him, or *negative feelings*, as my therapist would correct me, reminding me that being sad or angry didn't make me a bad person. I told her that growing up, having any feeling other than total contentment was bad in my house. She told me that I was evolving and growing as a person, and I might be ready for the rough edges and dark spots.

"Love isn't always pretty," she explained, which didn't completely make sense to me back when she said it, but with all this space, I was starting to see what she meant.

How do you think I'm doing? was what I wanted to text, but instead, I flipped out of my text messages and back to the map. I was too tired to think of a reply that was the perfect combination of clever and seething.

I backed up slowly out of the parking lot, turning onto the side road toward the highway. The warm breeze circulated through the cab, wrapping around me like a hug.

———————

Mama slept for the two-hour ride, save the few times she started talking in her sleep. Her brain just never had an off button. We were similar in that way, and probably many others that I didn't really want to admit. I just kept everything I was thinking inside; I suppose I could have learned a thing or two from Mama. But everything with her was always so loud and dramatic that it took up all the space between us, leaving little room for me to do anything more than make a face, or as of late, a snide remark.

Before she drifted off, Mama had left me the reservation info and the motel address, which was surprisingly easy to find without the help of my phone. It wouldn't have done much good anyway with the spotty signal I had been battling for miles.

I pulled the car into the motel entrance, parking near the main lobby so I wouldn't have to move again depending on where our room was located. Mama had a penchant for motels, even though there were plenty of nicer spots nearby. I guess that's what happens when you spend all your money on a ridiculous car.

"Mama, we're here." I tapped her gently on her shoulder, but she didn't budge, her head slumped over against her door, the faint rattling of her tongue against her uvula making a gentle, rhythmic warble. Even though it was pitch black out, the air felt like clay around us.

Mama sighed, as if she heard my thoughts, then chortled and looked as though she was settling back into the rhythm of her slumber. Instead, she popped awake, looking around.

"No! We can't stop now!" she yelled urgently.

"But we're here at the motel. It's late." I spoke to her like she was lucid, even though I was almost certain she was having another mid-slumber outburst. She wasn't usually this agitated.

"Of course, of course," Mama replied. "I must have been dreaming is all."

"I hope it was a good one, at least."

Her smile was hesitant as she started packing up items that had fallen out of her bag during our drive.

"I can do that, Mama. Why don't you just go inside?"

She patted around the inside of the door for the handle, then pulled it open gently, as if she had never opened a door before. Hobbling out of the car, she shuffled into the main lobby, then headed straight for the coffee and tea station by the reservation desk, rummaging through every single tea bag, then cup. I left the car in its shambled state to help her, but she just shooed me away.

"I'm certain I can make my own drink, thank you very much. Now where's the ice?"

"Mama, it's hot tea. See, look." I showed her the hot water sign.

She looked confused, then recovered quickly. "Of course it is! I just don't want it to burn my mouth, silly child," she said unconvincingly. The three tea bags bobbed up and down in her half-full cup of hot water.

I added a bit more water, dumped out two tea bags, and escorted her over to a large armchair. With her occupied, at least momentarily, I checked in, then ran out to grab enough things to get her settled in our room, hoping that a good night's sleep would erase the fog that Mama had somehow woken up into.

And I decided I would text Wyatt.

GRACE: Hey, I got your note.

Duh, dumbass, of course you got his note.
The three "I'm typing" dots appeared and disappeared a few times.

WYATT: I'm glad you texted.

More dots appeared and disappeared, so I just jumped in. I did appreciate his overthinking, which I could relate to at an almost cellular level.

GRACE: We made it to Dallas.
WYATT: Oh good.

It kind of felt like I was texting with a robot. The dots kept appearing and disappearing.

WYATT: Jesus, I swear I'm better at this. Maybe I need to give up writing this book. I can't even text properly.

I was relieved.

GRACE: Maybe you're just using all your words for the book?
WYATT: So I *am* bad at this. Fuck.
GRACE: It's okay. I'm only mildly judging you.
WYATT: I would be too! Well, keep me posted. I am kind of living vicariously through you.
GRACE: You do remember that I'm driving my 70-year-old mother to Memphis, right? You really need to get out more. 😄
WYATT: That came out totally wrong. God. Maybe I should stop now while I'm ahead. Or something. It's nice to hear from you.
GRACE: I will keep you posted. 🙈 Bye!

———————

I felt surprisingly well rested after the night in my full-size motel bed, all to myself. Mama, on the other hand, looked like I had left her out in the car to sleep all night long. "You look like—"

"Don't even say it, Grace." Mama flopped back onto the bed. "And since when do you speak to your mama like that?" She covered her face with a pillow. At least the Mama I knew was back.

"You always taught me to be honest!"

Mama whipped the pillow off her face and sat straight up, her eyes glaring at me through the puffy lids. "What time is it? And where in the blessed hell is my phone?"

She tapped around her nightstand, not remembering that I had to nearly carry her into the room and undress her myself, which I learned was no small feat. Her undergarments were like Spanx on crack. And she kept batting me away. I imagine it was similar to trying to change a toddler's clothes, except with more hooks. And expletives. She had at least found the wherewithal to change into her nightgown and crawl under the covers, her phone at the bottom of the purse I had frantically stuffed with whatever was left in the passenger side of the car.

"Nearly nine o'clock."

Mama shrieked. "Grace! Why didn't you wake me? We're going to be late. We've got to get on the road."

I was too tired to hide my annoyance. "Well, if I had an actual schedule of what we were doing, I could have awoken the dead from their sweet slumber." I added loud snoring noises for an extra effect.

"Save it. We gotta get moving. Pack up the car while I get ready. I've got a ten o'clock appointment I cannot be late for!"

"You need that entire hour to get ready?" I pointed to my under-eye bags. "But whatever you say."

Mama tossed the pillow at me, but I batted it away, grabbing my suitcase, which had never been unpacked in the first place, and laughing as she scrambled through her own to find clothes.

"Just grab my toothbrush, will you?" I yelled back to Mama as I walked out the door to the car. By the time I had grabbed a "complimentary coffee" in the motel office and sufficiently doctored it to my drinkable standards, she was standing by the passenger-side door, tapping her foot, waving my toothbrush at me.

"If we are late because of your coffee addiction..."

I snatched the toothbrush out of her hand, then rolled her suitcase over to the trunk, ignoring her. At that moment, I wished I had an addiction to something a whole lot stronger than motel drip coffee in a Styrofoam cup.

"Where are we going anyway?" I asked. "Just call and let them know we'll be a few minutes late." I slammed the trunk, then walked around to the driver's seat.

"It's not that simple, Grace." She handed me a paper:

Loralynn Johnson: UT Southwestern Medical Center, Oncology—Dr. Amovar 10 a.m.

"Mama. What? What is this?" I started shaking. She grabbed my hand. *Oncology? Maybe this is just a remission follow-up visit. But who does a remission follow-up visit in a different city with a completely different doctor? This is bad. Very, very bad. No, this has to just be me, reading into things and overreacting. It has to be.*

"Just drive. I'll explain on the way."

Chapter 8

A thousand things raced through my mind in the silence of our drive, my one hand on the wheel and the other pressing the tears back into the corners of my eyes. I wanted to badger Mama with questions, to scold her for keeping secrets. But instead, I cried— a combination of sadness, anger, and utter fear, all of which was better than panic.

"I'm sorry, baby," Mama said. "I would have told you, but then it would have ruined the whole trip."

I looked over at her, and she was pallid. Her lips were squeezed tightly together, quivering ever so slightly. That was not a good sign.

"Told me what?"

"Well, you'll get the official news soon enough, I guess." She turned away from me, toward the window, her breath fogging it up in short puffs. "The cancer...it's back." She whispered the last words, perhaps hoping that if she said them gently they wouldn't sting so much. But it didn't matter how you said that fucking word. I hated it. "Or maybe it never went away in the first place? But like Elvis said..."

"Mama, stop. What kind of cancer?" I tried to sound more inquisitive and confused than angry, but it wasn't easy, my head turning back and forth from her to the road, hoping for some sort of look in her eye that might offer some reassurance. She kept staring out the window, unfazed by my chicken-necking.

"It didn't seem to matter at the time, Grace. Either way, it's there." She finally turned her face toward me, and I could see the streaks down her face, where her makeup used to be.

"Why didn't you say something about this, Mama?"

Considering she would run to the doctor for any phantom ache or pain, worried that she somehow had whatever disease du jour she was obsessed with, I couldn't believe that she had kept this under wraps. And now it all added up: the gaggles of pills in her bag, her bald head that was still bald, all that money on this ridiculous car. Maybe even last night's confusing episode.

"What would you have been able to do anyway?" she said. "Just worry about me from thousands of miles away?" She was starting to raise her voice, which at least felt a little more normal.

"That's kind of part of the job, Mama."

"No, that's *my* job. Yours is to live blissfully un-aware that your mama is dying. Or in your case, just unaware." She laughed nervously, then shoved her bony elbow into my side, which hurt as much as her faux punch line. When I didn't budge, she dropped her arm back into her lap, then slid her hand over to mine, which was still gripping the wheel. She uncoiled my fingers, then laced hers into mine.

I couldn't breathe. "No one said anything about dying," I eked out, just barely, trying to wrap my head around what was happening. I carefully released my hand from hers to wipe the tears rolling down my face at a now rhythmic pace.

"Yet." Her overenunciated "t" was meant to be the period to our conversation, the spit flying out of her mouth onto the dashboard in front of her. How could she be so blasé about something like this? This wasn't appendicitis. Or a fucking broken toe.

"No 'yet,' Mama. No. This isn't how it works."

"Well, then, how exactly does it work, darlin'?" There was the defensive tone I had been waiting for, and it was just the motivation I needed.

"You tell people—your daughter—that you're sick and then they get to do something about it." Why was it so hard to help her? I wanted to believe that she thought she was doing me a favor, and that by keeping it to herself, she was trying to make my life easier.

"Like what? Call my doctor from your big office in Boston? And then what?" Her voice squeaked, and she started coughing. I handed her the bottle of water I had stashed in the cupholder in my door.

"I don't know. You didn't give me the chance." Now I was yelling too, and it felt good to put the energy that was building inside me somewhere other than my tear ducts.

"It's just what I do, Grace. You know that!" As if she didn't have a choice.

That was what always drove me nuts about Mama. Well, one of the things. She just decided that the things she did, that affected everyone else, were just character flaws. Or worse, biological traits that she had no control over. But no one is born keeping their pain to themselves. Or hiding everything from the people who should be allowed to care the most. "But you don't have to keep doing it. This doesn't have to be a thing."

Mama was flustered. "We haven't really *talked* for years. So why would I tell you anything?"

And there it was. The truth that we both knew but could never quite say. Shots fired. Direct hit. I mean, she wasn't wrong. Like an Easter Christian, I tried to be a decent daughter with the scheduled once-a-month Sunday phone calls and bi-yearly visits.

"You're right, Mama. Why would you?" The words came out more calmly than I had expected, which I think surprised us both. She slumped back in her seat, reaching for my hand again, which I gave to her this time, willingly.

I wanted to ask her why she thought I hadn't talked to her for years. Or better, why we had never really *talked* at all. But I knew that wouldn't do anything to change the fact that this trip was taking an unexpected turn, one I wasn't sure how either of us would be able to handle.

The rows of high-end cookie-cutter houses made me think my trusty maps app had done me wrong, but one last turn as directed by the voice in my phone and a huge medical complex emerged into the skyline in a *Wizard of Oz* Emerald City kind of moment. The irony of a huge liquor store within walking distance of the hospital entrance was not lost on me; in fact, a small part of me thought about dropping her off, then bee-lining it there so I'd be ever so slightly lubed up for her appointment. But anytime I imagined using alcohol to take the edge off—before awkward conversations or difficult situations—I thought of my dad, and everything I had learned about genetics and alcoholism. It was never worth tempting fate.

The hospital grounds were immaculate, with wild-flowers and a small body of water with a bridge, which did what I imagined was intended: distract me, if only momentarily, from remembering that I was about to take my mother to meet with an oncologist. And as we walked in, the gorgeous wall murals and open floor plan made it feel like one of those trendy co-working spaces where people pay lots of money to have the office they were trying to avoid in the first place. I actually caught myself scanning the reception area for a kombucha tap fridge and vibing with the hipster Muzak. Then I saw the big "Dr. Amovar, Oncologist" sign at the reception desk, and my fascination turned back to disdain.

Mama checked in and I sat, flipping through my phone to find some reviews of this place and this doctor. Five stars for both, which is pretty decent considering most online reviews I've seen just go on to rip people and places apart. No super happy patient decides they'll take time out of their day to tell the world how great someone was to them. They reserve that honor for close friends, family, and Facebook followers. Just read Yelp for a minute.

I could hear Mama slowly and passive-aggressively spelling her name for the receptionist. It was a "Yes, I have an American name" tone that I knew well. People assumed Mama didn't speak English because of her face, or was stupid because of her clothing. Both meant she was often spoken down to, usually in extreme slow motion like she was four years old. She plopped down on the chair next to me, the jewels on her pants clacking against the pleather chairs.

"Well, that is not promising."

"What's the old saying? Don't judge a doctor by their receptionist?"

"They sure as hell judged this old bag by her..." She was interrupted by a nurse-looking person.

"Mrs. Johnson." Mama waved her arm in the air and nearly hit me in the face with the fringe. The woman looked confused.

"Yes, it's really me. I promise."

The nurse looked unamused as she led us back to a sprawling corner office, framed degrees lining every wall. From the pristine state of the desk, you could tell no one spent much time in there, which was probably a good sign—more time with patients, less time checking emails?

"So, Mrs. Johnson, you have certainly come a very long way to pay me a visit." A tall Black man who could have easily played an American Idris Elba strolled into the room and shut the door behind him. "Dr. Amovar. Pleasure to meet you."

Mama was clearly flustered by his presence. So was I, mostly because I had never not waited for a doctor. Also, he was hot.

"Um, well, please call me Loralynn. This is my daughter, Grace. And she's the one who has come a very long way, all the way from Boston." My mom said it proudly, like she hadn't just shamed me halfway back to Massachusetts in the car ten minutes ago.

I shook his hand and smiled suspiciously. He was much too cute and cheerful for this job. He pointed to the seats in front of his desk, and Mama and I scurried over, nearly tripping over each other. Neither of us knew quite what to say next. I imagined how different it would be had we all been sitting down around a dinner table at a five-star restaurant, and not a mahogany desk at a cancer hospital. We both watched intently as he typed, then looked at his screen, then typed some more, his face devoid of any indication of what he was looking at. He could have been reading his Twitter feed for all we knew.

"I don't suppose there's anything new to tell you, which may not be what you're hoping to hear."

"Can I hear the old stuff?" I interjected. "Some of us missed that part completely." I was tempted to glare at Mama, but then I remembered where I was and who I was with.

"Well, if it's all right with you, Mrs. Johnson."

"Loralynn. Please. If you're going to read my death sentence, you might as well use my first name. Elvis knew it was his time, and now so do I."

He didn't even discreetly raise an eyebrow. "Mrs.... I mean... Loralynn... Um." Clearly, none of his expensive degrees and years of experience had prepared him for the likes of Mama.

"What she meant to say is: yes." This time I didn't feel bad about glaring at her.

He gave me a grateful glance and leaned back into his chair, hands crossed in his lap like he was about to deliver some bad news.

"It appears that your mother's cancer has metastasized to her brain."

And there it was. Actual bad news. I'm pretty sure the "m" word is worse than the stupid "c" word. I was instantly inconsolable, as if someone had turned a switch on inside me from zero to a hundred.

Mama looked unfazed.

"You knew?" I managed two words through my sobbing—nothing short of a miracle.

"That's what they told me at my last scan, but I figured it would be better for you to hear it from a professional, and a handsome one, I might add." She winked at him. His eyes widened as the level of awkwardness shot through the vaulted ceiling.

"How long have you known this? Why didn't you tell me?" All the questions I had were coming out of me all at once like a tennis ball machine that couldn't stop firing.

I looked at Dr. Amovar. "Is this why she's forgetting things? Getting confused?"

"Yes, those are definitely early symptoms—"

"Of getting old!" Mama added.

"It's possible, Loralynn, but these are rapidly progressing tumors. The meds your doctor in El Paso gave you should be helping a bit, but without chemotherapy and radiotherapy, you will start to see symptoms like blackouts and confusion."

"So that's why you had all those pills that you didn't want me to see! Dammit, Mama!"

"Maybe I should give you two a few minutes alone?" Dr. Amovar wheeled back from his desk, almost hitting the large floor-to-ceiling window behind him.

"So what does this mean?" I asked him, ignoring Mama, who hadn't even started to answer my questions. I figured I'd persist with the person in the room who did.

"It means that what she has is treatable, but not curable."

I leaned back into my seat and glanced over at Mama, who was fiddling with her jacket fringe. I said the words over and over in my head—*treatable not curable. Treatable not curable.* That was a sentence, not an explanation. Surely there had to be more than that. I opened my mouth to speak, but Dr. Amovar jumped in.

"But the good news is that you're here now." Even he seemed to regret his choice of words. Good news? Really?

"I'm not sure how that's good, Doctor, all things considered."

"We're the best cancer center in Texas. She'll be in excellent hands. The treatment protocols and access to clinical trials are truly unmatched." He sounded like an actor reading off a teleprompter for an ad, which felt a little cold given the current circumstances.

Mama jumped up out of her seat. "No way I'm staying here!"

Dr. Amovar reached across the table with an outstretched hand. Mama retreated toward the door as the doctor looked at me for some assistance.

"Mrs. Johnson, I mean Loralynn. With treatment you could add months, maybe even years, to your life. Without it, well…"

Months? I thought. *We're really talking about months?*

"I will not stay one more minute in this hospital. My daughter and I are on our way to Graceland. I'm afraid I cannot accept your...hospital-ity. Or whatever this is, exactly."

Wrong word. So wrong.

"Mama. Please sit. Let's just hear the options. We're here anyway. If anything, we don't want you getting sick on the road."

"Grace Louise. I have enough pills to last me until I'm dead and buried. I will not be hooked up to some beeping machine wearing some godawful pastel gown that has no proper zipper or buttons with my wrinkly ass hanging out. Sorry, Doctor." She had temporarily forgotten where she was. "Now are you going to drive me out of here, or shall I leave you to fraternize with the enemy?!"

"I'm hardly the enemy, Mrs...."

"Hush now, Dr. Amovar. I appreciate your time and opinion. Now we have a long drive ahead of us."

Mama marched to the door, the jewels on her pants tapping together as she walked, cowboy boots clomping on the pristine marble floors. She flung open the door and walked out. I went to offer my thanks and apology to the doctor, but he was busy scribbling a few things down on paper for me.

"Here, take this with you." He handed me some predictably illegible prescriptions. "Try to get her to take these daily if you can. They'll help keep things...together, at least for a little while. Then follow up with me as soon as you get back. This is only treatable if she gets treatment."

"Thanks for this, though I'm not sure I'll be able to get her to take anything else."

"You certainly do have your hands full. But it's good that she still has that fiery spirit. When it starts to wane...that's when you should start to worry."

I grabbed the papers and stuffed them into my pocket, then realized I should probably take the time to fold them given their level of importance. "Thank you, Doctor. Can I ask you...how long?" I struggled to make the sounds of those two words.

His face softened from what I had to believe was a tinge of humanity. "It's really hard to say, since I didn't personally do a full exam. I'm only going on her scans that are now a few months old, and well..." He swallowed heavily. "...I'd say, if you have things to do, or say, now's the time."

More words no one ever wants to hear. More words worse than "cancer," all coming at me in a singular conversation.

"Like I said, it's a very good sign that she's got so much..." He couldn't think of the right word.

"...energy?" I offered him.

"Something like that." He smiled. "It's times like these where we all have to dig a little deeper." I felt like he knew this was a lot, and I was grateful for that.

"If you only knew how far I'm digging, Doctor."

"For fear of sounding overly philosophical: the truth will set you free."

He sounded overly philosophical.

"Yeah, if it doesn't kill you trying!" I replied.

He laughed.

"I can see *you* are going to be just fine. But patients like your mother…let's just say don't let her fool you. She needs you. More than she probably even knows." His ability to peg Mama in such a short time surprised me, but also made everything he had said more believable. I wasn't sure how to feel about that.

He walked out from behind his desk and extended his hand to me. I reached out, but instead of shaking it, he placed his other hand over mine, and just squeezed.

"I'm so sorry, Grace." The words I actually wanted to hear. Even though they couldn't do anything to salve what I'd just heard, they were enough to help me through the door and out of the room to catch up with Mama. The elevator dinged, and I picked up my pace to catch it, missing it by just a few seconds— enough for me to catch a glimpse of Mama, leaning in the back corner, weeping.

I don't think I've ever purposely taken the stairs for anything other than a fire drill at work, but the thought of Mama crumpled up in an elevator with no one there to catch her was worth the impromptu exercise. The bell rang just as I pushed through the heavy stairwell door, but as I ran to meet it, I realized that it was actually closing, not opening. And Mama was already halfway out the door, her wig bouncing as she marched toward the car. I chased after her, breathless.

"Mama!" I stopped to breathe, hoping she'd hear me and do the same. I was wrong.

"Let's go, Grace. I do not want to spend one more minute in this place." She glared at the lobby receptionist as she flung the glass doors open.

I grimaced, teeth clenched, as I ran after her through the parking lot and back to our car. For a moment, I felt a tiny sense of relief that she had remembered where we parked, but then again, we were also driving a huge purple boat.

"Grace, unlock these doors. I want to leave now." She rhythmically rolled her fingers on the top of the car, her fake nails making a tapping sound that echoed more loudly than I thought it should.

"Just wait. Wait, Mama. Why the rush? Let's talk about this for a minute."

She stood up straight, then leaned in and stared right at me, which I think is the universal sign for "you're about to get a talking-to."

"We have an entire long car ride to talk. I don't want to talk now. I want to get on the road. According to Dr. Amovar, I don't have time to talk."

"That's not exactly what he said, Mama. He's just doing his job." I thought I should be angrier than I was. But killing the messenger didn't seem like a worthwhile use for my energy. I'd spent it all racing down those stairs anyway.

"Don't you even try to get me to stay, Grace Louise. I can see it in your eyes, and I will tell you right now that if you do, I will scream."

"Oh no! Not the screaming!" I said sarcastically, emphasizing each syllable. She wasn't wrong. I *was* going to try to get her to stay. "How is that different from your actual everyday talking?" She did tend to screech out her words, particularly when she was excited, which was most of the time. The concept of "inside voice" was something Mama would never actually understand.

"Now is not the time to be a smartass. I'm serious." She started sobbing again, but this time didn't have the elevator bar to fall back on. She leaned over the hood of the car to help hold herself up.

I unlocked the car and walked toward her, but she had already lifted herself up, and plopped onto the passenger seat. She snorted loudly, then choked, coughing into a handkerchief she had pulled out of her bag.

"If I could make you do anything, you think you'd still be wearing this getup?" I slid into the driver's seat and started the car. "So what if we just wait a few months? Graceland isn't going anywhere. But you…" My voice crackled. I was not prepared to finish that sentence.

"I'm not going anywhere in the next five days, other than to Memphis with you," Mama said firmly, slamming her door, which startled both of us. "I've spent too long hooked up to machines and gagging down pills for one lifetime." She pointed to the road, as if that would somehow will the car to move, but now I was crying, the car idling in the parking lot as the air conditioning blasted at both of us, and the pointing just pissed me off more.

"You don't get another lifetime," I snapped. What was so difficult for her to understand?

"Then we best make good use out of the one we've got," she said definitively. She lifted her arm, but instead of pointing again, she placed it firmly on my leg, and squeezed in a way I'm pretty sure only moms know how to do.

I sighed back the rest of my tears and tapped her hand before flipping the car into reverse as I pondered her use of "we." True to form, Mama never said anything by accident.

"Fine. You don't want to stay here, I'm not going to force you. But you at least have to take these pills." I tossed the prescriptions at Mama. "Dr. Amovar told me it would help."

She grabbed the papers out of my hand.

"You thought Wyatt was Jeff. They look absolutely nothing alike. Can you at least accept the fact that it's not just you getting old? I mean, that's happening too, but..." I tried to make a joke.

"Until I'm not able to make my own damn decisions, I will make my own damn decisions!"

I started to say something, because Mama was never known for her sound decision making, but instead, I just raised my hands in the air. She attempted to flatten the crumpled papers, then folded them like I should have done in the first place, putting them carefully into her wallet for safekeeping.

I pressed my foot on the gas, and the tires screeched, which was way more satisfying than I had expected.

Of all the times I would have welcomed Mama's silent treatment, now was not one of them. Sure, the banter about Ronnie and Sally and the rest of the crew at the Palisades had already gotten monotonous, but at least I knew Mama was okay. Now all I could hear were my thoughts over the roar of the engine and syncopation of the wind hitting the flaps of the convertible top. Oh, how I'd rather be having a silly argument with her about Priscilla's wedding dress.

I looked over to see if Mama had fallen asleep, but she caught me checking on her and straightened up, as if snoozing would indicate some sign of weakness. Then she started screaming. Again.

"RIGHT TURN! RIGHT TURN!" Mama grabbed the handle above her window with her right hand, then braced herself with her left hand on the dashboard.

I spun the wheel as fast as I could onto the dirt road to nowhere, then pulled over.

"What the hell, Mama? Was that really necessary? I am never letting you plan another road trip again.

Oh wait, news flash. Never doing a road trip with you A-GAIN." And not because you're dying.

She pointed at the sign "THRILLVANIA HAUNTED HOUSE PARK" that was standing high above a herd of cattle grazing on the grass near its base. As I looked around, I could see a rooftop peeking up from behind a tall, barbed-wire fence.

"No. Nope. NO. Turning around right now." I peeked over my left shoulder and started to turn the car back on the road.

She grabbed my arm.

"PLEASE. GRACE."

"I know what I want to do! Scare the crap out of myself after I've just had the crap scared out of myself." I understood the difference between the two, but my anxiety saw them both as an opportunity to rear its debilitating head. "And since when are you such a super fan of haunted houses, Mama?"

"Since forever, Grace, don't you remember?"

I didn't, actually, until she reminded me.

Halloween was Mama's favorite holiday, but not just any sort of Halloween, but an Elvis-themed Halloween that involved intricate costumes, topped off with hair, makeup, and lots of blood. It was the spectacle of the year, and all the neighborhood kids would wait in line to make their way through the house. My dad would hide deep in our basement with his booze and ham radio. I'd throw a mask over my face, head out to trick-or-treat with my friends, and pretend not to live there when they ended up on my doorstep. It never worked, and even worse, everyone at school would tell me how cool Mama was for the first week of November, which was more of a curse than a compliment. And once she got wind of it, there was no hope for it to ever stop. In fact, she made it bigger in an effort to outdo herself from the year before.

It didn't help that I was pretty much always scared, and Halloween made it a zillion times worse. My anxiety spiked every time October hit, and I didn't feel settled until November when Mama had safely packed away the Halloween decorations in the attic for another year. I had it in my mind to just go up there one weekend when she was busy shining her Elvis statues and toss it all out. But I never quite had the guts to follow through with my kid-sized threats.

"I honestly cannot think of anything I would much rather not do than this. Especially since we just left—"

"This is exactly the thing I need to distract me."

I suddenly realized that the doctor had not just delivered bad news. He had delivered a never-ending source of guilt.

"And a haunted house? Since when did you hate haunted houses?"

"Since forever, Mama." I mimicked her in my best fifth-grader voice.

Her look was still blank. "Even *our* haunted house? All the kids loved it!"

"All the kids…but me. Don't you remember me standing outside in a costume with my face covered, pretending not to live there?" Still nothing. "You were too busy worrying about being the talk of the town."

"For a week! Then they all went back to…"

"Being assholes."

It's true that Mama was not the most popular person in our small town, unless you judge popularity by stares and whispers. She got plenty, no matter where we were going or what we were doing. She would smile and wave, as if they were talking *to* her and not about her. I never saw her lose her cool, but instead of just blending in, she would just do herself up a little bolder and bigger the next day.

But when Halloween rolled around, the haters became fangirls. "Well, now I know. You hate Halloween," Mama said decidedly.

Or maybe I just hated how people treated her every other month out of the year, and Halloween just emphasized their fickleness. Her uniqueness was only good when it pleased them.

Back then, I blamed her. How could she be such a glutton for their judgment, practically rewarding it with free full-size Hershey bars?

But now, I understood that it was just something that brought her joy, and especially now, I didn't want to be the one to take that from her. Besides, facing old fears head-on, whether I wanted to or not, had become part of my new existence. At least

I had a choice in this one, with a high potential for exceptionally good stories to tell.

"Grace, I'm not going to force you into a haunted house." Her tone was serious, as if she was actually trying to reassure herself, not me, of her decision.

I couldn't believe she actually heard me. Or perhaps I had never been so clear.

"Thanks, Mama. But, actually, I want to do it. Or at least I'm going to do it. Not sure 'want' is the right word."

"Are you sure there...scaredy-cat?" She laughed, rubbed her hands together with excitement, then hopped out of the car.

"I'm so glad my childhood fear is so entertaining for you," I replied, trying not to change my mind out of spite. "I am the one with the car keys, just in case you might have forgotten that." I got out and slammed the door, walking around the front of the car to meet her. Oddly, I felt tears welling up, but it was too late to blink them away.

Mama reached for my hand and squeezed hard, her nails unintentionally digging into me. I squeezed back and didn't let go.

"There. You can hold on to me the entire time."

"Should I be worried that my wingman is a soon-to-be seventy-year-old woman with so much mascara on she can barely see out of her eyeballs?"

She tugged my arm, and I nearly fell into her, avoiding a huge cow pie.

I shrieked, then looked down and started laughing.

"That's some scary shit!" I blurted. Mama started laughing too, which made me feel like I think you're supposed to feel at a haunted house in the middle of Texas at noon: ridiculous.

We kept walking down the road, wondering if we had somehow missed the parking lot, and then realized we hadn't because it was behind a locked gate. Mama tried to enter a code on the box, as if she had some sort of telepathic powers.

"Of course it's closed. No haunted house worth going to would be open during the day!" She held on to the gate and pushed her face up to it like a kid peeking into a toy store window, longing for everything they couldn't have. "It doesn't look so scary in the light, now does it, Grace?"

I stood next to her and looked around the grounds through the chain-link fence topped with what looked like homemade barbed wire, trying to figure out if they were actually that worn down or if the damage was part of the experience. The skeleton hanging out of the hearse window was held together with silver duct tape that glistened in the bright sun, and I could see how in the dark it might look foreboding, especially with what I imagine would be real people, drenched in blood, waving at us as we walked by. But right now, seeing it all right in front of me for what it actually was—a bunch of old, dilapidated houses and an old broken-down car, I felt liberated, like the mask had been pulled off the villain in *Scooby-Doo* to reveal their little, harmless next-door neighbor.

"I suppose we've had enough scary things today?" She pulled the prescriptions out of her wallet.

I reached over to feel her forehead. "Are you okay? What is in the pills you're taking?" She batted my hand away.

"Shall we find ourselves a drugstore?" she said, marching back toward the car.

With pursed lips, I nodded at her, wondering if she had known all along that we'd never actually get to go in, but also feeling grateful for this unexpected glimpse of normalcy that I had only imagined as a fantasy: just a regular mother and her adult daughter, enjoying each other's company, trying to get the crap scared out of them at a haunted house.

GRACE: Hey. We're about to leave for Louisiana.

ASHA: That was fast.

GRACE: Was it, though? Feels like forever.

ASHA: I know you're deeply concerned about Puddles. He is fine. Also, the kids have renamed him "Harry." As in "Harry Potter." ⚡

GRACE: It is pretty magical that he's still alive, so that's fitting.

ASHA: You doing okay? I guess I should have led with that.

GRACE: Well, I just left the hospital.

ASHA: Are you okay?!

GRACE: Eh, I'm fine. It's Mama I'm worried about.

ASHA: Killing your mother is not an option, Grace. LOL. (Seriously, I'm totally kidding.)

GRACE: 😄 That might be easier given the circumstances. (I'm kidding too. Mostly.) This trip has suddenly taken a sort of bucket list turn. ☹

ASHA: Oh no. Can you talk? Call me when you can. We've got things under control here at home. 💟 I still need updates on this special friend of yours.

GRACE: Okay, okay. I promise.

ASHA: Does he like cats? 😊

GRACE: BYE, ASHA.

Chapter 9

I can't remember the last time I was in LOSE-I-ANA." Mama rolled down her window and stuck her head out like a golden retriever puppy, then retreated quickly when her wig started to lift off like a launching rocket.

"Well, first of all, Mama, it's 'LOU-I-SI-A-NA.' Five syllables. And I can't remember either."

"You don't think I know how to say the state that you're middle-named after?"

I shot her a glare. "Are you freaking kidding me?" I'm not sure how I went all these years not knowing I was named after the state.

"You have your daddy to blame for that." She rolled her eyes.

"Um, how is it that you were not involved in the naming of your firstborn child?"

"I wanted 'Grace.' So I just gave him the middle

name to get him off my back. I had to pick my battles."

"I can see not wanting to fight over a pizza topping. Maybe. But my name?!" My voice squeaked. It always did that when I wanted to yell but tried to contain myself. I thought I was named after some great-aunt. At least, I swear that was what they'd told me.

"I was half lucid, Grace." Mama's voice got quiet, which was way worse than it getting loud. Her words were pointed and enunciated. "They hopped me up on drugs to get you out of me, and I could barely say my own name let alone think about yours. And why do you care anyway? It's your middle name. I'm the only one who says it."

She had a point.

"Just be glad he wasn't super toasted. You could have been named El Paso," she joked.

I knew just as well as she did that he was probably more wasted than she was that day. "You know he would never have named me El Paso." And then it hit me.

"Is this why we're driving through this godawful state?"

"No! I mean, not exactly. We're here to see the Shreveport Municipal Auditorium." She paused as if that would somehow ring a bell in my head, which it didn't. "Elvis's first concert! Where 'Elvis has left the building!' became a thing. There's a statue and everything."

That was a pretty big deal. I had to give her that.

"And the cemetery is practically right around the corner," she continued nervously.

I let out a deep sigh, the air rushing out of my lungs so forcefully, the windshield got a bit foggy.

After Mama begged me to forgive Daddy, I never saw him again. But neither did she, because she reluctantly told him to leave, upon the counsel of her church pastor. And so, with no other family nearby, his brother came out and packed him up, driving him from El Paso to Shreveport. A few friends couldn't believe what she was doing, kicking out a dying man from the place he had called home for most of his life. Neither of us felt obligated to explain the circumstances. Revealing that Daddy had been an abusive asshole wasn't anything we wanted to get into, so we made up something about insurance and medical care and tried to avoid anyone who looked like they would ask too many questions.

Daddy's brother filled the car with everything they could fit. Not just medical supplies. He took the Civil War gun that had hung over our mantel for my entire childhood, the spoon rack Daddy made in high school in his wood shop class. Daddy even had his brother send out a towing company to take the '57 Chevy that had been sitting in our garage, awaiting a little TLC from him for as long as we lived in that house, the seats and trunk filled with empty wine bottles.

Daddy died two weeks later, buried by his Louisiana family in Shreveport. There were no goodbyes for either of us. Just a call from his brother and a death certificate in the mail.

Mama helped organize a memorial service for him in El Paso, mostly for his friends and old army buddies who couldn't wait to espouse his greatness in front of a mourning congregation. Neither of us did anything but watch the trail of men line up at the microphone to share their war stories, and bar stories, of a Daddy we never really knew. Or in some cases, knew all too well.

I sat and wept, sad that the reconciliation I dreamed up in my head would never be possible. It played out like a scene from a fairy tale. He would see me, so successful and happy in my life, and *boom!* Epiphany would strike him like a grenade, and he would apologize for everything that he'd ever done and do his best to make up for lost time. The day he died, he took that fantasy with him.

This trip was suddenly taking a morbid turn. First the hospital in Dallas, then the haunted house. And now the stop at my father's grave. This was not exactly what I signed up for.

My phone buzzed with a text message, which Siri automatically read out loud. I quickly turned the volume way down so Mama couldn't hear.

You have a message from Wyatt. "Hey, it's Wyatt. Just checking in. God, I sound like a parent. Next time I'm just going to call."

I giggled at the conversation he was having with himself and made a mental note to give him a hard time about it when I had a chance to text back.

"We don't need to stay long," Mama said. She handed me the directions, and indeed, the auditorium was on Elvis Presley Boulevard, only two miles from the cemetery.

I nearly missed the famous music hall, expecting the grandeur that seems to be implied by having a famous person's name in front of the word "boulevard." The park along what looked like a one-lane street was full of people lying under piles of blankets on benches, the storefronts only one street over covered in graffiti with wooden boards over the windows. Even Mama didn't want to get out of the car.

"Here, Grace, just pull up and you can take a photo of me pointing at the Elvis statue." The tall brick building was beautiful and looked like what one might find Googling "concert hall," but it felt as though someone had accidentally dropped it out of their pocket into the wrong neighborhood. The street butted right up to the several stairways leading into the building, and there wasn't a parking lot in sight. I slowed the car to a stop, then grabbed my phone, Mama leaning as close to the statue as she could get without having to get out, then relenting by opening her door to get a better shot. A man from the park with a suit and no shoes started walking toward us, and Mama quickly hopped back in.

"Hit it, Grace. Go!" she yelled, holding on to the side of the door as I jetted back down the other side of the boulevard and back onto the main road, both of us laughing and trying to catch our breath.

We both went silent as we turned into the cemetery, the old metal sign forming an arch over the entranceway. To our left was a small modern building with a large map on the outside. I pulled over and stepped out, peeking inside to see a large television hanging on the wall, and restrooms, which made me shake the door handle. No such luck.

As I scanned the first names and death years, the map had no shortage of Johnsons. "Found him. It's plot K-727."

I snapped a photo on my phone, then got back in the car, magnifying the screen to find his plot, which was farther back into the cemetery property.

We followed the main drive around, weaving through huge, willowy trees that provided shade over sections, all of which looked so haphazard with large statues and small headstones, some with fake flowers, others with flags. I caught a glimpse of some of the dates and wondered how Daddy could have ended up here with folks buried back in the 1800s.

I couldn't remember the last time I had been in a cemetery. During college, we used to run through one close to the BU campus, but I didn't actually know anyone buried there, so it didn't feel as morbid. Thinking about it now, it was kind of morbid.

I let Mama navigate, which meant we had to loop

around to find parking in the form of a grassy spot. The scent of freshly cut grass swirled past us, mixing with the newly dug soil that smelled earthy and sad.

Mama went first, walking up row K, counting numbers as we passed each stone. I followed slowly behind her, reading the names, then the years. I caught myself walking a little bit more tenderly on the grass, as if I would somehow awaken them with my heavy footsteps.

The sheer number of graves was overwhelming. We were surrounded by what would have been crowds of people, peacefully slumbering six feet under. It was hard not to wonder what they looked like, or how they died, particularly, at least for me, those folks who had lived such short lives. I'd never so instantaneously received a gift of perspective and gratitude than walking down a grassy row of gravesites. I suddenly felt so small, my personal woes like paper cuts to the real wounds of loss that had been experienced here.

Mama stopped abruptly. I nearly walked right into her as she stood, hands on her hips, in front of what appeared to be my father's grave. She started dusting off the modest stone, then dropped to her knees to pull the weeds that only a weed whacker could reach. And based on their size, they were not whacked often.

Loving son of Dinah, the stone read. Dinah? I never even knew my grandmother's name. That's how close we all were.

At first, I thought all Mama's sniffling was allergies, but when she looked up at me, her eyes red and glassy, I knew I was wrong.

"I should have been there to say goodbye."

"Would that have made any difference?"

"Maybe not to him. But for me."

"You did the right thing, Mama." Now I know it was the hard thing. Or at least I imagined that it was. Back then it seemed so obvious that Daddy needed to go. He had deserved to be kicked out a long time before that whole Fourth of July backyard barbeque incident, and maybe if he had, she would never have had to tell him to leave on his deathbed. Second-guessing what-ifs was a tough game to play, though, and I stopped myself from going there many times.

"Then why did it hurt so much?" I had never heard Mama talk about her sadness after sending Daddy away. I suppose it was naïve to think that even with the way he treated her *and* me, she wouldn't feel some sort of pain for making him leave.

"I know you loved him. At least enough to marry him. And there must have been good times." I believed those words, even though what he had done to me had erased any good memories I might have had, and I was left to question whether he ever loved me. And if *we* ever had good times. But with Mama, I knew it was different.

"He loved you too, Grace. I know it didn't look like that, but he was so happy when you were born. So proud of his beautiful daughter."

"But what he said, the things he did...that didn't feel like love."

"Your daddy did the best he could. He was so sick with all that alcohol..." Her voice trailed off. Was I just supposed to give him a pass because he was a pathetic alcoholic? "We were all in so much pain."

"But I was the kid. It wasn't my job to think about his pain. Or yours." I was barely able to say those words out loud. I had worked for so long—in therapy and on my own—to understand the why of all of this. I knew he was sick, that Mama was just trying to survive. But I couldn't ever figure out why it still hurt so much until this very moment, when I imagined me as a little girl, dancing around my father's crazy mood swings and violent outbursts, trying so hard to be perfect. I had been taught that I was responsible for the feelings of everyone around me. The memories began to swirl, of me trying so hard to make him happy with my good grades. And to make Mama notice me, singing Elvis songs and doing his signature pelvis move and lip quiver, which was cute when I was little, but then flipped to her thinking I was making fun of her when I was older.

By the time I hit middle school, I figured if Elvis wasn't going to work for me, then he was my enemy.

Oh, how hard I had tried, and it was never enough. I was never enough for them.

My chest started to tighten, and I knew what was coming. I ran away from the grave, down Row K, and back to the car, my feet pounding beneath me, unafraid of who I might accidentally awaken. Mama yelled for me, but I kept running. A safe distance away, I slowed to a walk.

Breathe in four, hold seven, out eight—trees, grass, acorns, flowers…

I moaned, and, predictably, the apologies started flowing.

I'm sorry. I'm so sorry. I repeated myself over and over. *It wasn't my fault. I didn't mean it…* I had never gotten to those words before, usually reassured by Jeff's stoicism, Asha's calming voice, or the bottle of Xanax rolling around in my bag.

No! Please don't. I held my thigh, and the memories of the night when I said those same exact words thundered through my brain. I had been practicing ballet near the shelves holding his military medals and accidentally kicked too high. The shelf came crashing down, the glass box of medals shattered, and before I could explain, he was chasing me with a wooden dowel. I could hear my eight-year-old self screaming how sorry I was at him, but he wouldn't listen, he was hitting me right across my thigh as I begged him, "No! Please don't!" My leg bruised instantly.

My breath slowed as I put the pieces together, finally making some sense out of what I had always thought were just nonsensical ramblings.

Mama finally caught up to me, hobbling on the uneven grass in her heeled boots that were not made for walking, at least in nature. She tried to offer me a wadded ball of tissues, but I pushed them away. She persisted, trying herself to wipe my face as if I were a toddler again. "Why didn't we ever leave?" I stuttered.

Her eyes apologized in a way words could not. I had never remembered seeing her face so pale, and I wasn't sure if she was about to cry or throw up. "Oh, Grace, I was terrified."

I had never heard Mama describe what it was like for her in our home so honestly, and even though it was terribly sad, her truth was comforting.

"I wanted you to have it all—the school, the lessons—all of it. And, well, I had absolutely nothing. You were so strong. I just hoped that someday, after you made a beautiful life for yourself, you would forgive me, because as bad as it was with your daddy, it would have been way worse for us alone." She had relaxed her jaw a bit, and it felt like she was speaking her truth.

"You don't know that, Mama." I didn't have the will for sarcasm, and the sadness that had been encased in anger took over.

"Oh, I do. You don't think I considered leaving every single day?" It sounded like we had both lost the will to battle each other in our old ways.

"How would I know?" I asked her.

Mama looked confused. "How could I not know why you left and never came back?"

All this time I believed that Mama was so wrapped

up in her own world of Elvis figurines and wild wigs that I didn't once imagine anything she did was strategic. I suppose I never thought of the alternative, and why would I? I was terrified too, and the only thing I could focus on was leaving. For the first time in my whole life, I felt seen by my mother, and I didn't know what to do with that.

"He was so funny, Grace—like you! Strong and handsome. We had so many good times. And then it just…changed."

But it hadn't *just* changed. He eroded slowly, over time. I remembered the Daddy she described, in fewer and fewer fleeting moments. Sneaking off for a Saturday breakfast at McDonald's that Mama forbade. Snuggling up between them in bed after a sleep-walking episode. I stretched to think of others, but drew a blank, only able to access the drunken tirades.

"It feels like you chose him over me." I was taken aback by my own truth-telling. So was she, it seemed, and she reached over and pulled me toward her, hugging me tightly.

She didn't lift her head to speak, and with her head in my chest, it felt like she was talking directly to my heart, which probably needed to hear what she had to say the most.

"Love doesn't work like that, darlin'. I love you so much. But even though your daddy's life was a tragedy, I loved him too. Because he gave me your brother. And you." She looked up at me, her makeup now streaked from her own tears.

I had always been too deep into my own pain to think about what it must have been like for Mama. No chance to say goodbye to the man that she had once loved. The father to her children. He was so easy for me to hate, but for her, it wasn't as clear.

"It's over now, Mama. It's all over." I kissed her forehead. She wiped her eyes, which just spread the mascara over more surface area on her face.

She cupped my chin in her hand and spoke with intention. "I understand if it's not. I really do."

I grabbed her hand from under my chin. "I think it's time, don't you?" It felt like I was telling myself this as much as I was telling Mama.

Her voice was shaky and soft as she sang "I'll Remember You," an Elvis song I hadn't heard in a while. This time I didn't mind it so much. Actually, I kind of liked it.

GRACE: So, I'm sitting in a cemetery.

ASHA: What the hell is going on down there, Grace?

GRACE: If I knew, I swear I would tell you.

ASHA: Loralynn sure has a weird sense of fun.

GRACE: This was after she tried to take me to a haunted house.

ASHA: Well, at least you know the trip can only get better from here?

GRACE: That's what I thought when we left the hospital.

ASHA:　Is she all right?

GRACE:　Define "all right," but yeah, it's fine.

ASHA:　And you? How are you?

GRACE:　I'm doing pretty well, all things considered.

ASHA:　Okay, well, if you need me to come down there and stage an intervention, let me know.

GRACE:　I might take you up on that just to watch. ☺

ASHA:　Don't tempt me, Grace. It would be like a vacation for me.

GRACE:　🫶

I started to text Wyatt back. *Hey, everything's fine…* Delete. I wasn't about to start in with that again, so instead I sent *Thanks Dad!* ☺ and figured that might help deflect from me having to tell the truth, at least right now, which was that actually nothing was fine. Nothing at all. This time, I was just going to allow myself to sit with that feeling.

Even though Daddy grew up in Shreveport, we spent very little time there. His relatives had always made the trek to El Paso to see us and never the other way around. And because of that, we rarely saw his mama, or really anyone but his brother, who was willing to make the long drive out to see his drinking buddy.

If Texas air was thick, then the Louisiana air felt like walking through wet cement, making your limbs and lungs get so heavy you could barely move. Even though the temperature was milder now, the humidity lingered, which seemed unfair. I'd grown so accustomed to an actual crisp fall in Boston, humidity without the hot weather felt like being shortchanged.

"It's those swamplands that get you," Mama used to say, which never quite made much sense to me until I got older and understood the landscape. "That's why there are so many dang snakes!" she would add, and I suddenly lost all motivation to visit.

Living in Texas for so many years did not stop Daddy from waving his gold-and-purple LSU flag proudly during college football season, which was quite a risky move considering we were in Longhorn country, not to mention a concealed carry state. I grew up hating it all because sports meant an invitation for Daddy to sit in his knockoff La-Z-Boy and drink copious amounts of alcohol.

I did remember the Red River, which snaked through Shreveport like a brown serpent, lined up and down with flashy casinos and riverboats. The bright lights around the big signs distracted me from the dirty fish smell of the dark water, the opaque waves crashing up against the docked boats as we drove by.

Not much had changed since then, except now I was old enough to venture into one of the many casinos that made Shreveport a popular destination for so many Texans. But the accountant in me would never indulge my curiosity, so instead, we zipped by as Mama snapped photos through the window, and I tried to find my bearings after a few days off kilter.

I'd forgotten what it was like to be around Mama. It always felt like being forced to ride a mechanical bull; it looks fun to bystanders, but for the person on top, it's just about holding on for dear life as long as possible.

My phone dinged, and I grabbed it to listen to the text, hoping it wouldn't be anything Mama shouldn't hear.

This is Wyatt's ghost texting to say that he has died of embarrassment and will make any further communication through actual phone calls.

I grabbed my phone to reply using voice-to-text, when Mama yelled.

"Oh stop. Grace! STOP. We have to stop."

"I've heard that before, Mama."

"Hey, you promised to try new things." I was never going to hear the end of that. But she was right, though I was feeling like I had just gotten the crap beaten out of me, my eyeballs so puffy from crying that I could barely see out of them. I needed some time to sit in silence and let everything that had been said between us reverberate in my head. No such luck.

"What part of me says that I would want to pay money to someone I don't really know to tell me what to do with my life?" I looked at the flashing

"PSYCHIC" sign, which should have come with a seizure warning.

"Isn't that exactly what that therapist you see does?"

"Touché, Mama." *And you know what she told me?* I had gotten a welcome respite from analyzing that whole shitty night with Jeff and the therapist, but now wasn't the time to go into it with Mama. There had been enough vulnerability for one day.

I made a hard right turn into the parking lot, tires screeching. Mama slid into her door and let out a fake yelp. I would never admit this to Mama, but I have always been tempted to stop in one of these places, mostly so I could authoritatively debunk them once and for all. I'd pass Madame Sue-Ellen's Shop of Spells and Mystical Knowledge every day on my walk to school, the crystal ball lamppost flickering in a Morse code rhythm, people going in and out like she was giving away free hambones with every reading, wondering how they could believe any fortune teller with the name "Sue-Ellen." But I never had the guts or the gumption to spend my spare cash on research.

Mama, on the other hand, worshipped at the church of all things mystical, with drawers and cabinets full of DVDs promising everything from a slimmer waist to a million dollars, both of which seemed fleeting. This was just a regular old Sunday morning service for her, which I suppose was why she decided to touch up her makeup before leaving the car.

"Next on our *Sixth Sense* Road Trip Tour…"

Mama didn't get it.

"I SEE DEAD PEOPLE. Don't you remember that movie? Bruce Willis. The little kid." I knew his name—Haley Joel Osment—but figured that would just complicate matters.

Mama's face looked blank.

"We've been to a hospital, a haunted house, a cemetery, and now…" I pointed to the house in front of us.

"Well, we didn't actually go into the haunted house. So…"

She missed the point entirely.

"Oh, forget it." At least I knew Asha would find it funny.

Mama was too busy fixing her makeup, which we had left in tissues at the cemetery trash can.

"If Elvis makes an appearance, he won't actually be able to see you, Mama." I grabbed the lipstick to give myself a little much-needed color. I looked as dead as the spirit she wished we'd be invoking.

"Why would Elvis make an appearance out here in Louisiana?" she said. "He would not."

Finally, she had found some sense.

"You'll just have to wait until we get to Memphis for that."

On second thought…

I pushed open a screen door that was barely a screen door anymore, half of it covered in rips and holes, which rendered it completely useless as anything other than a noisemaker. It slapped back behind me as we creaked toward what we assumed was the front desk. Every single inch of the small shack was covered in glass cases full of various oddities—crystals, rocks, statuettes of angels and devils—all carefully organized by color and size.

DING!

I looked up from examining the impressive collection of rose quartz to see Mama standing in front of a glass case with a cash register, ringing a small silver bell. She reached for it again, but I lunged over and grabbed her hand before she could make contact.

"Welcome! I'll be right with you!" a low, gruff voice called out from the beaded curtains behind the counter, and then a face peeked through, followed by the rest of a tall, elderly man in head-to-toe leather. The only thing missing from his ensemble was his horse and saddle.

"What can I do fer you ladies?"

"We fancy ourselves a reading, sir," said Mama. She had what you might call "Contact Southern," which is sort of like a contact high, but not nearly as fun. Whenever she was around anyone with a little bit of twang, she turned hers up to level eleven.

"It'll be fifty bucks for the two of ya together. Which I recommend. Lots more you can see and hear with a two-fer."

"Lots more dollar signs," I whispered to Mama under my breath.

"Sold!" Mama exclaimed. "What do you need to know to get started?"

He chuckled. "It ain't me who's gonna be doin' the readin'. Unless you want to know what size tractor you'd best fit on."

The man laughed at his own joke, as if he were delivering it for the first time. Mama counted her money on the counter.

"Just come around here and make yourselves comfortable." He pointed to the room behind the beaded curtain that he had just come from. "Turn off all your cell phones and other electronic devices. She'll be with you in a jiffy."

"What are we on, an airplane?" I whispered to Mama, who had immediately complied with his request. I was a bit more skeptical.

"The waves will interfere with the spirits," she replied matter-of-factly.

"Well, I'm risking it with airplane mode." Mama growled at me through her eyes. I guess it wasn't like my phone was blowing up with anything but text updates from Asha, so I powered it off and tossed it into my bag.

We found seats at a table behind the beaded curtain and sat next to each other as the whir of the large window fan blew hot air around the small space. The smell of bacon wafting through the room was confusing, but I quickly considered the alternatives. Bacon was just fine.

Apparently in Louisiana, a jiffy is exactly thirteen

minutes, and I know this because there was nothing in the room to do but stare at the clock on the wall as we waited. And waited.

"Mama, this is nuts. There's no one here." I was still whispering. "It's not like we're at the doctor's office with the flu, and we're being forced to sit for as long as it takes for someone to take our temperature." I pushed my seat back to stand up.

"Helllllloooooooooo!" I was interrupted by a tiny woman who looked not a day under eighty, her pink-hued gray hair wrapped in tiny, spongy curlers, all neatly tucked under a clear shower cap. She was wrapped up in a bathrobe that was just a shade darker than her hair, with "*Arabella*" embroidered on the front in Comic Sans. Where was the turban? The velvet robes?

"Marshall said there were two fine young ladies here to see me, and why golly, he was right!" She sat down in front of us at the table. "And I know you must be wondering where my turban and velvet robes are..."

My eyebrows went up.

"We're actually not supposed to open for another thirty minutes, but Marshall always forgets to turn the sign around. So here I am in all my morning glory for you two nice ladies to see."

Considering it was nearly dinnertime, I was a little worried that she thought it was morning, but also a little jealous she was still wearing a robe so late in the day.

"So what brings you to Madame Arabella?" Her voice deepened dramatically, as if she had taken a "What a psychic should sound like" webinar.

"Isn't that what you tell us?" I replied. Mama's eyes got wide, as if I had just spoken back to the queen of England.

Arabella grabbed my hand and peeked at my palm, then gently laid it facedown on the table. "Now what are you in a rush for? From what I can tell, you have got a long way to get to where you're going."

I could have read that in a fortune cookie. I was not impressed.

"You first," she said to Mama. "Your right hand, please."

Mama enthusiastically opened her palm toward her. Arabella traced the lines with her small, wrinkled pointer finger, taking a moment every few seconds to close her eyes and mumble something that I couldn't quite figure out.

"Mmhmm. Yes."

From the look on Mama's face, I could tell she was using all remaining willpower to not ask a million questions. Instead, she chattered.

"I'm Loralynn and this is my daughter, Grace, and we're..."

"Mama, stop. The waves, remember?" I said out of the side of my mouth. Mama clamped her lips shut and used her other hand to make a pretend zipping-shut motion.

"Sorry," she whispered, but Arabella was too

busy looking at Mama's hand to look up and ac-knowledge her.

"You are finally starting to listen to the many things being told to you. It is not easy to hear, but it is necessary."

Mama held on to every single word she was saying like a congregant at church listening to the Sunday sermon, even though the statements Arabella was making were just general proclamations. And though I wouldn't argue with anything she was saying, I could have told her that and saved us fifty dollars.

"Your life line is nearing a fork. The choices you make could be life altering."

Okay, so maybe it was a little specific to Mama.

"Now is not the time to be selfish. Or . . . difficult."

I looked at Mama knowingly, but she was too busy watching Madame Arabella, who had just folded up Mama's hand and squeezed it, then placed it on the table to rest. Mama looked disappointed.

"You have already made peace with the spirit world. The work you need to do is here." She gestured gracefully to Mama's heart, then placed her hand back on the table, picking up mine in one motion. As she had done with Mama's, she started inspecting my palm for a few seconds. Mama started to retract her own hand off the table when Arabella grabbed it and flipped it over next to my hand, which was now starting to sweat. I could see my palms getting slick.

"Look how similar these lines are. And you . . ." she

said, pointing to me. "I rarely see a line fork so early in a person so young."

"Is that a bad thing?" I asked, now slightly regretting my choice to stop here, even though the legitimacy of all of this was highly questionable. At least with a fortune cookie I got a freaking cookie.

Arabella looked up at me. It felt like she was searching around in my brain for secrets. I jumped, my body completely covered in goose bumps.

"You have lived a long life already. It has been exhausting for you. But you don't need to keep living that way."

She brought our hands together, clasping them with hers.

"Very interesting. You *both* are so afraid. Of what?"

Well, haunted houses for one. I wanted to see what she would make of that, but decided I didn't want to go there with someone I had just met a few minutes ago.

"Look at each other," she instructed.

Mama mumbled something, then turned toward me. I tried to do what Arabella had done with me, staring deep beyond the irises of my eyes, but Mama kept blinking rapidly, then looking away, pulling her hand from our fist of three.

"For glory be, how can you stare for that long? My eyes will clear dry right out," Mama complained.

"She didn't say 'stare,' Mama. Just 'look.'"

Her blinking slowed to a fairly normal pace, and I focused on the darkness of her eyes, the whites around her irises still slightly pink and streaky. They looked heavy, the corners of her beautiful almond eyes lower than I remembered, no bright eye shadow, heavy eyeliner, or layers of mascara to hide them. I stood, grabbing the table to balance myself.

"What's wrong, darlin'?" Mama asked. She looked away, dabbing her face with her fingers to see if there was something on it that might have startled me.

"I just saw…" I couldn't quite capture all the words that were swirling around in my brain. *Myself. I saw myself.* As terrified as Mama had been in her life, I'd been walking around afraid in mine. Not terrified of the father who had caused me pain or the mother who decided to keep us with him. Or even the husband whom I had chosen not as a lover, but as a safety net. I was scared of the feelings—the anger, the sadness, the disappointment.

"Sit down, child." Arabella gestured to the chair behind me. I lowered myself into it, then slid myself back into the table, still holding on to it for stability. "Now, close your eyes," she told us. She reached under the table and came up with a tiny bottle, which she opened, sniffed, and then tipped over, placing exactly one drop in my hand. She asked for Mama's hand as well.

"Rub!" she commanded.

We both clapped our palms and raced them back and forth against each other, the smell of peppermint and eucalyptus wafting into my nostrils and up through my sinuses. Arabella held my hands together, palms touching, then Mama's, breathing deeply for a few rounds until she let them fall. Then she dashed out of the room, the beads snapping as they hit each other on her way out. Mama sat at the table, her eyes closed with deep, slow breaths.

"Is the reading over?" Mama asked, sniffing her hands like a junkie. She peeked back into the doorway to see if another customer had arrived.

Arabella peeked back through the beads. "I have seen enough. The real question is: what did you see?"

Mama looked puzzled. "Well, you said something about 'selfish' and 'choices' and…"

"Sh, sh." Arabella held her hand up again. "That is for you to think about inside your head." She tapped the side of her own head for emphasis. "Meet me at the front desk!"

Mama scrambled through the doorway like a preschooler trying to get to the front of the line. I followed, not as desperate. We waited a few minutes for Arabella to emerge, seven minutes to be exact.

"Here you are." She handed me two sealed white envelopes, our names written on them in all caps.

We are not responsible or liable for any actions taken after the reading.—Arabella the Optimist was scrawled at the bottom.

"I'm handing these to you, because I don't want them to be opened until you get to your final destination." She shot my mom a saccharine smile.

"How do you know that this isn't our final destination?" Mama asked flippantly.

"Oh, darling, you don't need to be a psychic to know this is no one's final destination. Unless it's six feet under."

"Fair enough!" Mama exclaimed, straightening her wig, then walking right out the door.

I turned to follow her when Arabella tapped me on the back, clearing her throat.

"There's nothing to be afraid of, child. You've been carrying around so much, all alone. It's okay to let it out, so you have room to let someone in."

In all my years of reading books and getting therapy, no one had ever summed things up for me so succinctly.

She placed a little bag in my hand, and when I peeked inside, there was a small rock and tiny piece of paper. It begged for a Roshambo joke, but I was too impressed and slightly unnerved by her insight to chance pissing her off. So I held on to it, waiting for an explanation or some direction.

"My compliments. No charge."

I nodded.

"You're a tough one, Grace. But so is your mama. She can hear what you have to say." She walked slowly back behind the desk and through the beaded door. "And that boy. He likes you. Always has." She peeked through the beads. "The new one. Not the old one." My eyes widened.

"I'm melting!" Mama yelled in her Wicked Witch of the West voice, and I rushed out the screen door, which slammed behind me.

"I'm coming, I'm coming," I mumbled.

"What took you so long?" she asked. "We've got to get to Mississippi before dark."

"Oh, nothing." I patted the stone in my pocket.

"Well, then I guess we got our money's worth." She patted my leg. "See, it wasn't that bad, now was it. I only wish we could have had some sort of epiphany, don't you?"

I didn't want to disappoint Mama by telling her that I actually did have one, though I'm not sure I'd describe how I felt with Madame Arabella as an epiphany exactly. But her insights gave me a bit of clarity about the choices I had made and why I had been making them. Now I just needed to figure out what to do next.

GRACE: Do you believe in stones and all that shit?

ASHA: Like... kidney stones?

GRACE: 😆 No, like crystals. Quartz. That stuff.

ASHA: I haven't thought too much about it, but I'm totally loving this new Grace.

GRACE: I didn't say *I* believed in them. Yet.

ASHA: Well, it can't hurt, I guess. That is unless the rocks are telling you to do things. Then we have a problem.

GRACE: The rocks are not speaking to me. The psychic did that.

ASHA: 😲

GRACE: It was not exactly what I expected, but I guess I didn't really know what to expect.

ASHA: So many exciting developments. Next time, ask a friend to come with you!

GRACE: But then who will watch my cat?

ASHA: 😳

GRACE: 😍

Chapter 10

Oh, shit." Those are the only two appropriate words for when you hear the rhythmic clunking sound of your wheel's rim hitting the pavement. Mama hopped out of her door as I pulled to a stop on the side of the road.

"It's a flat tire, Grace!" she yelled from the back of the car.

"Dammit!" This couldn't have happened an hour ago while we were still in Shreveport and not miles from civilization? The only human we'd seen in the last two hours was a rest stop attendant who looked half comatose.

Mama got back in the car and reached down into her gigantic bag, pulled out her wallet, and handed me a wrinkled-up paper card that looked like it hadn't seen the light of day since she got her driver's license.

"Here, use my AAA card. I always knew it would come in handy someday."

I called the number on the back and an extremely unenthused woman answered. She sounded like she was speaking into a bucket, so much so that I spent the entire conversation going, "I'm sorry, what? I can't hear you" to everything she said. By the time I could actually hear what she was saying, I'm pretty sure a person could have arrived and changed our tire.

"Yes, looks like mile marker ninety-seven, by the large billboard for…Jesus?" I looked up at the huge sign above us. It was an advertisement for the Lord himself, as if he needed any promotion down here. She told me her guy was fairly close by, so it shouldn't take too long, but considering how long a "jiffy" took with Madame Arabella, I didn't get my hopes up. I did thank her anyway, considering she was the messenger to our own savior, so it seemed like a strategic move on my part to be nice.

"How long did they say, darling?"

"'*They*' didn't give me a time." I was frustrated at the woman, not Mama, but it seemed like the other way around. I felt bad that I had been so snippy. "I didn't mean it like that, Mama. It's just…" Annoying.

I had never done well with stuff like this, and while I know that no one should be expected to take flat tires on seemingly abandoned highways in Louisiana in stride, I probably had a more difficult time than most. Not even a matter of "doing my best," I always ensured that things went according to plan. And when things took a detour, it felt like everything was crumbling beneath me, my brain desperately scrambling to put things back together into a semblance of normal order. My therapist had helped me understand that this was at the root of my anxiety and certainly contributed to my panic attacks. Instead of trying to loosen my grip, I tightened the reins on all aspects of my life to the point where it often felt like I was holding on for dear life. Maybe getting away *was* what I really needed, even though I wouldn't categorize this as a vacation, even for one of my fancypants accounting clients looking for a write-off.

A honking noise that slowly grew closer and louder interrupted my thoughts. A deep voice calling us from Mama's side of the car followed a slamming door.

"Howdy, ladies! The cavalry has arrived."

I suddenly felt bad for doubting the AAA lady.

"Well, thank you, sir. We do appreciate it." Mama was batting her eyelashes at the older gentleman standing outside her rolled-down window.

He wore the largest cowboy hat I had ever seen, with more polyester on him than a rack at Goodwill. That seemed a little suspicious for a car mechanic, but given our circumstances, I wasn't about to judge his authenticity based on his outfit. He had the friendliest face, his eyes barely open from the intensity of his smile. And for someone near Mama's age, he seemed quite lithe and fit.

I elbowed her, and she jumped. "Yes, thanks so much! Do you need us to get out?"

"Not quite yet, ma'am. You should stay as comfortable as you possibly can while I take a look at what's going on. If you'll excuse me for a moment." He lifted his hat about an inch off his head, staring directly at Mama, then popped it back on as he turned toward the tire in question.

Mama followed him with her eyes at first, then leaned her head right out the window, without one ounce of shame.

"Mama! Mama!" I whispered, tugging at her shirt, half trying to stop her, the other half to keep her from falling out of the car.

She batted me away. "How's it looking? Hopefully nothing too serious!" she yelled back to him, then checked herself out in the mirror, brushing the wig hair out of her face, then stroking the rest of it over her shoulder.

I heard a couple of clanking noises, and then he appeared back at Mama's window. "I hate to be the bearer of bad news, especially since I just met you lovely ladies, but it's going to take a bit more than a simple tire change. I much prefer to get it into my shop and take a closer look, if it's not too much trouble."

I tried to catch Mama's eye to commiserate about the inconvenience, but she was too busy staring at the man to even glance in my direction.

"I don't suppose we have a choice, now do we…?"

"Cal!" He pointed to his name, embroidered on his shirt.

"Well, Cal, looks like we'll be spending the night in…"

"The beautiful city of Monroe." Cal finished her sentence without taking a beat.

"Like Marilyn! How adorable." Mama giggled.

She went to open her door, but Cal beat her to it, then offered her a hand, which Mama eagerly accepted. You would have thought he was escorting her to a ball; he rather gracefully helped her out and closed the door behind her gently, so it only made a light clicking noise. For the brief second that I saw his hand in hers, any question of his legitimacy as a car mechanic was answered immediately; his nails and fingertips were black from car oil.

Mama started talking to him immediately, about what exactly I couldn't be so sure, as I gathered up what we needed from the car and hopped out my own side, then walked to the trunk to grab our bags.

"Oh, good golly, allow me!" He left Mama to come help me grab our luggage, then rolled it over and stashed it in the cab of the truck.

Then Mama and I both watched from the side of the road as he gingerly maneuvered our car onto the tow truck bed.

"If you accidentally paint the whole thing white, we promise to look the other way," I yelled to him, only half joking.

"I rather like the purple," he replied. Mama gave me a knowing look.

"Makes it easy to spot on the side of the road!" I shot her one back. Even. "I'm Grace, by the way." I figured if we were about to squeeze ourselves into his tiny tow truck cab before he possibly kidnapped us, I wanted him to know my name.

"Oh my, how rude of me." He reached out to shake my hand, and I grabbed it. His grip was firm, and his hands rough, like he had been using them for work his entire life.

"Loralynn," Mama said, stretching out her hand toward him.

"Sisters is my guess." He grabbed her hand and kissed it.

Mama grinned.

"Funny, we get that all the time," I replied. Or at least we used to. But it was never funny. At least not to me. Much to my chagrin and Mama's joy, I was often confused for her sibling and not her child. I quickly figured out that it was a compliment to her, not to me, and so I learned to just smile and nod, while Mama gushed about her extensive beauty routine. Mama even had a stint as a Mary Kay lady, with the face creams as her top seller when really none of our white neighbors would ever have skin like hers, no matter what overpriced product they used.

We climbed into the cab, Mama sandwiched between us in the middle. Cal took off his hat and placed it in the back of the cab, then brushed his hand over his hair, doing his best to smooth it out.

"Now there's not much around these parts, which you probably already guessed, but we do have a small hotel in the center of town, with a nice little restaurant and bar. It's no Holiday Inn, but it does out-of-towners just fine."

I was worried that "Holiday Inn" was his idea of a fancy hotel.

"Sounds lovely!" Mama's voice cut through like a whistle, but thankfully dropped down as they started chatting like old pals. I had no idea she knew so much about Louisiana history, but she certainly wasted no time impressing Cal, or scaring him with conversation about the Louisiana Purchase, and other Louisiana-related historical facts. He seemed genuinely interested in what she had to say, even though he was probably quite familiar with Louisiana's state bird, which I learned was the pelican.

Cal peeked over at Mama as much as he could safely while driving, and each time, she smiled and giggled, surprised that someone was so interested in what she had to say. Every now and then, a few pieces of his slicked-back silver hair would fall onto his forehead, and he would take his hand off the wheel to push it back. I could imagine him as a young twenty-something, doing the same thing as the wind blew through the open cab window, and I wondered if this had always been his profession or if he fell into it later in life. The way Mama was looking at him, she probably didn't care about any of that, just that he was quite enthralled with her company.

There was no shortage of widowed gentlemen at the Palisades, and Mama's dress and demeanor certainly garnered plenty of attention, albeit not always the kind she wanted. Her appearance never failed to cause some sort of reaction from everyone who got within ten feet of her, though women were always the worst offenders. They just couldn't understand why any woman would wear such low-cut tops and tight pants and not be after something, as if older men had so much to offer. Mama laughed when they called her an "Oriental hussy," impressed that they even took the time to notice that she was Asian. She refused to say anything to them, but instead would saunter by and plop down at the table with the most eligible senior citizen bachelors to rub it in their faces.

Mama mentioned a few gentlemen callers over the years, but after I mistakenly tried to give her advice about the retired vacuum cleaner salesman who made her pay for all their movie dates, she kept any of her dalliances private. I never heard much about them beyond their names, and if she was feeling especially generous, how their wives died.

I didn't get the sense these dates materialized into anything, because I could only imagine one type of person who could walk into that home, filled to the low-beam ceiling with Elvis figurines, and feel anything but fear. He would have to be literally blind, or blinded by his own delusions. That's not to say I didn't think she deserved happiness for having to deal with Daddy all those years. I just figured she'd have to change way more than she would ever want, and living alone with her Elvises in peace was worth more than any new man in her life.

"Just about here now," Cal said. "It'll only be a minute for me to drop off your car and I'll get you over to the Homestead."

I knew I should have been worried, with a name like that, but I didn't really have much choice. Their chatter picked up again, interspersed with Mama's laughter and his deep guffaws that blended with the hum of the truck, lulling me to sleep against the window.

I'm not quite sure how I did it, but I slept through the entire unloading of the car at Cal's shop and didn't budge until we pulled up to the hotel.

"This is perfect!" Mama made it sound like we had just pulled up to the Four Seasons.

I jerked awake, doing my best to subtly wipe the drool off the corner of my mouth. Peeking up to look through the window, I saw what looked like someone's house, poorly kept at that, with a trailer to the side that had a flashing light out front that said "BAR." The hotel, if you could even call it a hotel, had a brick face crumbling in spots and a few of the shutters missing slats, though the bushes and flower beds were immaculate. I wondered if the effort spent in maintaining the greenery would have been better spent on the aesthetic of the building. Every time the vacancy sign flashed, I imagined it felt like adding insult to injury, if hotels actually had feelings.

"Clever name!" I said sheepishly. It was like naming your dog "Dog."

"It's the only one in Monroe, so it doesn't cause too much confusion," Cal replied.

I flung open the door, ripping my bag out of the overflowing back seat, and dragged myself into the front reception area. Mama hung back to talk to Cal, which looked more like her talking at him, but he didn't seem to mind. He could clearly take care of himself.

As I was rummaging through my bag for an ID and credit card, a friendly voice greeted me. "Welcome to the newly renovated Homestead Hotel." Her face was stunning and friendly, even with what looked like absolutely no makeup on her smooth chocolate skin. And her natural hair bounced like springs off her head in a perfect Afro.

"Oh, um, hi." She caught me off guard. I looked down at my two-year-old skinny jeans I thought were pretty damn cool at the time. Her ensemble wasn't over-the-top, but it was clear she had style—from the distressed high-waisted pants to the off-the-shoulder crop top à la *Flashdance*.

"Hey there! Checking in? Do you have a

reservation?" Her voice was bright and warm, with only the slightest of twangs. I'm not quite sure why I expected her to sound like she dressed: way too cool for Monroe, Louisiana.

"Oh, no, sorry. We just broke down a few miles back, and Cal suggested we stay here until he can fix our car."

"Oh, bummer for you. But not for us! We're glad to have you. Is it just you staying with us?"

"No. My mama too. She's out there." I pointed to the window, and we both peeked. They were still talking and laughing.

"They'll be out there for a while. Cal is quite a talker. He must be thrilled for the ear."

"More like the other way around. I think he's taking one for the team." Mama was talking with arms waving, while Cal just stood there, arms crossed, nodding. He let out the same booming laugh that he did in the truck, and I didn't feel bad for him anymore.

"Our rooms all come with complimentary earplugs, which you are more than welcome to pocket for future use."

"Oh, we're past that point. How about some sedatives?"

She laughed. "Well, from the looks of it, it seems like they're doing just fine. I'm not sure I've ever heard Cal laugh like that before. He's such a sweet man, but it always feels like he's carrying a weight around with him."

She sounded smart and sincere, which was something I hadn't heard in a long time.

"I'm Courtney, by the way." She reached her hand out, and I shook it vigorously, then retracted it quickly after realizing how enthusiastic I was being.

"This here is my place. It took me forever to fix up. You can't imagine what it looked like before."

"Did the inside match the outside?"

She nodded. "That's my next project. That and the bar. I can only do so much here by myself. Is a double room okay?"

"Sure, I'll take whatever you've got. And bar is…" I grinned nervously.

"I know, the dumbest name ever. I can't take credit for that. But it is easy to remember for drunk people." We both laughed. "I just need an ID and a credit card, and these keys are yours."

She held up two actual keys, a rarity with hotels anymore, and I slid the plastic across the counter. She asked for my address and phone number.

"Boston! I knew you were my people! I moved down here from New York."

"I'm actually from Texas. But I jetted right after college."

"I hear you. I grew up in this *hellhole* and couldn't get myself out of here faster." She whispered "hellhole" as if we were in church.

"So, if you don't mind me asking, what brought you back?"

"Daddy. He got sick, and it was either I move back

or get him a full-time nurse, and, well, I just couldn't afford that."

"Oh, I'm sorry." I instantly felt terrible for prying. The look on my face must have said that to her.

"It's fine. I won't bore you with the details." We both peeked out the window again. Mama was still talking at Cal, now slightly closer to the hotel entrance, but not by much.

"I don't mind, really. It's been pretty much Mama and me in a car for a whole lot of hours. It's a nice break."

"Well, how about you get settled in your room. We'll all be at Karaoke Night at the bar later. It's much better told over a stiff drink, with well booze."

"Mmmm, I love no-name gin."

I smiled at her, then tucked my ID and card back in my wallet.

"You're just down the hall on the left. Bright purple door, you can't miss it."

I laughed. Of course it was.

GRACE: More! Exciting! Updates! From! The! Road!

ASHA: My eyes. All those exclamation points.

GRACE: So, we got a flat tire...

ASHA: This is seriously turning into a Lemony Snicket sequel.

GRACE: It's actually not that bad. I could use the break from driving anyway. We'll be back at it tomorrow.

ASHA: What's that I hear? A spark of optimism. Have you checked your temperature?

GRACE: I'm completely healthy, promise. Except I don't remember the last time I had a vegetable.

ASHA: Sounds like the perfect vacation to me. You're not changing diapers, are you?

GRACE: Not yet.

ASHA: Yep, perfect vacation then.

GRACE: Haha.

ASHA: Miss you! 🫶

GRACE: Give Puddles a squeeze for me.

ASHA: You mean Harry? Of course.

GRACE: 👋

I will never again judge a hotel by its exterior. Or a room by its door. The inside looked like what you would have found searching modern bed-and-breakfast decor on Pinterest. The simplicity was an unexpected yet welcome surprise. Courtney had amazing taste, and it showed. The refurbished vintage bedroom set was droolworthy, and juxtaposed with very contemporary bedding, it felt extremely sophisticated. I felt a little bad throwing myself on one of the double beds to get my bearings. The slight scent of lavender on the pillowcase was a lovely touch.

"If you want to freshen up, Mama, go ahead. The owner, Courtney—that girl you waved at when you came flying in? She said there's karaoke at the bar if you're interested."

Mama stuck her head out of the bathroom. "Oh, I know that. Cal was talking all about it." She said "Cal" like she had known him for years, and it didn't completely bother me. "And you know how much I love karaoke!"

I didn't actually know that, but considering she was the kind of person who sang Elvis lyrics in conversations with complete strangers, I wasn't that surprised.

"I'm going to head down now, Mama, if that's okay by you. If I lie here too much longer, I'll fall asleep."

"Suit yourself, old lady!" she yelled over the bathroom fan. I needed to move quickly to avoid another two-hour headache-inducing nap, this one caused by sheer exhaustion, not day drinking, which right now felt like the exact same thing.

I grabbed my phone to text Wyatt back.

Dear Wyatt's Ghost, I'm writing to let you know that we made it to Louisiana. Please tell actual Wyatt to call whenever. I would love to catch up with him.

I instantly regretted using the word "love" but figured it was part of my new mantra of actually sharing my feelings and not second-guessing them. Too late for that part, but at least I had only gotten to second guesses and not thirds and fourths as usual.

I shoved my phone in my pocket and then headed out. The heavy purple door slammed behind me, and I looked down either side of the hall to try to figure out which way I needed to go to find the bar, as Courtney walked by with a huge pile of towels.

"Need anything?" she asked, trying to see around the towels to the hallway in front of her.

"A drink?" I replied. I didn't really *need* one but I also didn't want to sleep the rest of the evening away in my room either. "I feel like I should be asking you that. Here, can I take a couple of those?" I grabbed a few towels off the top of the pile.

"Oh, thanks. I'm not sure why I hate taking two trips. Some things you just never grow out of. If you don't mind walking down to the linen closet with me, I can join you. My shift is officially over."

I followed Courtney down the long hallway, past room doors painted in a rainbow of colors, which finally led to a small linen closet, aptly named "STORAGE."

"Mama was insistent on keeping the rainbow doors," she said, as if she knew I was going to ask her. "So when she passed, I didn't have the heart to get rid of them, even though they don't really match the decor."

"I'm sorry about your mama. I actually like them. Plus, they're easy to find when you're wasted."

She laughed. "Maybe that's why my mama liked them so much. Well, that and she worked hard to buy this place on her own, with no help from my dad. She wanted this to be her success. Or mistake, if it all flopped. She was the only female business owner in this town for a long time, and she had to fight to get everything, from a business lawyer to the damn liquor license!"

We stacked the towels on a large shelf already full of fluffy white towels, then locked up, continuing down the hallway to the end, where we were met by a glass door that said "BAR" on it. I could hear the chatter over a loud rumbling bass. For what looked like a pretty small establishment, there was a whole lot of noise coming out of it. And for good reason. The place was packed. Tables full, folks sitting at the bar and standing behind them, everyone facing out to watch the person yelling a Credence Clearwater Revival song into a microphone on a small platform being used as a stage. Most of the crowd was singing along, with a few stragglers attempting to have an impossible conversation.

"Come this way. There's bound to be a few poorly sung ballads coming up, so we might actually be able to chat without having to scream."

She made her way back to the bar, and pointed to a small four-top hidden in a little nook. It had a "RESERVED" sign on it, so I hesitated. Then I remembered that she owned the place, so I sat down, taking in the scene.

"What can I get you?" she yelled at me.

"Gin and tonic?" She jumped behind the bar, then grabbed a few bottles. A few seconds later, she was standing in front of me with a plastic cup and a lime positioned precariously on the nonexistent lip.

"Cheers!" I said. The only noise that came from bumping our cups together was the jostling of the ice. She joined me as the karaoke DJ put on a song for his break that gave our ears and throats a little respite.

"Ah...better than a ballad. So how's everything with the room? I put you in one of our newer suites. It's one of my personal favorites."

"It's definitely the nicest place I've stayed, possibly ever. Clearly you've been working hard."

"Oh, I'm so glad. Being busy has been good for me. At first, I missed home, and I thought about leaving a ton of times."

"This is definitely a jump from New York City."

"It didn't help that my dad and I didn't really get along, and for a while, I felt like things were getting worse, like maybe he would have been better off without me. But then we sort of had it out, and I sank all my frenetic energy into this place, and things are looking up. Parents." Her shoulder shrug punctuated the one-word sentence.

Speaking of which, Mama walked in, as if on cue. I waved at her from the table, and she weaved her way through the tables and groups of people.

"Courtney, this is my mama, Loralynn." Mama reached out to shake her hand, then sat down next to me.

"It's a pleasure, darling. Now where can I get one of those." She pointed to my plastic cup. "Long Island iced tea!" Mama didn't even wait for Courtney to ask her what she wanted.

Courtney waved down the bartender, yelling Mama's order over to her.

"Mama! Is that really the…" Mama cut me off.

"As long as I live and breathe on this earth, I will be the mama, and yes, it is really." She said the last part to Courtney.

"And there's my daddy. I'll be right back, with him and your drink, Loralynn."

A large Black man with slightly darker skin than Courtney's had rolled into the front door of the bar in a shiny silver wheelchair. His head was covered by a worn-out LSU hat, and the visor shadow made it difficult to see the family resemblance, except for his bright white smile, which looked identical to his daughter's. He carefully balanced a small oxygen pack on his lap, and as he made his way through the bar, he fist-bumped the customers.

"Hey, Bill!"

"Looking good!"

You could hear their voices over the high-pitched singer who was wailing an old Patsy Cline tune. If anyone was truly listening to her, I think they might have called 911.

Courtney dropped Mama's drink and another round for me at the table, then ran over to get her dad, pushing him right up to the table next to us. I scooted over to make room as she walked around to sit across from him.

"Well, how did I get so lucky to sit at a table with all these beautiful ladies? Allow me to introduce myself...I'm Bill, Courtney's sad old in-valid daddy."

"Hardly any of those things, from what I can see." Mama reached out her hand. "Loralynn. And you look quite dapper yourself, sir." She picked up her drink and started slurping it down through the two tiny straws.

Mama wasn't just being polite. He had a neatly pressed button-down shirt on, tucked into a pair of dark dungarees. His cowboy boots looked newly shined, but my guess was that, sadly, they hadn't been used for walking in a while. And from the way he was greeted and his welcoming demeanor, you could tell that he was well liked. I didn't even really know him and I already liked him.

"I'm Grace. Nice to meet you."

Courtney got the bartender's attention again, then pointed to Bill, while Mama craned her neck, nearly standing up out of her seat to eye all the people walking through the door.

"Expecting someone, Mama?" I said, rather loudly, and not just to cut through the Patsy Cline song. It was still better than listening to drunk people sing.

"Indeed I am," she told the whole table like they cared, dropping back down into her seat and wiggling her hips to get comfortable again.

"Well, he's one lucky fella!" Bill said.

"I'm just hoping he's a singer so I'm off the hook," I said to the table.

"Party pooper!" Mama shot me a glance, then

waved at Cal, who had just walked in, shaking hands with the same crowd Bill was so friendly with earlier. He waved back, then made his way over, still wearing head-to-toe polyester, but now with a jacket and a fancier hat. Based on what the crowd was wearing, he was overdressed, which was actually quite sweet when he could have easily phoned it in and no one would have been the wiser. I had only heard Mama's earlier conversation with him in brief snippets as I rolled in and out of consciousness in the cab of his truck, none of which I thought was particularly enthralling, but it appeared to be enough that they both were eager to continue it.

A few people attempted to stop him to talk, but Cal seemed dead focused on making it to our table.

"Well, look who decided to show his sorry old face. Apparently it takes a lady to get you to come out of your cave these days, Cal?" Bill said.

"Not just any lady, Bill." He grabbed a chair and pulled right next to Mama, tipping his hat just as he had done earlier, in case there was any confusion about his commitment to his brand. I could only imagine how sore Mama's face was going to be the next day, her smile from ear to ear without a break in the curve.

"What'll it be, Cal?"

"Oh, you know me. A sweet tea will do," Cal said. "Now who's up next?" He pointed to the stage.

"You better pick a song, Mama, so you get a good spot in the lineup!" I looked at Courtney, who was trying to get the bartender's attention. "So this is why you offer the complimentary earplugs?"

Everyone laughed as the bartender brought over Cal's drink, and another few rounds for all of us. Mama picked up her cup, tapping it against Cal's and then drinking all of it down as we watched, the others with fascination, me with a tiny bit of horror. She ran up to the stage and grabbed the huge karaoke book. With just a few page flips, Mama was already pointing out her number to the DJ and walking up on stage, Cal close behind her.

The twang of the guitar was all too familiar. Mama held the mic as she waited for the intro to end. She looked like a natural, at least wardrobe wise. As impractical as her clothing was for everyday use, it was perfect for the stage. I listened to hear which Elvis song she'd picked, spinning a veritable wheel in my head to see where it would land. With a few tinny plucks of the electric guitar, I mouthed the opening lyrics to "Are You Lonesome Tonight" with her, even catching myself swaying back and forth as she sang with abandon, though way more in tune than I had expected. It was probably one of her top three songs, and I figured she would work her way up to her number one once she got warmed up.

"So where are you and your mama heading?" Bill asked, taking a small sip of the concoction that Courtney had brought back to him. I grabbed from the line of drinks in front of me and slurped it down way too easily, picking up the next in my hand as he talked. He seemed like the kind of guy who was everyone's dad, and for a moment, I imagined what it would have been like to have someone like him in my life.

"Memphis!" I said. "Mama's been dreaming about seeing Graceland her entire life, so I'm taking her there."

"Such good girls we have here," Bill replied. "My Courtney came down here to take care of me, what, now a year ago, and I can't get rid of her."

Courtney grabbed his hand. "How could I leave? I would just miss you barking orders at me all day long, Daddy."

His laugh was deep and hearty, bellowing loudly enough for people to peek over at our table and smile. If Bill was happy, it seemed other people were too. "It's bullshit being stuck in this damn thing," he said, pointing to his ride, a pretty souped-up wheelchair. "But I s'pose it's better than sitting in my bed all day just rotting away. It's coming for me either way. I'd rather it take me down tryin'."

I could see Courtney's face dampen, and I knew how she felt, at least in a tiny way. He sounded just like Mama, who had been fighting this cancer for years now, and was determined to live exactly how she did before. This scared the shit out of me, but part of me believed it was her attitude that kept her going.

Mama beckoned me to come up to the stage as

the piano arpeggios of "Can't Help Falling in Love" started, but I just waved and smiled, pretending that I had no idea what her gesture meant.

"I wasn't a good daughter." I'm not quite sure why I picked that exact moment to tell two strangers that I was, in fact, not the kind of person they probably assumed I was. "In fact, I kind of hated her." I looked down at my drink, wondering exactly what gin was in my glass, then slugged it back and slammed the glass on the table. Courtney handed me another and I wasted no time chugging that one down too.

Bill started laughing again. "Oh, darlin', if you don't hate your parents at least once in your life, then you don't really love 'em!" I thought of all the times I had screamed "I hate you!" at Mama and how satisfying it was to slam my door while saying it. But that's what you're supposed to do as a teenager, then let go of all those resentments as an adult. I hadn't quite gotten that memo.

"I appreciate you letting me off the hook, Mr. Bill." His kindness felt undeserved, and I was inclined to correct the inaccuracy. Damn gin. My cheeks were feeling flushed, but I decided to ignore them, grabbing the next glass in the lineup that was growing longer thanks to a very attentive bartender. I decided to sip this one. "But I wasn't some kid pissed that she got grounded for getting home past curfew. We're talking 'get me the hell out of this madhouse because I never want to come back, so I didn't' hatred." I probably should have been embarrassed, but I was already too many drinks in for that. "It's been like twenty-five years of this."

"Darlin', you are preaching to the choir. This child right here was a pain in my very large backside. Always shooting off her mouth and getting in trouble. It's a wonder she ever made it through college and kept a job for longer than a hot second. She ran off with a joke of a man and we didn't hear from her for years. Years! Thank the Lord she finally kicked that jackass to the curb. You see all this hair?" He pointed to his bald head, then winked over at Courtney. "That's because of her."

She rubbed his head. "You never looked good with hair anyway." Then she looked at me. "My daddy is a little dramatic. Years? Well, maybe it felt like that. We all have our shit to work out."

I'm not sure why it was so hard to believe that Courtney, or anyone else, for that matter, had shit to work out. I mean, I knew I wasn't the only one in the world going to therapy, but she just seemed so together, and so happy and content in her life. I just imagined people like that were born into happy families.

"What if you were just shitty?" I replied. I hadn't ever verbalized exactly what I felt about all the years of trying to avoid the once-a-month phone calls and yearly visits. And even though I knew it was just my subconscious trying to skirt around all of the pain and sadness, instead of allowing myself to deal with what I was feeling, part of me had decided I was just a terrible person.

"So you had to work out your shitty shit." He laughed. "You can sit around and worry about all the time you were away. Or you can get busy enjoying the time you have right now. Every new minute is like one old year." He clinked my glass, which I was ill prepared for, and I nearly dropped it on the table. Gin's fault again, I suppose.

He had a point. Not dealing with these old feelings had cultivated a beast I couldn't quite handle, infiltrating my work life and my marriage. I just didn't know when I could let Mama off the hook. And maybe more importantly, myself.

"You make it sound so easy. I'm not sure there are enough minutes left for everything I need to make up for with my mama."

Courtney jumped in. "You don't need to pay for the sins of your past. They're not like college loans."

I laughed at that analogy, but it made more sense than anything any therapist had told me.

"You get to leave the person who did all of that stuff back when it happened. She sounds young and hurt. Maybe you both were." Courtney's face was more serious. Even Bill had become silent, and I knew that her words went beyond empathy; she had lived all of this herself. They both had, and in that instant, I felt a little envious about where they were in their relationship. I wanted that, more than I thought I did.

"I was. I think Mama was too," I replied, swallowing back the present tense.

"No parent wants to live with the thought that our own shortcomings caused our children pain." Bill placed his hand on top of Courtney's and just left it there. "There's a good chance I don't make it to next month, and that will be a blessing. Lord knows that pretty thing doesn't need to be stuck down here in Bumbfuckle, Louisiana, taking care of her sick, fat daddy." He sighed.

Courtney pushed his arm as a fake punishment, but he didn't budge. "If there's anything I've learned through all of this, it's not to live in regret. If you can believe it, that's worse than living here."

We all laughed and tapped our plastic glasses together. Poor Louisiana.

"I need a couple more of these. Then things will start to get interesting." This time, he caught the bartender's eye. I looked down at the table, which was covered in empty cups, more than I even remembered there being, but I was too buzzed to even try to count.

The bartender came over with a tray full of drinks, placing them on one side of the table, then grabbing all the empties. Bill grabbed a cup, then gestured to me to take one. There was very little liquid at the bottom. Shots? I looked at Courtney, and she shrugged, then picked one up herself.

"Don't think about it. Just do it, or you'll get a speech from him about having fun and 'back in our day…' that you won't want to hear."

I was quite familiar with the "back in our day…" speeches, so I took her advice and took the shot. Tequila. Blech.

"When are we gonna get some Captain *and* Tennille up in here?!" he yelled down to the stage.

"Them's fightin' words," said Cal, who ran over to the DJ, then flipped through the binder rather quickly. It was clear he too knew exactly what he was looking for. He showed the DJ, then hopped up onto the stage next to Mama, their feet tapping to the beat and their bodies swaying along as the music rolled out of the tiny speaker next to them, as if they had planned their act while I was sleeping in the tow truck.

"You gonna go up there?" Courtney asked.

"I'd typically say there isn't enough alcohol. Or earplugs. But I did promise Mama I would be a little more daring this trip, so I think I might, though when I said that, I was thinking spicy foods, not necessarily karaoke."

"Well, if there was ever a time, you're in front of a room full of strangers who are all about four drinks in. And that's an extremely low estimate, looking at this crowd."

"I appreciate your confidence in my singing ability." We both laughed.

"Let the tequila do its job!" Courtney exclaimed, then gave me a fist bump.

I stumbled ungracefully up to the stage. Mama and Cal were singing their achy breaky old hearts out as I flipped through the huge book of songs. I hadn't ever sung karaoke, at least in front of an actual crowd. Even though I had a great singing voice, or so I was told by my high school and college choir director, I never thought it was good enough. I'd get extremely nervous doing any sort of solos, so I relegated myself to car and shower performances.

As Mama and Cal entered the last verse of their song, the DJ beckoned me over to show him the number to mine. I debated just walking away or trying to get Courtney to sing with me. I looked up, hoping to catch her eye, but she and her dad had been swarmed by guests and were too busy with pleasantries to be watching me.

The audience cheered for Mama and Cal, who looked adorable with clasped hands raised in victory. I almost felt bad breaking them up as I stepped up onto the stage, hand outstretched to take the microphone from Mama. Instead, she started talking into it.

"Everyone! This is my only daughter, Grace Louise!" She said it like I was a famous person they should all know. The crowd cheered, and I tried grabbing for the mic. Mama leaned away from me, still talking. "And she is driving her poor old mama to Memphis. We should all be so lucky." Someone yelled "hear, hear" from the back of the bar, and the rest of the audience chimed in.

Mama placed the microphone in my hand, and I stood motionless, the stage lights brighter than I had expected, but also quite effective in blocking my ability to make out anyone's face. The orchestral introduction to "Always on My Mind" started to swell behind me, and I cleared my throat, then opened my mouth, hoping actual melodic sounds would come out.

I guess the combination of gin and tequila was working overtime, because standing there with the microphone at my lips is the last thing I remember.

GRACE: Yooooooooooo.

ASHA: Dude. Do you know what time it is? Is everything okay?

GRACE: Nope.

ASHA: Nope you don't know what time it is or nope everything is not okay?

GRACE: That. 😃 🧴 🐾 ⚡

ASHA: On a scale of one to wasted, how drunk are you currently?

GRACE: So not drunk. 🙄

ASHA: 😆 Okay, Grace. Go to bed! And FFS don't text anyone else.

Too bad I missed that last part.

GRACE: Yo. Yo yoyoooo.

WYATT: Hey! I was going to call you, but figured it was a little late. Senior citizen schedule and all.

GRACE: 😵😵😵😵😵

WYATT: How's Louisiana? Them's my stomping grounds!

GRACE: Our car borked down.

WYATT: Oh shit!

GRACE: Tisokay.

WYATT: Good. That sucks.

GRACE: Ducks. Ducks. DUCKS.

WYATT: Are you okay over there?

GRACE: Yeppp. So great.

WYATT: All right, well, good night.

GRACE: 💜 💜 💜 💜 💜

The one thing about being pretty much legally blind without glasses is that when I wake up in the morning with my contacts still on, there's a moment, albeit a brief one, when I think I've been cured. And that's not just because I had a wicked hangover. I blinked my dry eyes open a few times, then pulled the contacts out. At least I'd had the forethought to leave my glasses next to the bed. That was the only thing that was reassuring to me. Well, that and my bra was still on. Actually, everything was still on, except my shoes, which were lined up carefully next to my bed. Then it hit me. Mama. Oh god, Mama. How many of those gin and tonics did I have? And then shots of tequila? I busted open the bathroom door, hoping, for once, that she was just in the middle of her extensive morning ritual. But the room was dark, and empty, so I scurried around the room trying to find my bag and my phone.

Bzzz. Bzzz. Bzzz. I tossed all the blankets off the bed, then back on it again to try to locate where the noise was coming from. I followed the sound like a hunting dog to my purse, which was hung on the hook behind the bathroom door, shaking from my phone.

"Well, good morning, sunshine!" Mama's cheery voice was not what my headache needed.

"Mama, where are you? What happened last night?"

"I'm at breakfast, darling. Have you looked at a clock?"

I honestly hadn't looked. She kept going.

"Well, it's ten thirty and I got hungry waiting for you to rise from the dead."

"Oh, you could have woken me up."

"If you had seen yourself, let's just say that was not an option I was willing to take. I'll be back soon and will bring you a platter."

"Just coffee, Mama. Lots of coffee."

She chuckled. "Based on your performance last night, I already ordered you a whole pot."

She hung up, leaving me to wonder what the hell she was talking about—performance? Then I looked down at my phone. Shit. I needed coffee. I brushed my hair and tossed my shoes back on, then peeked out the doorway and tiptoed down the hall to find the coffee Mama had promised me. I nearly bumped into Courtney, who was carrying a tray with a covered plate and a hot pot of coffee.

She caught herself before everything went flying. Impressive, actually. "I was just heading your way, your mama's orders. I see you found your shoes. And your bag." She eyed the phone in my hand, then kept walking past me toward my room.

I followed her, trying to keep up. She was walking fast. "I cannot remember the last time I, well, couldn't remember. Was it awful?" I hesitated, because I had a feeling it was, but I was hoping that perhaps no one else could remember too.

She stopped dead in her tracks, then turned around and made a face—*the face*—then nudged me toward my room.

I ran past her to open the door, making room on the desk for the tray. She placed it down gently, then handed me a cup of coffee. I wasn't sure what was better—the warmth of it in my hand or the smell of it wafting up into my nose.

She walked over to the armchair in the corner of the room and plopped down. "Define awful."

Wait, seriously.

"Oh no." I took a giant gulp of coffee, the liquid scalding my throat.

"Oh yes. Well, sort of. When you got to the emotional rendition of 'As Long As I Have You' I figured I needed to stage an intervention." She shook her head, then chuckled, which gave me a good sense as to what she meant by emotional rendition. More like embarrassing rendition.

"How bad was it?"

She took a deep breath. "There was some sobbing... during the musical interlude between verse two and the bridge."

"Like actual sobbing?" She couldn't mean actual sobbing, right?

"It was hard to watch. That's why I video recorded it for you." She pointed to my phone, which I had placed on the desk to free my hands up for coffee.

"No."

"Go look." Oh god, what other embarrassing things were on this damn phone?

I grabbed my phone, then flipped through the app icons and tapped on photos, half hoping that she was just joking with me. But nope, there I was, on stage, singing my heart out. I pressed play.

Okay, singing is pretty generous. Then I heard a voice on the recording. Mama.

"Grace! That's my Grace!"

She sounded remarkably sober for someone who had been tossing back Long Island iced teas like a rich stay-at-home mom eating bonbons.

The screen went blank, but the talking continued. I couldn't make out the question or the questioner, but I heard the answer.

"I've been waiting so long for her to come home to me. And now I have to leave."

The voices muffled, and recording stopped. I

tossed the phone on the bed, then sat down next to it, resisting the desire to play it over and over again like an audio form of self-injurious behavior.

"Every year I'd tell myself that this would be the year to just hash it out with Mama once and for all, but then I'd just find something to get annoyed by and decide this visit wasn't the time. It's been a lot of visits and a lot of years of wrong times."

"If you keep looking back, you'll never truly be able to move forward," Courtney said. "I've been there, and it's a sad, dark place."

"Forward looks pretty freakin' scary too." I looked over at her, then down at my feet. My head couldn't take all the sudden movements.

She slid forward in her seat, and I could feel her trying to get me to look at her. I peeked up, and was surprised at the intensity on her face. "For them. But not for you. It's okay to be selfish, you know. Seems like that's what your mama would want for you. My daddy too."

I looked down again, the shame creeping up from within me. "I feel like I've been selfish my whole adult life. I've gotten really good at thinking only about myself."

She got up and sat down next to me, then turned to face me, forcing me to do the same or feel terribly inconsiderate.

"There's a big difference between selfishness and survival." Her tone was so forgiving.

"It's hard for me to separate the two sometimes."

Deep down I knew that leaving was keeping me safe, but Jeff would always remind me that she was family, never quite fully grasping our complicated dynamic. Then I'd feel terrible for not seeing Mama, for not going home more often.

"I can only imagine. But take it from this actually selfish person, you did what you had to do. But now, well, you don't have to do it anymore. It's not like you can turn it off like a switch, though. Just takes time—"

I jumped in. "—which I feel like is running out so quickly. You should have been a therapist." I got up, then wobbled over to get my coffee, which was still steaming.

"I guess I paid enough to one that I could have just gotten my own degree," she replied. "I'm in no position to help people."

I laughed, which was permission for her to giggle too.

"You know what I mean. Take it or leave it. But I hate seeing people beat themselves up. At least when they don't deserve it."

"At least one of us thinks I don't deserve it." I grabbed a piece of toast off the tray and started munching.

Courtney got up. "Take your time. No need to rush out of here, at least not until you're properly caffeinated."

She squeezed my hand on the way out, then closed the door behind her. I smiled, thinking about the randomness of life, and how I would have never met her if it hadn't been for the stupid old car and its flat tire.

I took another few sips of coffee, then flopped on the bed and stared up at the ceiling. I needed to get moving, and yet I just wanted to lie perfectly still for another few hours, preferably with the lights out. I guess that's basically the definition of a hangover.

"Mornin', sugar!" The door swung open.

I sat straight up. "Mama, why so loud so early?"

"The door was open. I figured Lazarus had risen. I see you got breakfast. But clearly not enough coffee." She handed me my half-drunk cup.

I sat up, but needed to steady myself. "Mama...did you see me..."

"Oh, darling. You were a star!" She clapped her hands together rapidly with complete disregard for my poor, throbbing head.

"I think you mean idiot." I was going to need way more coffee.

"I did not. I've never seen you so..."

"...drunk?" I handed her the cup, then walked over to get more toast. I was worried that the coffee was going to hit my stomach like a bomb.

"Well, that is true, but I was going for 'free.'" Mama rifled through her makeup case, as if her voice and clapping weren't noise enough.

"I guess. I just wish it came without this shitty headache."

She pulled out a little bottle of Advil, which I

immediately grabbed from her. "I heard what you said, Mama." I took three pills with the coffee, which had cooled off, but was still too hot to take pills with, then grabbed my suitcase to start packing. Mama had already finished, at what I can only imagine was some ungodly hour. I can't believe I didn't hear her.

"I said a lot of things last night, Grace." I could see her try to think of all the things she had said, then jumped in for fear that she might hurt herself.

"That you waited so long for me to come home..."

She looked confused.

"Courtney filmed my stunning performance last night, and forgot to hit stop on the record button."

She still looked confused. Technology was not her strong suit.

"And now you had to leave."

She finally remembered. "Well, I meant it."

"Then why did you never reach out to me? It always felt like you were choosing Elvis over me." Apparently booze is an honesty elixir, even after it's been in your system for a while.

"I could never!" She might as well have called me a liar.

"Then why did it feel like I had to work so hard to get your attention? All your Elvis stuff, so carefully tended to, and then your own daughter, miles away...I needed you too!"

My words echoed around the room, the downside of modern decor. No heavy carpets or curtains to soak up my truth talk. Mama was stunned into silence.

She breathed for a few beats, then cleared her throat. I knew what was coming, and it wasn't going to be pretty. If only the Advil were stronger.

"I guess I never tried because I thought seeing me would just bring up all the bad memories for you."

That wasn't at all what I expected, and for a moment, I felt bad for thinking otherwise, maybe because she wasn't wrong, and she said it in a way that didn't make me feel wrong. It wasn't her constant jabber or garish outfits that made visiting so hard. It was the sting of the past that I felt every time I was with her that had made me so resistant.

"Does it feel like I'm rejecting you, Grace? Because I'm not. I'm so proud of you. Look at all you've accomplished. And you found yourself a good man."

I had to tell her.

"Mama...Jeff and I...well, he met someone else. Our marriage is over." I could barely say the words out loud, squeezing my eyes shut to prepare for the barrage of questions that I had hoped to avoid by not telling her. I let out a deep breath and opened my eyes. She looked calmer than I expected. Way calmer.

"Oh, honey, why didn't you say something?" Her tone was soft. She walked over and hugged me, which was unexpected but welcome.

"It didn't seem like the right time. And I already feel like enough of a disappointment."

She pulled away and looked up at me, her arms still around my waist. "To whom, exactly? Because not to me. Besides, it's his fault that he's walking away from something so wonderful."

I wanted to just nod and accept her empathy—the whole gift horse thing and all—but I felt the urge to tell her the truth. That was new.

"It wasn't all him, Mama. I mean, he cheated, but I think I was the one who had left a long time ago, which I know doesn't even make sense really."

She cupped my chin in her hand. "Oh, darlin'. Sure it does. I understand why you were with him. But people change." I couldn't quite tell if she was telling that to me or herself, but I didn't care. All along I'd been waiting for her to judge me like all the other divorced kids of her Palisades friends, as if I held the ability to fix my marriage in the palm of my hand and I was just taking the easy way out. But she didn't. Instead, she just stood in front of me, rubbing my cheek in silence.

———————

Mama helped pack me up while I finished the toast on my plate. As delicious as they looked, the eggs were probably not the best decision considering the state of my stomach, which was still pretty angry about the tequila. I let the hot water pelt my back for longer than I probably should have, but skipped drying my hair and putting on makeup to get back the time I spent trying to steam the liquor out of my pores.

I had just finished packing up the contents of the

bathroom when I heard a knock on the door, and then Mama's high-pitched giggles and Cal's low guffaws.

"Good morning, Grace!" he said enthusiastically. Mama nodded him off with a "she's got a hangover" look, and he lowered his tone immediately. "Your car is all set. Good as new." He jangled the keys in his hand uncomfortably.

I glared at Mama, now wondering if they had been laughing about my memorable karaoke performance, then took the keys from him. "How much do I owe you?"

"Well now, there's no charge." He smiled up at Mama, and she winked.

"No, Cal. I can't let you do this."

"Please, Grace. It's really my pleasure. Now let me help this young lady with her suitcase." He ran over to Mama, who was attempting to drag her suitcase out of the room by the large zipper. She followed him out the door.

"Thanks so much, Cal," I yelled to him, rolling my own suitcase out, then quickly heading for the car to give myself some space to think.

I waited in silence, rubbernecking in the rearview mirror to see if Cal and Mama were close to finishing up their endless goodbye, which alternated between her awkward giggles and his sweet hand kisses. The urge to cry welled up behind my eyes, and instead of forcing it back, I just let it go, down my face, tears dropping onto my lap before I could find a napkin. I tried desperately to grasp onto a singular moment that was causing the waterfall, but it felt more like a truth-telling catharsis than a reaction to anything specific, though I didn't feel "set free," like good old Dr. Amovar said I would. At least not yet anyway.

Cal escorted Mama out to the car and carefully placed her suitcase in the open trunk, slamming it harder than was necessary. He opened her door, and she slid in, popping up to kiss him on the cheek before he closed the door. She reached over to wipe the bright pink lipstick off his cheek, but he stopped her, holding her hand on his face for a second before squeezing it and stepping back from the car.

"Goodbye, Grace. Take good care of this one. She's not as tough as she looks."

I smiled, then let him back away from the car before I pulled out of the drive. Mama handed me a paper with directions on it and only said one thing to me before turning back to her perch.

"Mississippi Coliseum." I had no idea where that was, or what it meant, but from her tone, I had a feeling I was about to get schooled in more ways than one.

Chapter 11

I wracked my brain for what was awaiting us at the Mississippi Coliseum, and while I had heard Mama talk about it, I couldn't quite pinpoint the context. It was just under two hours from the Homestead, but even though we had driven on the same Highway 20 for pretty much the entire trip, the change of landscape was so obvious that there was no "Welcome to Mississippi" sign required.

The Louisiana swamp changed to Mississippi kudzu almost immediately after we crossed the state line. On our few trips into Mississippi as a kid, I remember admiring the beautiful draping leaves on all the trees, at which point Daddy would tell me they were actually hogging all the sunlight and smothering the trees with a blanket of leaves. I couldn't quite believe that something so beautiful could be so dangerous.

The heat remained like a force field surrounding us, which was unseasonable, even for Mississippi, but the air conditioning blowing at us on high, with the convertible top down, made it bearable.

As it was the state capital, I expected to see my fair share of official looking buildings peeking up from behind the kudzu-covered trees. In my mind, Jackson was Mississippi's Atlanta, which I discovered very quickly was completely inaccurate, and worse, an insult to the state of Georgia.

The Coliseum concert hall is the flagship of the Mississippi State Fair Grounds, which was easily seen from the entrance. If it was like the Texas State Fair we'd made the pilgrimage to every fall when I was a kid, it was quite a lively place to be during fair season. But in October, it was basically a huge abandoned parking lot with a round auditorium in the middle. Signs for basketball games and Monster Jams lined the empty parking lot as we pulled up to the front entrance. The consolation: I got my pick of spots.

Other than being round, this Coliseum would've been a disappointment compared to the famous one in Italy. Instead of stately columns and the famous arched openings, the brick building had a copper cone roof that made it more reminiscent of a carousel. However, instead of animals hanging down on poles, there were large windows around the periphery that reflected the sun, making it look majestic and rather out of place next to the John Deere tractor parked on the edge of the lot.

"Are you sure it's even open, Mama?" I asked, not quite clear what we were doing here.

She didn't answer, but instead swung her door open, barely giving me a chance to put the car into park. She hobbled ahead of me to what she was guessing was the main entrance.

I looked down at my phone, pondering a text to Wyatt that wouldn't make me sound like a relapsing alcoholic, and decided I would just give him a call later. It could have been much worse than a bunch of heart emojis. I think.

Mama made her rounds, walking up to every entrance and shaking the handle of each door, pressing her face up against the glass, then moving on to the next to see if it was unlocked.

I kept my distance, but stayed behind her so it would be obvious to anyone who might be watching that I was with her in a "yep, that's my crazy mother" sort of way. The man sweeping the steps glanced over with a confused look, then returned to his task. Instead of stopping to ask him for the entrance, she continued along the pavement surrounding the hall looking for an unlocked door, which she finally found. She swung it open and walked right inside, forcing me to increase my pace.

"Mama!" I whisper-yelled, uncertain as to what exactly I would encounter when I entered the building. I told myself that if they didn't want anyone inside, they would have locked all the doors. This didn't necessarily make me feel any better, especially since the groundskeeper had stopped what he was doing to walk our way.

I followed Mama through the same door, but by the time I had reached it, she was already long gone. It wouldn't be too hard to find her, considering we were the only people in there, but since we were the only people not supposed to be in there, I wanted to find her before anyone else did.

I can imagine the Coliseum might have felt like one when it was first built, the ornate interior matching the noble exterior, but now it felt more like a museum, with its rich history honored by the signed photos of celebrities lining the walls, along with more candid concert images. Scanning them quickly, I recognized many of the faces, from television, movies, and music, but none seemed to make this a worthy stop. And the empty concession stand and concierge booth, along with the dark, unlit hallways and stairwells, were starting to spook me in a slightly warmer version of *The Shining*.

"MAAAAAMA!" My voice echoed through the building's lobby, but still, no sign of her anywhere. I had it in my mind to check the bathrooms, which I wished I had done in the first place, given how quickly she had disappeared inside. The restroom signage was rather aggressive with large arrows and very specific directions every few steps. "Restrooms! Turn right." "Just a few more steps to restrooms!" Though, if the Coliseum was anything like other venues, the snaking line of women during an event would be enough for anyone to figure out where to go.

I peeked into the theater through the small, oval windows on the closed doors to see a grand stage and a large red velvet curtain pulled shut. And sitting down in the front row, right next to the aisle, was Mama, her wig the only visible part of her from the seat. Replace the microphone stand at the center of the stage with a pulpit, and it could have been Sunday church.

A few overhead lights were on, though I'm not sure Mama would have been bothered by sitting in complete darkness. I pushed through the doors and ran all the way down the aisle, rendering myself almost completely out of breath. Every inhale tasted like popcorn. Still, Mama didn't budge.

"Hey. I've [breath] been [breath] lookingforyou." I exhaled the last three words before gasping for air. Clearly the gym membership at work that I had never actually used was doing me a whole lot of good right now. I sat across the aisle from her, looking up at the stage to see if I could figure out what she was staring at so intently.

"When your brother died, I didn't think I'd ever be able to go on. Your daddy soaked his sorrows in alcohol, but me, I had nothing. No one." She let out a huge sigh, and I could see her stare soften. She moved her head and scanned everything that was in front of her, eying up the dark spotlights above us, then leaning in to examine the floor.

Nothing?! No one?! I mean, I wasn't a BFF she could confide in, but she did have something to distract her.

"You had me, Mama!" I felt exasperated, as if we had been existing on two different planes in two different universes. I wasn't asking her to replace the loss of my brother with affection for me. "I would have taken whatever space you had open in your heart!"

That shook Mama out of whatever dreamlike state she was in. "You were a little child, Grace. And it was the day after your birthday. It wasn't fair. To any of us."

I could see she was remembering the pain, her face empty of emotion.

"I was putting away your brother's things and this concert, the one right here at the Coliseum, came on the radio, and something clicked in me. I mean, I'd heard his songs before. Everybody had. But on that day, when he was singing for those tornado victims, it felt like he was singing to me."

I'd heard that concert over and over as a kid. Mama would scream, "I love you, Elvis!" to him like she was in the crowd. He'd answer back, "I love you too," like he was talking to her and not the woman in the crowd who had yelled it to him. Now her obsession with it finally made sense, but young me couldn't quite wrap my mind around why she was so focused on professing her love to someone who would never really love her back. Was it his voice?

His tender smile? All the time I spent trying to do something and be someone to get her attention when it was never about me. There was nothing wrong with me. I felt the weight of that realization in my gut, a dull pain spreading across my abdomen.

"Elvis gave me hope, Grace, when I needed it the most. You 'member what I used to tell you? There's a lot you can do with a little bit of hope." Her voice went up at the end of the sentence, her eyes bright as though she had just shared the most amazing, life-changing secret with me.

I nodded, doing my best to breathe away the stomachache. It was actually working.

"I bought a few ceramic pieces of him, to put around the house, so when I'd find a little binky under the couch, or when they came to take your brother's crib away, I could just look at Elvis, and in that moment, I was in his world, not mine."

I started to say something, but she cut me off.

"I couldn't go out in town without people whispering about me. I was the Chinese lady, now with a dead baby. Except no one would actually come up to me or ask me how I was feeling. Daddy's friends came to the funeral, but then he went back to work with his buddies, and I was left alone with you. I couldn't be sad because I had you to take care of, Grace. So after trying to do my flat, boring hair like Priscilla's, I decided to try a wig, and a wig became boots, and the boots became these pants you hate so damn much. And at first, your daddy even liked it, maybe because he needed an escape too. Then his liquor did him better in that department."

I couldn't remember a time when my dad liked anything to do with Elvis. Or Mama and me, for that matter. And I felt a little jealous that I was never privy to that part of him, considering I was so young when my brother died.

"But me? I could put on an Elvis record, pretend for a few minutes that I was happy. You deserved a happy mama, Grace!"

Now Mama was the one who was exasperated, trying so desperately to make me understand why, I think, to panhandle for my forgiveness. She could have just asked for it.

"I didn't care what kind of Mama I had." My voice cracked. "But you felt so wrapped up in all of this." I waved my arms around, then let them flop down next to me. "I wanted you, Mama. And it just felt like you were always—"

"Somewhere else," she interrupted. "It's because I was. Oh, Grace…" Mama sobbed, dabbing her eyes and blowing her nose in an old handkerchief, the realization overwhelming her in a way I'd never seen. I wrapped my arm around her and pulled her head into my shoulder.

I never expected her to ever get it, and as much as I had hoped Daddy would come to his senses about me, I had wanted Mama to do the same. I just didn't give her the chance until now. I didn't give myself the chance until now.

"I know, Mama. It's okay. It really is." I was sobbing now too, doing absolutely nothing to try to stop myself from crying.

"I always thought we'd have time, Grace, but you grew up so fast, and I didn't know how to stop a train that had long left the station. After you were gone, well, I just figured you'd be better off without me anyway." Mama's floodgates had opened, and her honesty was pouring out with abandon, but she was wrong, and I felt terrible that she had suffered with those thoughts for so long.

"Mama, it was never like that." She offered me her handkerchief for the tears rolling down my face, but I still had enough sense to use my sleeve instead. "I was never better without *you*. I just wanted you to know that you are loved without all of this." I waved my hand from her head down to her toes. I took a deep breath, then swallowed hard. "But what I really want you to hear is that you're loved with it too." I needed to hear myself say it.

"It's hard to separate that all out now, baby. After all these years, I s'pose I am who I am." She shrugged, then dabbed her eyes.

"I guess I can't really imagine you any other way." I tried to think about what she would look like in a cardigan sweater and a pair of capris and FitFlops, like a suburban mom Halloween costume, and I chuckled.

Mama stood and took a deep breath. "Well, now you know where it all started." She blew a kiss at the microphone as I got up out of my seat and shuffled up the aisle. "Now let's get the hell out of here before they toss us out on our behinds."

She started back toward the entrance. "Wait, Mama. We have to get a picture."

"We both look like water gophers, for crying out loud." She turned and walked back, knowing full well I didn't care what the hell we looked like.

"Water gophers aren't even a real thing, Mama. Now come here. I'm taking a selfie."

"Let me at least put some lipstick on!" Mama rummaged around in her bag, finally grabbing the applicator and holding it up, victorious, then started to apply it without a mirror. Impressive.

"What in the hell do you two think you're doing in here?" a man in a uniform yelled at us from the side entryway door, then turned and left as quickly as he had come in, making me think he was about to call for reinforcements.

"Just leaving, sir!" I yelled. "Mama, quick. Forget the lipstick. And smile!" She rubbed her lips together to spread what she had applied.

I snapped a couple of photos of us, our grins looking more worried than happy, then grabbed Mama's hand. We raced out the adjacent exit, then straight to our car, splitting up once we got there to hop into our seats. We both exhaled, then started laughing hysterically.

Mama rummaged around in her bag for her next paper map, while I peeked at the photos. There we were, a tall daughter with her tiny mama looking up at her proudly, our eyes crimson and swollen. Her wig was tilted slightly to the side, covering a part of her forehead. My hair looked like a small rodent had made a nest in it. At a quick glance, I would have deleted that photo right off my phone. But right now, it felt so incredibly perfect.

GRACE: So, hey!

I debated the exclamation point but figured I'd go in excited.

WYATT: Hey there.

He was not as excited. Unfortunately.

GRACE: So, I'm so sorry about those texts. As you probably guessed, I was a little tipsy.

That's an understatement.

WYATT: No apology necessary. I was actually a little jealous. All those misspellings and no *corrections after the fact. Pretty bold.

GRACE: Nothing a few bad gin and tonics couldn't do for you. They're the gifts that truly keep on giving. But seriously.

WYATT: Tisokay. 😆

GRACE: Har har.

WYATT: Where y'all at now?

GRACE: We have finally crossed into Mississippi.

WYATT: Good news. You're so close.

GRACE: I'll keep you posted.

WYATT: 🖤🖤🖤🖤🖤

GRACE: You win.

WYATT: 💪

Chapter 12

I was waiting for Mama's speech about the grandeur of a Mississippi sunrise, but she was too tired to do anything more than roll out of the motel bed and into the outfit she had carefully laid out the night before. I felt surprisingly well rested for someone who'd been nearly pushed off the bed by her senior citizen mother's bony ass all night long. Maybe I was finally getting used to having her all up in my business in my sleep too.

Mama's chatter picked up once we hit the road and was the playlist for pretty much our entire three-hour drive from our motel in Jackson to Tupelo, which mostly consisted of a looped conversation with herself about Elvis's birthplace. I couldn't help but think that she found comfort in the sound of her own voice like her own body's version of Prozac.

Tupelo was hardly as iconic as Graceland, but it

held a special place in Mama's heart. She would talk to anyone about Elvis's humble beginnings, whether they were listening or not, which usually ended with someone asking whether that's where Tupelo honey originated. Mama would gruffly sigh and reply, "No, it's where *Elvis* originated." The conversation would continue about bees, and Mama would walk away frustrated by their ignorance. She eventually took to learning where Tupelo honey *did* originate to arm herself with the fuel to steer the conversation back to Elvis, except most people were more interested in the fact that the honey was from the Ogeechee tupelo tree, found in parts of Georgia and Florida. Even I had to admit that the city being named after a tree that wasn't even indigenous to it was much more fascinating to me than Elvis, but I never said that to her face.

We passed signs for Philadelphia, Louisville, then Columbus, and I started to wonder if someone in Mississippi was drunk on moonshine when they named their cities. Weren't there enough names, and indigenous trees, for that matter, to go around so that they didn't need to steal from other states? It had to make explaining where you were from a little difficult, and from what I could see, terribly disappointing.

"I think this is it," I said, pulling up cautiously to a small wooden building that looked more like an outhouse than anything else. Mama started grabbing at the door handle before I stopped the car.

"This looks like it, all right," she said. "Let's park."

I pulled into the lot and parked, surprised at how many spots were taken at this early hour. Mama hopped out and started walking.

I looked down at my watch: 9:53 a.m. Dammit. "Mama," I yelled. "It's not even ten o'clock yet. Get back in the car, will you? You look ridiculous."

"Oh, honey. I think you pronounced 'fabulous' wrong."

I couldn't help but chuckle as I watched her flap around in the stuffy Mississippi air. "Mama. As I might have mentioned at least four hundred times, Elvis is not there. They moved him to Memphis. It's just a house."

"Just a house?" she screeched, as if I had used the Lord's name in vain at the Assembly of God church that was also sitting on the property. Apparently it was Elvis's childhood church, and it was only slightly larger than the house. The people had already formed a line outside the tiny shack of a home, and I suddenly felt bad for trying to shame her back into the car.

"Mama, I think you have to get your tickets there first," I said, pointing to a big, more modern brick building and the people gathered near it. She did a little shimmy shake to back herself up, then giggled with embarrassment as she caught most of the people in line staring at her. I unbuckled myself and followed her over. Instead of getting in the ticket line, she had stopped to examine his car, or as the sign said, "A car similar to the one Elvis's family had driven from Tupelo to Memphis." A few of the other visitors were doing the same, a couple of them fully decked out in Elvis attire from head to toe, with vintage Elvis t-shirts, baseball caps full of buttons, and my favorite part, the infamous gold Elvis sunglasses, making Mama look sorely underdressed. She made a point to compliment them loudly.

"I'll take your photo, Mama. Get in front." I waved to her, but she gestured toward me instead.

"Surely someone else will take our photo. Get in here, Grace!"

I handed the superfans my phone and stood next to Mama, waiting for her to dramatically wave her arms, but instead, she just planted one around my waist and the other on her hip, her smile as full as I had ever seen. So I decided to wave my arms for her, which made her laugh out loud and do the same.

"Here you go! Looks like they're opening up, finally." Our photographer pointed over to the building we had passed.

I looked down at my watch: 10:05. Only slightly better than Louisiana time.

"C'mon, Mama. Let's go get tickets." I called her over, but she was too busy soaking in every sign and memorial. It was as though Mama's shelves had been transformed into a garden of sorts.

I decided to let her be and get in line myself, which was moving quickly as more people started to file in. The woman behind the counter looked like she could have been with the gracious couple we had met outside. "Welcome to Elvis's Birthplace," she said with enthusiasm. She snatched up my cash, then returned the change with a brochure and two tickets, at which point Mama ran in.

"Thank you!" I chimed, then noticed a couple of Elvis figurines sitting on the counter next to her, their heads bobbing back and forth. I was about to point out to Mama that they had the word "Tupelo" on his big gaudy belt, but she was too focused on getting her hands on the tickets.

We exited through the same door we'd come in, then walked around a paved path with a fountain Mama seemed surprisingly uninterested in. Instead, she was waiting patiently outside of his house, which I learned was quite a generous description.

I suppose I wasn't intimately clear on how small Elvis's house was, but when the sign said "Shotgun Home," it made sense. You could shoot a gun from the front to the back, right through the entire house. A few steps up led to a tiny porch, and then just two tiny rooms before you could walk right out the back, which gave a striking image of what growing up poor in Mississippi might feel like, and emphasized the remarkability of his rise to fame. As much as I knew about Elvis, I had never had any empathy for him; I was too busy being jealous to think about the reality of his "humble beginnings" Mama rambled on about.

I snuck up behind Mama, who appeared to be in

the middle of a very serious conversation with the historical society volunteer. I reached for her, but then decided I'd sit instead, opting for one of the two chairs not blocked by velvet ropes.

I didn't expect to be moved by any of this, really. I had never felt any connection to a person through their home and the objects inside it. Maybe it's because anything I ever really loved or cared about had been taken away from me in anger.

"Well, you can hand over that emerald ring I gave you," my dad would tell me, at which point I'd never see it again unless Mama could find a way to sneak it out of the box in his closet when he was too drunk to care about anything but the bottle in his hand. And so to mitigate the loss of my once precious possessions, I decided it was easier to just not care about them.

But as I watched Mama examine every inch of the home and all its artifacts, I understood why her collection was so important to her. The link between everything had suddenly become illuminated for me, and I saw what I hadn't seen before—not because it wasn't obvious, but rather because I couldn't bring myself to admit it. The hope that had been bestowed upon her the first time she heard Elvis sing was carried through her life in those ceramic figurines. And when hope was not readily within her grasp— her parents passing, her child passing, her husband passing out, night after night—she'd grab an Elvis or order one, and that hope would be completely restored.

"It's exactly what I pictured," she said, doing a 360-degree turn to take the home's modest glory in.

"Do you want to go into the church too?" I asked.

She looked at me curiously. I answered my own question. "Of course you want to go to the church." Actually, *I* wanted to go to the church, though my excitement caught me off guard. Still, a building so special that they moved it was definitely worth seeing.

We were welcomed by an enthusiastic woman wearing an Elvis t-shirt, tucked neatly into a pair of blue jeans that looked like they had been pressed that morning. She acted like a church usher, walking us to an empty pew, while a young Elvis impersonator finished up a hymn. Mama was so taken that she nearly sat down on top of me.

"Good mornin', everyone," the woman said in what felt like a loud voice, but was probably just the acoustics of the very small wooden building. "My name is Ramona, and you are sitting in the Presley family's church."

Mama applauded, blissfully unaware that she was the only one clapping. Ramona looked pleased to find an enthusiast in the crowd, sharing a bit of the history directly with Mama, who looked more relaxed and content than I had seen her in a while. Once the short movie about the transportation and reconstruction of the building was over, she walked over to us.

"Where are you fine ladies headed?" Ramona sat

down on the pew in front of us, then leaned over the back to chat.

"Graceland!" Mama said. "Have you ever been?"

"Two glorious times," she replied. "But I have to say, the true fans always like it here better."

Mama looked rather confused, and you could tell she, a self-proclaimed true fan, was trying to figure out what about the two tiny buildings would over-shadow his home in Memphis. She looked over at me, and I gave her a tight, toothy grin that said, "Sorry, you are looking at the wrong person."

Ramona could tell she was struggling and leaned in. "Elvis made Graceland." She paused. "But Tupelo made Elvis." She sat back as if to give her revela-tion space. Mama totally drank the tea, and even I couldn't help but think about what she said. There was more, apparently. "You are going to swing by the hardware store. After you eat at Johnnie's, right?"

Mama looked confused. "Grace, are you writing all this down?"

I wasn't, but I grabbed some old receipts out of my bag, feeling a little important that Ramona had decided to bestow her infinite Elvis wisdom on us.

"The hardware store is where Elvis's mama bought him his first guitar! And it's right down the street, just a few minutes. The very counter, can you imagine?"

Mama shook her head, completely enthralled

with Ramona's knowledge and enthusiasm, while I grabbed my phone, deciding it would be much quicker to just type it in than writing it down.

"But you gotta get you a doughburger at Johnnie's Drive-In first...where Elvis used to eat?"

She kept asking us like we had heard of these spots, which I'm pretty sure Mama hadn't. Though Mama didn't seem to mind in the least bit, basking in her little Elvis club of two and a half.

"You can actually sit in the Elvis booth where he used to eat. Better get your camera ready." She pointed to the phone in my hand, then looked at her watch. "I'd head straight over and get there right when they open. It's a popular table, and you can't make reservations." She laughed at her own joke, which made me giggle too, even though I was only guessing why it was funny. I figured a place known for doughburgers was not on OpenTable.

Mama grabbed Ramona's hand and squeezed it tightly and let go, then started walking down the aisle.

"Mama, wait. Let's get a photo. Would you mind snapping one, Ramona?"

I handed her my phone, and Mama scurried back. "Good idea, Grace," she whispered in my ear as Ramona counted down like she was snapping pics with an old Kodak camera. She handed it back with a bunch of photos—clearly this was not her first photo rodeo—then walked out of the church ahead of us, greeting more guests as we headed back toward the entrance. Mama had her eye on the prize: a seat at the Elvis booth. I had to pee.

"I'll meet you at the car," I yelled, pointing to the restroom sign. Mama gave me the universal sign for "hurry the hell up," so I stepped up my pace, wandering back to where I bought the tickets. There was actually way more to the birthplace than I had expected—a bridge, an amphitheater, a museum. Mama's Elvis fandom always felt so unique, when in reality it was how she expressed her fandom that was all hers.

"Restrooms?" I asked the woman whom we'd met earlier at the ticket counter. I picked up one of the bobblehead figurines while waiting for her answer.

"Just through the shop, where you'll find a lot more of those, in case you're looking for something in particular."

I thanked her, then made a beeline for the bathrooms. On the way out, I stopped to examine the rows and rows of figurines, all neatly lined up, like at Mama's house. I suppose I should have been triggered, but instead, I was fascinated. I'd never seen so many of them before, most of which I recognized, making it difficult to spot any that Mama *didn't* own. That was until the replica of the statue in Shreveport caught my eye. It was cast in brass, giving it the same exact shine as the real one where we'd taken a photo. Against my better judgment, I grabbed it, paid quickly, and shoved it deep into my already full tote. The walk to the car was shorter than

I expected, so I was surprised that Mama wasn't there.

"Excuse me. Have you seen a woman? Short," I asked the woman from the shop, who was now taking her smoke break. She looked unshaken by my terribly generic descriptors. "Gigantic wig?"

"Ah, yes. She went into the museum a few minutes ago."

I smiled to thank her, then decided I'd rather sit outside and wait for Mama. The bench near the entrance seemed like a good place to hang out and flip through my phone. There had to be a couple winners in these photos to send to Asha. Mama was predictably smiling so hard her already super high cheekbones pressed up into tight balls right under her lower lids. And as I looked at my own face, in photo after photo, the smile I hadn't seen in a very long time had become predictable too.

GRACE: I have lost Mama in Tupelo, Mississippi.

ASHA: Oh my god. Grace. WHAT? Hold on. I'm hiding in my room so I can call you.

GRACE: SHIT. No. She's fine. I meant that I can't find her. Well, I technically know where she is but... God, I'm really off my game.

ASHA: I'm glad she's alive because I am not. 💀

GRACE: I'm sorry!

ASHA: It's fine. Just take good care of my children. 😆

GRACE: I would feed them all the sugar. And make them listen to Elvis.

ASHA: I am never dying.

GRACE: Clearly.

ASHA: So where are you now?

GRACE: Tupelo.

ASHA: Oh, like Tupelo honey. 🐝

GRACE: ✋

ASHA: That's what happens when you inadvertently kill someone with your texts. So how are things in Tupelo?

GRACE: Well, other than I've been waiting for Mama for who knows how long on a bench? Pretty good. I even bought an Elvis figurine.

ASHA: Now I'm really dead. 💀 💀

GRACE: It's actually...kinda cool.

ASHA: So long as you're not shopping for wigs. 🐢 I feel like figurines are the gateway drug to...

GRACE: No wigs. Promise. 💟 OMG finally here she comes. Okay, next text from Graceland. Whoo!

ASHA: Yay! It's like you ran a marathon or something. Except not at all.

GRACE: In a way it feels like that. The bad and the good parts. Bye!

———

If I had known before we got to our car that Johnnie's Drive-In was within walking distance, I probably would have forced us to do that instead, especially considering the amount of southern cuisine we'd been partaking in over the last week. A little exercise would have done us both good, though that might have been a dangerous endeavor for Mama in her shoes. They were more for cat-walking than actual walking. And even though she managed better than some women half her age, I didn't want to risk any kind of hospital visit, especially since we were within striking distance of Graceland.

We arrived at the infamous Johnnie's right as they unlocked the door, making us the first ones in line, scanning the menu over the counter full of greasy fried food that neither of us needed, but both of us suddenly wanted.

"I think I'm going to steer clear of the pimento cheese this time," I said to Mama, who was too busy looking for the booth where Elvis sat. The teenager behind the cash register smiled nervously. "Mama, what are you having?"

"Oh, just order me something, Grace. It's not the time to worry about food."

"Mama, considering we're standing in a restaurant, I'm pretty sure it *is* the perfect time to worry about food."

I looked at the teenager, who was eagerly awaiting our order.

"What do you recommend?" I asked her, as if I had been transported to Tavern on the Green.

She looked at me as though she didn't understand

the question. "Um, we're kinda famous for the doughburger. And the barbeque." She pointed to the sign above her head that said "Johnnie's Bar-B-Q Drive-In."

I laughed nervously. "Okay, great, so we'll take a doughburger and barbeque plate."

"You get two veggies with that," she replied, not even skipping a beat.

I opened my mouth to ask her about the offerings, which was her cue to rattle them off to me. "Mashed 'tatoes, mac 'n' cheese..."

"That's a vege...?" I started to ask her facetiously, then remembered where I was. "We'll take some tots and...funnel cake fries?" I was waiting for her to tell me that they weren't considered a vegetable and force me to choose something that was actually grown in the ground, but she did not. Instead, she yelled my order back to the kitchen while grabbing the cash out of my hand. She looked surprised when I dropped a few dollars into the tip jar.

While I was ordering us a couple of heart attacks, Mama had situated herself in a booth, appropriately marked "Elvis Booth" with a golden sign. The wall next to it was covered in small shelves holding up rows and rows of Elvis memorabilia. Mama must have felt right at home.

"I can't believe it wasn't taken," Mama said to me as I grabbed some napkins and a few ketchup packets, then realized that I probably didn't want ketchup with funnel cake fries. Actually, I probably didn't want the funnel cake fries. But, hey, it's considered a vegetable in Mississippi.

"That's what you get when you have a hankering for barbeque at eleven in the morning."

Mama was too busy snapping photos of the sign to take offense at my sarcasm.

"Here, Grace. Come sit by me and get a photo."

I moved over to sit next to her at the same time that the cashier was bringing our drinks. Surprisingly, she offered to take a photo of us together.

"It's actually better if you sit on your own side." Like Ramona at Elvis's birthplace, clearly this girl had taken her share of tourist pics. "This is the oldest restaurant in Tupelo. Since October 17, 1945."

She snapped a bunch of photos, then let us know she'd be back with our food. I guess a few extra bucks goes pretty far in northern Mississippi.

Mama waved her hand at my phone. "Let me see!" she said, and I obliged, opting to just flip through them rather than give it to her. She had a penchant for clicking buttons that ended up doing things like deleting important information. She smiled bigger at the sight of each photo, even though the most recent photos were just a bunch of the same.

Our food arrived almost as quickly as our drinks had been delivered, and before I could even open a napkin to put on my lap, Mama was diving into the doughburger, which I learned was a burger with flour filler, a trick they used back during war times to stretch the meat. Yay, Wikipedia.

"I have never eaten anything as delicious as this," my mother crooned, her voice loud but garbled with food. "I can see why Elvis loved it here." A few people who had walked in for pre-lunchtime barbeque turned to see the weirdo proclaiming her love for a flour-filled meat patty with such fervor at eleven a.m. as I slumped in my seat while shoveling fries into my mouth by the fistful.

"Mama!" I whisper-yelled, something I had perfected over the years when anyone in my life came remotely close to embarrassing me.

In this case, Mama was right, the food was pretty freaking delicious, though I'm not quite sure she needed to announce her affection to the entire dining room.

"Mama, did you see this?" I held up a small figure that was different from the rest of the tchotchkes stuffed on the surrounding wall of the inside of the restaurant, a little hand-painted piece of Elvis, Priscilla, and Lisa Marie.

"Oh, honey, I've got one just like that, except mine only has one Elvis, not three."

"Um, Mama...there's only one..."

Mama shrieked. "Grace!"

She was holding on to the table in front of her like it was the edge of a mountain cliff and she was about to fall over. Her eyes were closed, and for a second, I thought she was going to faint. I jumped up out of my seat and slid in next to her. She opened her eyes, like a deer caught in headlights.

"Mama, what happened? Are you okay?"

I wrapped my arm around her, and she slowly loosened her grip from the table. Her rapid breathing probably wasn't helping her calm down, so I tried to reassure her the best I could, given I was pretty much freaking out inside too.

"I've got you. I've got you now." She melted into me, and I just held her close, trying to figure out what to do next. The young waitress brought over some wet towels, which I placed on Mama's forehead. I couldn't believe she let me, considering how much time she spent putting on her makeup in the car, which made me think this was pretty damn serious.

"The lights just went off. They just went off on me…" Her voice trailed off, and I remembered what her doctor had told me about the blackouts and what they meant. And from the tears coming down her face, it was clear that she remembered too.

"Mama, seriously, I think we need to see a doctor." We hobbled back to the car together, my arm underneath hers for what I thought was stability.

"I'm perfectly one hundred percent fine!" She stopped in the middle of the lot.

"Except you're not. You have brain cancer, Mama. I need to make sure you're okay before we get in the car for another long drive."

"It's barely a two-hour ride! Don't be ridiculous!" she yelled.

"We're going to the doctor, and that's it. No discussion!" A couple getting out of their car looked over in our direction, but didn't seem fazed by the escalating drama. "You know there's something wrong, and yet, what, you're just going to pretend like everything's okay? Not this time."

She turned and looked straight at me. "Why do I feel like this has nothing to do with my 'passing out'?" She used air quotes as if I had just imagined what happened.

I shuffled over next to the cars so I wouldn't be standing in the middle of the parking lot getting chastised by a woman who looked like a walking caricature, then thought about what she said. And what I had said. She was kind of right.

"You're right! It doesn't. I mean…" I stumbled.

"You cannot force me to do anything! If I want to stay, I'll stay." She sounded infantile, at best, but also confused by her own choice of words.

"I'm not trying to tell you what to do. This is me being worried about you!" I didn't care so much about the people in the parking lot anymore. Maybe I should have, but I was tired of Mama just dropping bombs and leaving shrapnel everywhere she went.

Mama started talking through her teeth, which was always worse than her yelling. She pointed at me with her tiny wrinkled finger like she was pressing a button repeatedly. "Sometimes we make decisions that we just can't explain, Grace. And they might not be what other people think are right, but they're right for us."

"*For you.* Not for us." My voice started shaking, the fear of losing Mama and the pain of having to fight her at every turn was unsteadying. I turned to walk away from her, realizing that would just take me back to the restaurant, so I tried to sneak past her so she might get the hint to get in the car. It didn't work. "Don't I count in this equation? There's not just you to think about here."

Mama stuttered, trying to keep up her level of obstinance with me, but she couldn't do it. Maybe she was getting weaker, which I tried not to focus on. I wanted to believe that our time together had started to sink in.

"Oh, Grace, you know I love you. So much." She grabbed my waist and hugged me so tight I couldn't help but believe her.

"Love isn't so selfish, Mama." The words were getting harder to say through my tears.

"I imagine it might feel that way for you. But I've got my reasons."

I gently pushed her back so I could see her face, now with fewer layers of mascara on her eyelashes, the remnants on my shirt. "You've got to go to the hospital, Mama. You just have to."

She paused, and for a moment, I thought she might actually concede. But then I remembered who was standing in front of me. "I can't, baby. I know you won't understand, but you can't control everything. I saw more Elvises than I should. I had a little blip, but we're so close."

"I understand seeing more Elvises is your ultimate fantasy, but in this case, it's not a good thing." I couldn't believe she was so blasé about what had just happened, like she had just gotten a bad case of the hiccups from her doughburger.

"I can still make decisions for myself," she said, doing what looked like her best headstrong toddler impression, though it felt like she was trying to convince herself more than me. That made it a little easier for me to give her a hard time.

"I know you can. But sometimes you need to let other people in. You don't have to do everything on your own."

Mama's face softened, which surprised me. I figured she'd come back with something like "you of all people," like it was the pot calling the leopard-print kettle black. But she didn't. "How about I promise to go to the doctor the second we leave Graceland."

I couldn't believe it. "Compromise? Who is this woman and what has she done with my mama?"

Mama smiled, then grabbed my hand. "I'm going to miss you so much, Grace Louise." I had to think twice about what she said. And then I got it, sort of grateful I had been a little slow on the uptake to give myself time to digest the weight of what she was saying. I don't think she meant it to hit me like a wrecking ball.

"What are you talking about, Mama? I'm not going anywhere," I replied, walking over to my side of the car and hopping in. She smiled softly, picking up the subtext that I was doing my best to drop, then got in and buckled up.

I backed out of the parking lot, thankful for the opportunity to look out my driver's-side window, away from Mama, so she wouldn't see the tears running down my cheeks.

Chapter 13

The tufts of cotton on the plants along the side of the road, nestled in between rows of catfish farms, didn't seem real. Except for the fluff, the bushes were completely barren, looking like they were pulled right out of a Dr. Seuss book.

My phone signaled our welcome into Tennessee, but I didn't need Siri's help to tell us. The farmland had quickly been replaced with Waffle Houses, White Castles, and Walmarts. And then our own destination, which would likely feel like seeing a mirage after all these miles.

Mama had booked us a night at the Guest House at Graceland, so we could be fresh for our visit in the morning. She had mistakenly assumed it was actually on the Graceland property, and was confused and disappointed when I explained to her that it was just nearby. I couldn't figure out how, after seventy years, she could be so naïve about things. Or maybe it was just her optimism.

"Mama, look! The first Graceland sign we've seen this entire trip."

She rustled a bit in her seat, then mumbled something that sounded like, "Oh, well, that's just lovely, honey."

Then she snuggled back into the side of the door, her head resting on a travel pillow she insisted on bringing. I wanted her to ask me to pull over so she could take a photo. Or at least get annoyingly excited, like she always did about the most inane things. Instead, she was curled up into what seemed like a slowly shriveling ball.

Since I knew Mama so well, that should have been the clue. But it wasn't until she started shaking violently that I got the message loud and clear.

Mama. Oh shit. "MAMA!" I swerved off the highway onto the shoulder, unsnapped my buckle, frantically Googling "What to do when someone has a seizure" while trying to call 911 from some random location across the Mississippi-Tennessee line.

"Yes, hello. Um, my mother is having a seizure and I'm stuck on the highway." I tried to sound calm, but I think that only made me sound like a serial killer. I'd heard enough true crime podcasts where they analyze the 911 calls, and the ones where they're calm are always worse than the ones where they freak out. But as the panic set in, I realized there was no chance of me sounding calm. I had gone from zero to ugly cry, and I was having difficulty forming words.

"Mi-le mark-er? I'm not sure." I frantically scanned the greenery out my window for anything that looked like one, hoping I was just too upset to see it right in front of me. "There's nothing. Wait! That green 'Graceland' sign." I squeezed everything, closing my eyes as if I was a beauty queen waiting for an announcer to call my name. "You know it? Yes. Yes. I...I don't really know. No, she's breathing. Yes. Yes. Okay, thank you so much."

Unfortunately, WebMD's advice for dealing with a seizure was not friendly for someone driving down the highway at seventy miles per hour, or even sitting in the car on the side of the road. *Place her on her side?* Not happening. *Don't put anything in her mouth?* Is that really something people try to do? *Use your watch to try to time...* I tossed my phone back in the bag. I couldn't remember ever feeling so helpless, Mama shaking in the seat next to me as I gripped the wheel, gently rocking back and forth, knowing enough not to try to touch her. "Please be okay. Please please please," I whispered, trying to slow my breathing.

Mama jerked up out of her seat, confused and unsteady.

"What in the...?" She was breathing hard.

"Oh thank you! Thank you! Mama, just relax. It's going to be okay," I blubbered, trying my best to sound believable. I could hear the sirens in the distance, roaring louder as they got closer and closer, until they stopped right behind us. I didn't want to have to explain what I had just seen to Mama. It was frightening enough as a bystander, but to be the person actually experiencing it? Traumatizing.

"Ma'am, is everything okay?" Two EMTs in uniform ran up to the passenger side of the car. The man held up his ID as I leaned over to help Mama roll down her window. She tried to speak, but it sounded like gibberish.

"Oh, how swirly whirly. Everything's keeny peach. Gracie's golden!" Mama sounded drunk.

I smiled weakly, then flopped back into my seat, head leaning back onto the headrest, eyes closed to get my bearings back.

"Well, we're going to check you out to make sure everything truly is *keeny peach*, as you say, ma'am. Are you able to walk?"

Mama didn't answer. Instead, she was dozing off, her head now resting uncomfortably on the door.

"I'll take that as a 'no,'" the EMT said. They hustled over to the ambulance, then returned with a gurney, which they helped her onto like they had choreographed it beforehand. The female EMT came over to talk to me after they had gotten Mama into the back of the van.

"Listen, she's got cancer. In her brain." I tried to speak quietly in case Mama could hear me, not that she'd have any say in what I told the EMT at this point.

"We'll take a look. Do you want to come back there with us?"

I shook my head. "Nah, I'm just going to sit here for a minute, if you don't mind."

"Well, it's a good sign she's up and moving. So that's something."

"Yeah, she's something, all right." Mama waved at me from the back of the ambulance. Or maybe she was swatting a fly. I couldn't tell.

The EMT smiled, then nodded, walking briskly back to the ambulance behind us, saying something over her shoulder walkie-talkie that I couldn't quite understand, though did it really matter what she said? I knew Mama needed to get taken to the hospital. But what I was really worried about was whether she'd actually be leaving this time.

Anytime she had gone in for her chemo treatments or checkups, the thought of her not coming home had never crossed my mind. I couldn't let it. And well, I was never privy to all of it. She kept everything fairly hush-hush, in true Mama style, always asking me about what I was up to, as if there was anything new to report in the world of accounting. No major crises that needed to be averted, unless you call the mystery of the missing lunches a newsworthy event. On those obligatory calls, I'd ask her how she was doing, and somehow she must have sensed, perhaps from my "uh-huh" and "yeah," that I couldn't be bothered with more than "fine." More like, I'm not sure I would have been able to handle more than "fine." I needed to know that everything was okay with Mama, so I could relax and keep her at a very long-distance arm's length.

I watched from my car as the EMTs started an IV, then covered her with a blanket, both of them taking notes on different clipboards. I rolled down my window.

"I'll just follow you. Is that good?" I yelled. The woman walked toward me.

"We're headed to Memphis South. She's stable enough that we can get her pretty darn close to your destination, actually."

"You mean Graceland? Well, only if you feel as though that's the right place for her."

"From what I can tell, she's definitely in the right place." The woman's face was stoic and professional, but I could see the smile in her eyes. "Just follow along behind us as best you can. We're going full sirens upon special request."

As the EMT who was sitting with Mama shut the doors, I saw her holding her buckle straps tightly, like a roller coaster was about to take off. I waved at her, but she didn't see me, her eyes closed tightly, as if she was making a wish. Or maybe she was, just like me, scared as hell.

I drove into the emergency entrance, then diverted over to the parking lot as the ambulance pulled up to the sliding glass doors, waving at the EMT who jumped out of the driver's seat. He was moving much more quickly than seemed customary for special request full sirens, and when my eyes moved to the back of the van, I understood why.

Doctors and nurses were racing out of the hospital building to help bring Mama's gurney in, while the female EMT, straddling Mama, was pumping her chest and yelling to the team.

"Mama!" I screamed, racing over behind them, her gurney zipping down the hall, growing smaller and smaller as it got farther away from me. "Wait! Please!" I made it halfway, then felt myself crumbling into the ground.

"Whoa, whoa there. I got you." An older gentleman with a light blue lab coat caught me and helped me over to a chair. If he had been wearing red, I might have expected his name tag to read "Santa Claus." Instead, it said "James."

"I need to get back there. My mama..." I started to point to the hall, then decided my hands would go to better use stabilizing myself in the chair than giving someone who worked at the hospital directions.

"Of course you do, miss. But by the looks of those puddin' legs, I might need to push you back. Let me get us a set of wheels and we'll see what all the fuss is about. What's your name, darlin'?"

"Grace. I'm Grace. My mama's Loralynn Johnson."

I sat, gripping the arms, trying to get myself together, though part of me felt somewhat reassured that if I was going to lose myself to a panic attack, sitting in a chair directly outside a hospital emergency room would be the ideal location.

James disappeared for a minute, returning with a large metal chair with a black pleather seat. "Now climb on in—carefully, you hear—and slide this band on your wrist. That way I won't get in trouble for rolling back a stranger into the ER." I stood, then turned and sat, propping my feet onto the footrests, and slipping the wristband onto my arm while he pushed me down the hall where I had seen Mama disappear, then through a couple of double doors that opened magically as we pulled up.

I took it as a good sign that no one was yelling, but the cacophony of beeps, mixed with the smell of excrement and bleach, did little to ease my racing brain. The first and only time I had ever been to the ER was when Jeff cut himself with a knife and ended up needing a few stitches. The physician's assistant seemed disappointed that his deep cut was the result of him trying to cut through a pesky sweet potato. It did seem less heroic than, say, fighting off a potential pickpocket. Or even butchering a steak. "They're quite hard to cut," he told her unconvincingly. *Sorry he doesn't have a javelin through his head,* I remember thinking.

But this visit, no one was sitting around judging Mama for her poor choice in cutlery. They were all crammed in her room, taking notes and talking with each other in whispery voices you might use at a movie theater when you don't want to come off as rude but you still want someone to hear what you've said.

After a quick chat with someone at the nurse's station, James pushed me right over to Mama's room, and I took comfort that no one was yelling "CLEAR," like I had watched Dr. John Carter on *ER* yell a hundred times.

"This is Grace—the young lady's daughter." Everyone turned, and I stood up out of the seat to greet them, then plopped right back down after seeing Mama, a tube down her throat and wires attached to every part of exposed skin I could see.

"Hi. Her name is Loralynn. She has cancer that has metastasized to her brain. She had a seizure in the car, but I thought everything was…" I started crying, actually sobbing, not even worried that I was being stared at by what felt like the entire staff of the ER.

"Grace, I'm Dr. Williams, the head of the ER here." She looked like one of the interns, a young Asian woman barely Mama's height, with big dark-rimmed glasses and her hair tied up in a messy topknot. For a second, I forgot where I was and felt incredibly uncool. She seemed kind and genuine. "Your mama is stabilized for now, and we've intubated her to help her breathe while we figure out exactly what's going on. We'll be sure to get our director of oncology down here to see her immediately."

"She was fine just a minute ago! She had a seizure

and then she was a little woozy but…" At some point I'd be able to complete a sentence again.

"We're going to take good care of her. I'll get all her doctor information from you when you're feeling a bit better. For now, why don't you have a seat in here and we'll get you something to drink."

"I don't think you've got anything hard enough for me, Doctor." She smiled and shook my hand.

"That all depends on what you're looking for, and who you ask." The team giggled and exited the room behind her. One of the staff stayed behind and dropped a couple of small apple juice cups into my lap.

"I know this is not exactly what you were looking for, but they do taste pretty good."

I smiled up at her.

"Just hang tight. We're definitely going to admit her. I'll have all that info for you in a bit."

I pulled out my phone and dialed Asha. It went to voice mail. She never answers the phone. "Hey, Ash, it's Grace. Mama's in the hospital. Again. It's back. The cancer. *Her* cancer. God, I shouldn't be telling you all this over voice mail. I'm sorry. Um, anyway, call me when you get this."

Then I texted Wyatt.

> **GRACE:** Hey. So…Mama's in the hospital. Which I guess means I'm in the hospital.

My phone rang immediately, and I jumped. It was Wyatt.

"Oh, hey. You didn't have to…" I tried to sound all nonchalant like I hadn't just been through the most traumatic thing in my life and needed to talk to someone familiar. But I really needed to hear his voice, more than I had known until this moment. All this time we had been texting, and I felt like, in some ways, I could have taken or left this new relationship, but with my heart nearly busting out of my chest, that clearly wasn't the case. It was weird feeling elated and desperate at the same exact time.

"Of course I did. I hate the phone as much as anybody, but some things are sacred. Are you okay? Is she okay? That's probably the worst thing to ask. Of course you're both not okay." His voice trailed off as he scolded himself, but it was clear to me that he cared, not just about Mama, but about me too.

"It's really not the worst thing. I'm just happy to hear your voice."

"Same. I'm sorry, Grace. What happened?"

"She had a seizure in the car…and was mostly okay when the ambulance took her…but then I got here…and they were pumping her chest and…" Crying again. Fuck. Breathe. "She's intubated now and they're going to take a look and see what's going on. Which means, I think we'll be here for a while. In Memphis. We fucking made it to Memphis."

"Oh, shit. Grace. That fucking blows. Can I say that? I just did, but anyway, dammit. Apparently I curse a lot when people are in hospitals."

I chuckled. "I appreciate that. More than you know. Dammit."

He laughed, but then stopped abruptly. Even I felt a little weird chuckling, given the circumstances, but it felt good to have an emotion other than fear for a few minutes. "Are they taking good care of her? And you?"

"I could go for a measuring cup full of whiskey right about now."

"It's Memphis! Don't they have booze in the vending machine there?"

I giggled. "I'm going to go check right now. And report back." He had a way of acknowledging the situation and calming me down, sort of like a hostage negotiator. "Thanks, Wyatt."

"I'm here if you need me. Well, I'm not there...but you get the idea. Call me anytime, Grace."

I hung up, then slumped back in the chair, ripping open an apple juice and throwing it back in one giant gulp. The nurse was right. It did taste pretty good.

I could just about see Graceland beyond the fence through the dirty hospital window in Mama's room. I had asked the nurse to pull her bed as close as all the machines and cords would allow.

"How can they have a hospital so close to Graceland with such filthy windows?" I asked, channeling my inner Loralynn. I dipped the bathroom paper towel in the water and cleaned up the spot right near where she would look out if she turned her head. If she could turn her head.

"It's just part of the scenery," the nurse replied. Just part of the scenery? Mama would have been horrified.

I could imagine Mama wiping the window clean herself and me being completely grossed out by it.

Oh, what, Grace? Am I going to catch a disease or something? She'd pretend to lick her finger, and I would stick my tongue out. *I can't get much sicker than I am right now.*

There was something terribly unfair about seeing Mama's beloved Graceland for the first time through a dirty hospital window. On one hand, it was like being at a party but not being allowed to have any cake. But then it felt a bit poetic, wiping away the grime to get a glimpse at hope. This was not an unfamiliar theme in our lives, but it seemed like an insult to her illness that we would have to do it literally.

"Do you by chance have any spray?" I asked the nurse who was taking Mama's vitals. I realized it was her job to take care of Mama, not help me take care of the hospital, but I wanted that window to be immaculate when Mama woke up.

"You must be Grace!" a petite woman said as she entered the room. Her bright pink lab coat was buttoned only once, in the middle of her stomach, and just barely at that, looking like she had left her own coat at home and was borrowing one that belonged to her miniature schnauzer. Her hair, which was the nicest bad wig I'd ever seen, was even higher than Mama's, and that was saying something. It added a couple of inches to her height, making her barely five feet tall. Her shiny iridescent clogs reflected off the horrible lighting.

She saw me noticing and mistook it for admiration. "Mermaid. That's what they're called—isn't that great?...and also a little weird, now that I think of it, since mermaids don't wear..." Her voice trailed off as she tried to comprehend what seemed to be quite a conundrum.

My confidence waned. Oh, who am I kidding? I had no confidence to begin with.

"I'm Dr. McMenamy, but you can call me Dr. Mac. My friends call me Big Mac." She let out a "ha!" which sounded like someone had read it at the end of a sentence in a text message.

"All right, so we got in touch with your mom's doctors in El Paso and in Dallas, and I've got a good sense of what's going on here. It certainly doesn't take a pink panther like me to tell you what's happening up in your mama's brain." I would have described her more like a Kirby, but whatever.

"She's got a lot of cancer up in there, and without some treatments to beat it back, she's going to start having a lot more of those seizures. That's just not good for anyone."

I nodded, trying to process all the information without crying. Again.

"We're going to stabilize her and give her an intense course of medicine. Depending on how she responds, you can probably be on your way in a week or so."

"A week?!" I didn't mean to sound so exasperated. Or maybe I did.

"It's possible it could be less, but I don't like to overpromise and underdeliver. However long it takes, she has to continue when she gets back to wherever it is you're getting back to."

"I don't disagree with you, Doctor. She's just..." I couldn't quite find the right word to describe Mama's level of stubborn.

"I've got a few patients like your mama. I'll do my best to convince her. Now you should go get some grub. The cafeteria ain't half bad, as you can tell." She patted her belly, then extended her hand out to me to shake it before leaving.

My phone rang. "I'm going to let you take that, even though they're anti–cell phones up in here." She pointed to no less than three signs with cell phones and a huge red "X" through them.

I smiled and nodded.

"Hey, Asha," I said as I answered.

"Dammit, the one time I don't have my phone glued to my hand. What's going on?" I was relieved to hear her voice and the normalcy of her response. She wasn't freaking out—just curious.

"She nearly passed out in Tupelo, but refused to go to the hospital, then had a seizure in the car, and then coded during the ambulance ride. She's stable now, but they've got her intubated. I've never seen her so quiet, and it's kind of freaking me out." I finally took a breath. It felt good to just spit it out, but also good to hear myself say it out loud to let myself off the hook for all the feelings I was feeling. This wasn't just a strep test or a couple of stitches.

"At least your mom is consistent." And that's why I love Asha: concern with a side of humor. She knew exactly what I needed.

"Diagnosis: a pain in the ass." We both laughed, and it felt a little weird, but good. Like my body had been waiting for someone to give it permission.

"All moms are. It's part of the job description, especially when they get older. So now what?" I tried to run through the laundry list of things they were doing to Mama, but I figured she didn't need to know every detail. And the rule follower in me was worried I'd get yelled at for still being on my phone.

"They're giving her some treatments, and then if she's stable, we can finally get to Graceland in a week or so. But they want her to do treatments when she gets back to Texas." I said it like I had no skin in the game, when really, all my skin was about waist deep. Thankfully, Asha didn't critique my delivery tone.

Clearly Asha knew Mama quite well. "Do you think she'll listen?"

"I don't think this doctor will take no for an answer." And thank goodness for that. I was not sure

I had the willpower or the patience to try to convince Mama to continue the treatments after the trip.

"And how about you? How are you holding up?"

I paused, deciding how honest I wanted to be. I was not quite sure my eyes could take any more tears. "Well, these are the first sentences I've been able to finish in the last few hours that haven't been punctuated with crying. So, much better."

"Progress! I'm sorry. This fucking sucks." For a second, I worried about her kids hearing her, then remembered she didn't care about cursing around them. Cool mom.

"I just didn't want it...It can't end like..." So much for not crying.

"Grace. It's not ending like this," Asha said definitively. I wasn't sure if I was ready for the tough love, but that wasn't about to stop her. "I know that is not the thing to say because I do not know for sure, but I'm saying it anyway."

"I said a lot to her—about Daddy, about Elvis—but I don't know if it was enough. She still probably thinks..." I ran through all the stops on our trips—the conversations we had—and as honest as I thought I had been, I didn't know if it was enough to make things feel right between us. Would I ever know if it was enough?

"...that you're her daughter who she loves very much?" That was not exactly what I was going to say. She kept going, not even giving me a chance to protest. "You're so damn hard on yourself. She was in the house. She saw what happened. It can't be a surprise that you did what you did—move away, marry Guy Smiley..."

"What do you mean?" I jumped in.

"Sorry, we've been on a *Sesame Street* bender here."

"No, I mean how is Jeff a part of this?" I couldn't quite figure out what she was getting at.

"Isn't it obvious? Jeff is the complete opposite of your dad, which was probably good, but that's not love. That's saving yourself from being your mom."

Shit. All this time and therapy and wracking my brain, and Asha let me off the hook in one simple declaration. I remembered what Mama had said when I told her about Jeff's affair, and how at the time, I couldn't quite grasp what she meant about understanding why I was with him. Now I did.

"You did the best you could with what you had, Grace. But now you have more. You can do more. You deserve more."

I breathed in Asha's words, thinking of all the times I'd told myself that there had to be more, that I deserved to experience true love just once in my life, as scary as I knew it might be. I wanted to feel dizzy with passion and sick to my stomach with longing, finally daring to take a risk on something that might not be a sure bet. And I wanted Mama to be there to see it all, to know that my dad hadn't won.

"I can't lose her like this," I sobbed.

"You wouldn't be able to lose her in any situation, Grace. There's no ideal way to lose a parent. So just cut yourself a little slack. Loralynn is a fighter, and she is not going down like this. Not without seeing Graceland. There's no way in hell." She sounded so convincing. I wanted to believe her. I really did.

"I've said that before..."

"Stop. I love you, Grace, but stop. What you've done—what you're doing—is more than a lot of kids would do." She was not messing around. I'd never heard Asha do this to anyone before, let alone me. She was the one who would never really take sides, always trusting that you knew yourself best. Not this time, though.

The old Grace would have said, "Is it, though?" but new Grace knew better, and agreed with her. "I know, I know."

"So just prepare what you're going to say to her when she wakes up. And go get some rest. You know you can call me anytime if you need anything, okay?" All good ideas, especially the rest. Mama always said that if I'm feeling sad or tired, it was probably the tired talking. I needed to listen to her. And Asha.

"Okay, okay. Thanks for the intervention, Ash. I miss you." My friends had been my chosen family in lieu of an actual one, or at least, one that I connected with beyond obligatory gestures, though now Mama was feeling familial too.

"I miss you too. Bye."

I hung up and walked to the side of Mama's bed near the big dirty window, and lay down on the couch next to it, the city lights now glowing across the vast darkness. Feeling the lump in my pocket made me jerk back up, and I pulled out the little bag with the rock from Madame Arabella. I'd completely forgotten about it. The soft, smooth blue stone was wrapped in a note.

Blue Lace Agate: Use to release repression and suppression of feelings caused by past fears, judgments, or rejections.

Um.

The calm, centering properties also aid those who are unable to stop talking, or who speak before thinking about the consequences of their words.

That sounds familiar.

Use for sore throats, stomach issues, and seizures.

Whoa.

Maybe we did get our fifty dollars' worth. Now where was that prediction she gave us? I couldn't remember where I had put the envelopes, which I guessed wouldn't do me any good now, sitting here in the hospital she probably told me I'd be sitting in. This rock was going to have to do for now, which sounded ridiculous running through my head. But really, this whole thing was ridiculous. Two weeks ago I was sitting in my office trying to convince a client that his new eighty-inch screen television as a business expense was a stretch. And here I am hoping a rock given to me by a Louisiana psychic can help Mama. Or perhaps it already had been helping.

I grabbed her hand, placing the stone in it, and clasped my hand around hers until I slowly dozed off. More than anything, I wished that I was being kept awake by the purr of her snoring and not the beeps and pumps of the machines that were giving her life.

After a couple of nights on the hospital couch, I decided I needed an actual shower, at least for the sake of the staff who had to smell me every single time they walked into the room. They were all too polite to actually say anything, other than that I should get some rest, but the look on their faces said, "Get a fucking shower, woman" quite clearly. I reeked of a combination of bleach and chlorine courtesy of the blanket that felt like I was sleeping under a Brillo pad. The deodorant over armpits washed with hospital bathroom hand soap was not helping. And my neck would never have full range of motion again. Who needs to be able to look left anyway?

Since Mama had already booked us for a couple of nights at the Guest House at Graceland, I just extended my stay indefinitely and finally got that much-anticipated shower and some sleep that didn't involve permanently damaging my neck. About 72 percent of me wanted to scold the hotel for false advertising on behalf of Mama, who had been confused by the name, but I had hope that she would be able to do that on her own in the next few days.

My back, on the other hand, was not super pleased

with the choice of mattress, so I added an extra Advil to my daily pill regimen. I spent most of my time in silence, sitting with Mama in her room, then sitting in the car on my drives to and from the hospital. It was a stark contrast from the rest of our trip, with Mama's chatter and self-talk as our soundtrack. Even during her catnaps, she would shout out, interrupting whatever music or podcast I had playing in the background, with some wacky command that about one out of every five times made scary sense. I tried not to think about what her dreams, or nightmares, were like—a weird brain cancer and chemo cocktail that I hoped had her dancing with Elvis and not pacing around the outer rim of hell completely barefoot.

The rotation of hospital staffers kept telling me she was doing well, and the meds were working, but I wanted to hear it from Mama. As much as I understood that I could believe them, she still had a tube down her throat and was lying motionless in her bed, which didn't really say to me, "The meds are working, Grace!" Hearing her sing some Elvis would at least instill some confidence. I wasn't much on trusting the word of strangers.

I was drifting off into an afternoon nap, which signaled my level of sleep deprivation, when my phone rang. "Hey, Wyatt." I said it, then realized I sounded kind of drunk.

"Hi there. Figured I would check to see how an actual night's worth of sleep in a real bed was treating you." I had kept him up to speed on all the goings-on, and he had been a heavy influence in getting me out of the hospital room. "Doing okay?"

"I was just about to take a nap, actually—no Bloody Marys involved."

He laughed. "I could go for a couple of those right now. With the right company, of course." His voice changed, and for the first time in all of our conversations and texts, I felt like he was flirting with me.

"How long's the drive from New Orleans? I think I can scrounge up a measuring cup or two." I was feeling a little bold. "But seriously, I'd probably be a terrible host."

"Yes, clearly you should be worried about my needs, seeing as…your mother is in the hospital. Speaking of, how's the old whippersnapper?"

"Not whipping or snapping just yet. I'm trying not to freak out." Everyone at the hospital warned me that she would look worse than she was, but it wasn't her appearance that was off-putting. It was the deafening silence every time I walked into her room, other than the beeping and whooshing of machines.

"I'm sure it's hard. You're handling everything so well, Grace. She's lucky to have you." His voice lowered. I loved how he could go from silly to serious so handily.

Any other time anyone would have said that to me, I would have flopped my hand over in a "pshaw" kind of manner, and explained to them in coded language that my family was kind of messed up, and

I hit the road, making me the least eligible candidate for child of the year. But I was starting to give myself a little credit, and letting the words Mama told me over the last week sink in.

"Thank you. That means a lot." I let those words stand. No silly quips to take the edge off. It felt foreign, but right. But there was more I wanted to tell him, and I didn't want to wait any longer. "So I was wondering…" I started, but he also began talking at the same time.

"So, is it weird for me to say…I'd love to see you again? I know that's probably the last thing on your mind right now, but I feel like I would regret not telling you while I have you."

I started shaking as all the butterflies flew out of my stomach and into all of my extremities. "I'd love it too," I said calmly, even though I wanted to reach through the phone and squeeze him. "You bring the measuring cups, and I'll bring the vodka." I sounded so cool and collected.

"Deal!" he exclaimed. "Now get some rest. Because you know when Loralynn wakes up, she's going to be rarin' to go. Bye, Grace."

"Bye." I clicked the red button on my phone to hang up, excited at the thought of seeing him again. Then I imagined Mama racing around in a tizzy to pack up her bags and free herself from the shackles of hospital imprisonment. I flopped back onto my pillow to try to rest and fast-forward to the end of the week.

On Sunday morning, exactly one week after Mama arrived at the hospital, I walked into her room armed with my extra hot soy latte (Memphis has Starbucks!). But instead of beeping and pumping, Mama's room was graveyard silent. And her bed empty. Someone would have told me if something had happened to her, right? Well at least, a bad something.

I raced out of the room without an ounce of chill and headed straight to the nursing station.

"Excuse me. Do you know where my mama, er, Loralynn Johnson has gotten to?" I asked with the tone of a person who knew her mama was indeed alive and not wrapped up in the morgue waiting to be claimed, even though the thought crossed my mind at least three times while I asked it.

"Let me check," the nurse replied, without even looking up from her computer. Isn't it her job to know where her patients are?

I breathed a loud sigh, and the nurse looked up as if I had just contaminated her personal space with my exhaled germs. "When did she get…?" I wanted to say "excommunicated" but I knew that wasn't correct.

"Extubated? Last night. She was doing so well, we obliged her request for church. With an escort, of course."

"Are you fucking kidding me? Mama asked to

go to church?" The adrenaline was still coursing through my veins, and, clearly, my mouth.

The nurse's jaw dropped so low I thought it was going to hit the counter.

"Let me try that again." I smiled, trying to look more like a confused, lost daughter and not the asshole I probably sounded like. "Could you direct me to the chapel, please?"

"Down the hallway, where you came in. Then back to the first floor. You'll probably hear the organ."

I raced off before she had finished speaking, the hospital hallways bustling like a Vegas casino, except the noise was from heart monitors and breathing machines, not the ringing slots. Thankfully, the signage was clear because I couldn't remember anything the nurse said, other than the fact that Mama was not on a table somewhere getting her organs harvested for donation. Oh, the joys of an anxious brain.

The chapel looked surprisingly like a chapel, with wooden beams, stained-glass windows, and rows of pews—though everything on a much smaller scale, including the door. I would have probably walked right past it if I hadn't heard the tiny pipe organ blasting chords without any sense of rhythm.

I scanned the room, desperate for the sight of my mother to help calm me down and return my heart from my throat. And then I spotted her. *Mama!* I felt a huge release, which led to an uncontrollable burst of sobbing. I was suddenly grateful for the blaring pipe organ that covered my blubbering, and what felt like the audible clunk of my heart returning to my chest.

I sniffed back the tears and did my best to slow my breath, tiptoeing along the back wall, then into the last pew where she was struggling to get up off the soft, cushioned bench. Her full face of makeup couldn't cover her exhaustion, and for the first time, she looked old and sick, which scared me.

She wriggled her way up to standing, looking over at me with tenderness and relief as I slid in next to her, my hand atop hers on the pew in front of us, trying not to give away how upset I had just been. I let out a sigh, like I had been holding my breath for the last week. I needed my other hand to brace myself on the pew, overwhelmed by a sense that things might just be okay, when it never felt like they were, always waiting for the next shoe to drop.

"You scared the crap out of me, Mama," I whispered as the organist murdered "How Great Thou Art." Apparently I will never escape Elvis songs. "And don't you think Jesus would let you skip a day?" That sentence came out louder than I had anticipated, and the man two aisles in front of us turned and shot us a look of disdain.

Mama patted my hand and kept singing until the musical interlude started. "Considering I had a near-death experience, all the more reason to go." She didn't even bother whispering, and when the man looked at us again, she winked. "The nurse assured me she would tell you as soon as you got in the room."

"More like after I saw your empty bed and nearly shit myself." I did the sign of the cross to absolve myself from cursing in church.

She giggled, then went back to singing what felt like verse ten.

What was most disconcerting about the whole scenario (and there were many disconcerting parts) was that Mama had traded in the hospital gown for actual clothing and she looked...normal. No flare sequin pants or platform shoes. No low-cut polyester tops or large bangle bracelets that clanged on her wrist like Christmas bells. If it hadn't been for the teased, jet black wig sitting slightly off center on her head, I probably wouldn't have recognized her.

"Are you okay? What are you wearing?" I couldn't help it. I needed answers.

"I couldn't take that nasty gown any longer."

"Okay, it's not actually the lack of the gown. It's this." I pointed to her clothes.

"Lost and found."

"Ew."

"After it's there for thirty days, they wash it all and put it in this sort of bo-tiquey closet that patients can 'shop' from."

"But your suitcase. I left it in your room! Also, I think it's more for patients who are, like, indigent?"

"Of course they told me about my suitcase! But...it

was all that crazy stuff. Not very hospital church friendly, I suppose."

She had a point. Her clothes would never be considered church friendly, even at some hippy-dippy Unitarian joint with a rock band in the smack-dab center of San Francisco.

"Besides, I thought it was time for a change, since everything else seems to be changing. Do you like it?" She used her hands to Vanna White the simple white blouse and black slacks she had on, her voice blending with the haphazard organ that I was suddenly very thankful for.

"I think the more important question is…do you?" I couldn't remember the last time I had seen her in anything so plain. She kind of looked like a waitress.

"Maybe now you won't mind being seen with me in public." She pressed that last sentence out in a low tone, looking intently toward the pastor in front of us.

"That's not it, Mama. Really."

"Lying in church? I taught you better than that, Grace Louise." She turned toward me with a sharp grin.

The singing stopped, and the pastor instructed us to sit down while the organ continued playing. "But I'm not lying." I had given up on whispering. "It was never the clothes, Mama."

I said it out loud again so I could fully digest the words. "It was never the clothes."

My frustration with Elvis was a way for me to channel my sadness. The wigs, the outfits, and the shelves full of collectibles were an excellent cover. It was much easier, and more appropriate, *as my therapist used to say,* to be annoyed at a dead musician than my own mother. Elvis couldn't reject me. Or tell me I was wrong. Not that Mama would have done either of those things, but the threat that she could was enough for me to keep my bitching aimed at the King.

Another song started, the introduction more like a pipe organ accident.

"Amazing Grace, how sweet the sound." Mama's voice started shaking. She squeezed my hand. "My throat hurts from that thing…" she whispered.

Against my better judgment, and with reckless disregard for the people with good hearing around me and absolutely no alcohol in my system, I joined her. "Who saved a wretch like me. I once was lost…" My singing trailed off, but the words played over and over in my head.

Before this trip, I could hardly take so much as a peep of an Elvis tune leaving Mama's shiny pink lips, let alone sing one myself, but I guess the karaoke beat that out of me. Though to be fair, I didn't even know until much later in my life that Elvis had sung this hymn. It was my bedtime song, the one Mama would croon every night to me as I fell asleep, and later when I was older, in the kitchen after I slammed my door bitching about all the homework I had to do.

I'd heard these words a hundred times, but they had never meant so much to me. I was so lost in a world that I had created, blinded by my own pain, that I was missing out on the life I actually wanted. I had let my fear make my decisions for far too long. Fear that I couldn't do anything but crunch numbers. Fear that I wouldn't find someone who I fell head over heels for. And then if I did, fear that he'd leave me.

I guess I just believed that if I kept my head up, worked hard, and did my best, ignoring the sadness and hurt that had pummeled my existence, I'd be okay. The only problem is that when you do all that, you're not living. You're just surviving. And suddenly, it all catches up with you, and you realize that an "okay life" is not the life you want or deserve.

The organ crashed through the exit hymn as the pastor walked down the aisle, shaking the hands of the few dedicated attendees, and nodding at the staff. The aide helped Mama out of the other side of the pew and down the side aisle.

"You coming, amazing Grace?" I looked over at Mama, who was waving at me as she marched to the beat of the barely recognizable song, wearing clothes unlike any I'd ever seen her in.

"Yeah. Of course. I'll be right there." I slid the hymnal back into the pocket in front of me.

I hadn't had high expectations for this trip. Hell, I didn't really have any expectations at all. Just plain old perseverance. And I certainly didn't expect any kind of epiphany, much less one sitting in a hospital chapel down the street from Graceland.

But I suppose the King, well, he works in mysterious ways.

My phone rang the second I stepped out of the chapel, set to the loudest ring possible to alert me to any news of Mama. I fumbled around to quickly shut it off. It was Jeff.

I was tempted to just decline yet again, but that was old Grace. Even after everything he had done, it felt unfair to keep avoiding him. And he deserved to know about Mama.

"Head on up, and I'll meet you there!" I yelled to Mama, walking in the opposite direction of her room. I pointed to the phone, and she just winked, walking slowly with the aide following behind her. I would address the wink later, knowing full well who she thought it was on the phone.

"Hello?" I said weakly, trying not to call attention to myself in the corner of the hospital hallway, especially since I was standing right in front of a big "no cell phone" sign.

"Oh, hi. It's um, me. Jeff." As if I had forgotten who he was. "Thanks for picking up. I was about to be the worst kind of human and leave you a voice mail!"

I started to think about how many times I'd wish calls would go to voice mail so I could avoid talking to people, which I think is the actual worst kind of human.

"Everything okay?" I brushed my feet back and forth on the floor, hoping he just wanted to ask me where his spare car keys were or something.

"Oh, yeah. I'm doing pretty well. Work is the same and…" He started talking about how the chef had double booked a party, but I interrupted him.

"Did you really call to tell me about work? Mama's in the hospital, and I should really get back to her." I decided it was time to drop the guilt bomb and move things along.

"Shit! I'm sorry! Is she okay?" He sounded genuinely concerned, which he always was when it came to Mama. And truthfully, to me too.

"She's fine. Well, now, at least. Should be leaving soon." A voice came over the loudspeaker announcing that lunch trays were on their way. Proof that I was not lying to get out of talking to him.

"Good, good!" He paused. "I'm sorry, Grace. I really am." I guess the pleasantries were officially over.

"I believe you, Jeff. You're a good person. You always have been." It was true. Jeff hadn't done anything wrong. And really, I hadn't either. I just didn't believe he was *my* good person. "I'm sorry too."

"What are *you* sorry for? I'm the one who…" His voice trailed off. I couldn't blame him for not wanting to finish that sentence.

"Sorry you got swept up in all of this."

"Swept up in what? In loving you? Because I did

love you. Still do." He said it softly, as if he was saying it to himself.

"I know you did. It's not that. It's a lot of old family shit and wanting to feel safe and not being on red alert all the time." And it had worked for a while, but it wasn't enough. I was done just surviving in my marriage, and my life.

"You always looked better in blue anyway. It really brings out your eyes." He chuckled awkwardly, then went silent. I didn't even try to muffle my deep sigh.

"It's not anything that you did, Jeff. You cared a lot about me. I know you did. But this just isn't right for me. Not anymore. And I think you kind of already knew that." I started to feel my chest tighten, and I looked around to find the closest seat, which at this point was probably back in the chapel. Not an option. I closed my eyes. *You're safe. You're safe now.* No breathless sobs. No panicky "I'm sorry's." Just relief.

"Okay, okay, I hear you. I do." It sounded like he was trying to convince himself. "I'm proud of you, Grace!" Only Jeff would say something like that in the middle of a deep, heavy conversation. That's why I'd liked him in the first place. And why I still did, maybe in the way it should have always been. As a friend.

"Thanks, Jeff. You know what? I am too," which is something only new Grace would say, and that's exactly why I said it.

With all the hiccups and bumps we'd encountered along the way, I was surprised our exit from the hospital went so smoothly. Mama immediately ditched her scavenged waitress uniform for her old clothes, then said her goodbyes to the staff like she had known them her whole life. I suppose a week asleep with a tube down your throat could feel like a lifetime. It certainly felt like an incredibly long time to me. Once Mama was awake, she made fast friends with everyone who entered her room, from the nurse on duty to the cafeteria worker delivering her grits and eggs. Everyone was pleased and from the looks of it, surprised that Mama had bounced back so quickly. They had only been introduced to an unconscious Loralynn Johnson. Had they known Mama prior to her series of seizures, they would have had no doubt that she would be back on her feet, dancing some variation of the grapevine to any song that came on the radio, quicker than most patients they had ever seen.

Dr. Mac stuck to her guns, which I feared could have included actual ones during her off-duty hours, and urged Mama to follow up with her own doctor upon her return. They were like two old friends, a couple of wasabi peas in the pod, comparing wig manufacturers and nail polish colors between homecare instructions. I'm not sure Mama would have listened to anyone else.

I kept running through my packing list in my head as I drove to pick up Mama. The only time I really ever forgot things was when I was tired or distracted, and this time I was both. My phone buzzing interrupted my attempt to remember where I had put my hairbrush.

"I was just going to call you!" I said to Wyatt. I'd wanted to let him know that Mama had been discharged from the hospital. I spotted my brush sticking out of my purse and decided that my hair could wait.

"I felt a disturbance in the Force. A good one, that is." I could hear him smiling on the other end, and I imagined how his happy face looked.

"There is! Mama is getting out!" I was having a hard time focusing on the road and talking to Wyatt. I nearly rammed into the car in front of me, which had braked hard for what seemed like no reason. I beeped.

"Everything okay? Do not get into a car accident while talking to me. I don't want to be blamed for delaying Graceland. Well, that and...I want you in one piece when I see you again." He wasn't even trying to be coy, which kind of made me happy.

"And when will that be?" I asked, begging for the banter to continue.

"Whenever you'd like. I'll let you make that call." He paused. "But first, Graceland!" He did a Loralynn-style woo-hoo, which made me giggle.

"Yes! One exciting thing at a time, sir." I was actually feeling excited about Graceland. Or maybe it was the thought of seeing Wyatt. Either way, I was borderline giddy.

"Please send photos. I would love to see the happy! Now go before you get into fisticuffs with a bad Memphis driver." He laughed at his own joke.

"Oh, just you wait," I said. "Bye, Wyatt."

I hung up, then pulled up slowly to the light at the hospital drive. And for the first time in a really, really long time, I felt like I was exactly where I needed to be.

———

The hospital halls seemed a bit brighter since I knew I would be busting Mama out in a matter of minutes. I peeked into Mama's room, and found all her bags packed and piled onto the bed, but no Mama. Then I heard what sounded like two little old ladies cackling down the hall, which was an accurate statement.

"That treatment wasn't so bad now, was it, Miss Loralynn?" asked Dr. Mac, who was clearly slowing her pace to stay next to Mama. She looked up and waved at me.

"You were indeed correct, Doc. I've had more painful meals that I wish I could have slept through," Mama replied. When she saw me, she moved a little faster, much to Dr. Mac's delight. "I'm all ready to go, Grace Louise! Just doing a lap so I didn't have to sit in that room one minute longer."

"Hi, Doctor. How'd she do?" I asked, walking next to her, back into the room to start grabbing bags. Mama followed.

"I did great, of course! Didn't I, Dr. Mac?" Mama grabbed her makeup case, which she nearly dropped from the weight.

"You did, indeed, my dear, but you still need to take it easy." The doctor walked over to help her with the case, as my hands were full with her suitcase and a few other plastic bags I was afraid to look in. The way Mama worked, she had probably packed extra pairs of hospital socks and graham crackers.

"Did you hear that, Mama? Take it easy." I smiled at Dr. Mac, knowing full well we were about to get a talking-to.

"You won't get an argument from me. I'm on my best behavior these days." She walked over to me and kissed me on the cheek. What meds did they slip into her treatments?

Dr. Mac looked pleased. "Now you girls go enjoy yourselves. I hope Graceland is everything you imagined."

"I'm sure it will be even better." It already had been, and we hadn't even made it to Graceland itself.

"All right, Mama, I just need to make one little stop before we go, okay?"

"Well, I suppose I've waited *this* long. What's another…?"

"Hour. Tops. I promise it won't take long."

We zipped off the floor and out of the hospital

doors. I piled the bags into the trunk, not even taking one peek at what was in them. The drive out of the hospital parking lot was liberating, like we were leaving more than some dirty sheets and half-eaten cafeteria pancakes behind. I looked down at my phone, then back to the road, making sure I didn't miss a turn anywhere. I had turned Siri's voice off, so it was just me and a maps app to get me where I needed to go. Mama had started guessing where we were going to stop.

"Waffle House? I suppose I could do for something. Those eggs were a tragedy." Then I'd pass it and she'd move on. "Walmart? Why do all the stores start with a 'W'?" Mama was enjoying the conversation with herself. We finally pulled up to our actual destination.

"A costume shop?" Mama seemed very surprised.

"I'm sorry it doesn't start with a 'W,' Mama. I tried."

"Well, what does that have to do with anything?" I wasn't sure if she was completely unaware of her mumbling or if she was confused by the costume shop.

"You'll see." She stepped out of the car.

"I'm still very alive and breathing, Grace. You better not even be thinking of pawning off my possessions!" She marched up to the front door of Mr. Lincoln's Costume Shoppe and walked right in.

It was exactly how I would have imagined a costume shoppe, especially one spelled with the additional "pe," to be. It was more like a house than a shop, with the walls of each tiny room overflowing with everything from masks to makeup, from floor to ceiling, and in every possible nook and cranny. There was barely room enough for two people to walk through.

A man called out from what sounded like a closet and emerged wearing a simple striped shirt and pair of brown pants with suspenders, looking... well, not like an owner of a costume shop. "How can I help you folks?" he asked in a quiet, steady voice, dusting off his hands and walking forward to offer one to us.

"I called ahead. I'm Grace. Are you Mr. Lincoln? You were going to put something aside for me." I shook his hand. Mama had already taken off to another room.

"Oh, right. You're lucky I had that here. It's one of our most popular costumes... for obvious reasons. You need anything else?"

Mama waltzed back in just when he offered.

"From the looks of it, you do not. That's quite an authentic Priscilla Presley look."

I couldn't tell if he was being nice or serious, but Mama's big smile indicated that she didn't care, so neither did I. She was sporting a bright pink go-go dress, with the skirt dusting the top of her knee-high go-go boots. At just over five feet tall, even a mini-dress was long on Mama. Her wig added a solid six inches, the teased bouffant reaching just below my shoulder.

"Alrighty then, why don't you come with me, and,

ma'am, you just wait here. If you can find a cleared-off chair, it's yours. We won't be but a minute."

I followed him back where he had come from to greet us, which dead-ended at two dressing rooms with doors. We passed the large mirror and platform on the way in.

"Go on and get dressed and we'll see how it fits you."

The garment bag was hanging on a hook in the room on the right. I walked in as Mr. Lincoln closed the door behind me, and I could hear him trying to make conversation with Mama. Even though the sign did say they dry-cleaned each costume between customers, I did not want to think about how many people had worn this. I slipped off my shoes and out of my clothes, hanging them on the hook next to the garment bag, then slowly unzipped the bag for the big reveal. It was exactly how I had hoped.

"You good in there?" I could see Mr. Lincoln's brown orthopedic shoes outside the dressing room door.

"I think so?" I replied, opening the door and walking out toward him.

"Oh, that is good," he said. "You're nice and tall. But here, let me fix a few things."

He pulled the belt, then tucked in a few things around the neckline. Once he was done, he stepped back to look at his handiwork. I could see where the costume could have come off as sexy on a curvier woman, with the low cut "v" front showing a slice of cleavage without the snaps done. But on me, it looked like Elvis, which is exactly what I was going for.

I readjusted the wig, then fiddled with the sleeves, trying not to be bothered by the itchy fabric that was a little stiff from some sort of chemical process that had hopefully washed off any sweating situation from the previous renter. I didn't even mind the wafting smell of Febreze, which gave the whole thing a very on-theme *Blue Hawaii* scent.

I tried to remember Elvis's moves, most of which I was quite familiar with thanks to countless videos I had been subjected to over the course of my life. I didn't necessarily plan on performing any pelvis rotations or rubber legs in public, but it felt sort of fun to at least give it a try. The more I moved, the more I liked it, and the hesitation that I might have used as an excuse to change my mind and do something less embarrassing, like wear a pair of Elvis sunglasses, was replaced by confidence and not really caring what anyone else thought. Except Mama, of course, who looked like she had been frozen in time, her mouth hanging open like she had just seen real Elvis come back to life.

"What in God's holy name are you wearing, Grace Louise?!" She shrieked the question out so quickly, it sounded more like a bunch of sounds—the only truly intelligible thing being my name.

I sauntered over to her. "Hey, Mama," I said, doing my best Elvis impression. It wasn't the worst attempt I'd ever heard, but still very high on the creepy scale.

"Are you doing what I think you're doing?" Mama still looked more horrified than excited, which wasn't exactly the reaction I was hoping for. Or even expecting. I decided I would just roll with it.

"That depends on what you think I'm doing."

"Wearing *that*...to Graceland?" I was starting to worry. I thought for sure she would be thrilled.

"I'm certainly not going to rent it to just wear in the car, that's for sure." I started to perform his signature hip slide.

With that, Mama let out her loudest WOO-HOO yet. It was so loud, in fact, that Mr. Lincoln inched his way out of the dressing room area as if he had just run into a mama bear in the wild. To be fair, I could see how one might think that. Her excitement could lean toward dangerous.

She clapped her hands together vigorously. "The last time I saw you in an Elvis costume you were as tall as my knees!"

"And now you're as tall as my knees! It's the circle of life." I laughed. Even Mr. Lincoln let out a chuckle.

Mama looked around for something to throw at me.

I kept trying to contain my usually nonexistent cleavage from popping out of the V-neck. "Are we really doing this?" I asked her.

Mama cheered, then started moving her hips to the bossa nova beat in her head. She shuffled her way out of the store and ran straight to our car, not passing go, and certainly not collecting anything but a mint from the counter.

"Thank you. Thank you very much," I said to Mr. Lincoln as I walked by, pointing at him like I knew what the hell I was doing. I caught a hint of what I believe was a smile on his face.

GRACE: I've broken her out!

ASHA: Yay! Is it the big day? Finally?

GRACE: YES! I didn't think I would be this excited.

ASHA: Well, an entire week like you've had, I'm pretty sure a visit to the Memphis Highway Rest Stop would be exciting.

GRACE: Ew.

ASHA: Okay, I didn't mean it that way. Gross.

GRACE: Wait until you see photos of us. I did something a little crazy.

ASHA: You mean crazier than what you're doing right now? I'm afraid.

GRACE: It's all good.

ASHA: Have fun! I wish I were there, mostly because that would mean I wouldn't be trying to force someone to wear pants and eat perfectly good macaroni and cheese.

GRACE: 🖤

Chapter 14

For all the grandeur that is Graceland, I thought the surrounding area would be a little more majestic. But our ride down old Route 51 looked more like the harbinger of mediocrity than music royalty. Even for fall, the air was stuffy and uncomfortably warm, neither conducive to wearing a polyester jumpsuit in a car where air conditioning had been restricted. Instead, Mama insisted on riding with the windows down so she could "take it all in." Like a Labrador retriever out for a Sunday drive with its owner, head sticking out, air blowing his ears (or in Mama's case—wig), and flappy skin pushed back tightly by the wind.

"Make sure you get a photo of that Dollar Store, Mama. And that gas station."

She waved her hand back at me, not even turning to shush me verbally. I sensed that she was surprised at how seemingly normal everything looked, now that she was driving through it.

I caught a few people staring at us at the red lights, but I just smiled and waved, even though I really wanted to flip them off. Mama didn't notice anyone, which I thought might be because she was too busy taking photos of gas stations and strip mall delis to look at the people in the car next to us. But I also figured she'd had her share of rude gawkers so that it didn't even faze her anymore. I suppose that was the best way to deal with them without getting permanent rage.

"Here. Grace! GRACE!" Her voice jumped several octaves as we neared the parking lot, with Elvis's private airplanes parked just off the side of the road. The metal gates were up just a bit farther, on the left. The large complex gave the whole place a Disney vibe that I wasn't expecting. The practically full parking lot seemed to agitate her, as if she had just learned that Elvis was not exclusively hers all these years. She shook the door handle even before I had put the parking brake on.

"Mama, it's not even open yet. And we have VIP passes, so just take it easy on that damn door, will you?"

She let go of it slowly, then started brushing the skirt of her dress with her hands, doing her best to smooth out invisible wrinkles. The sound of the polyester swishing under her palms filled the space between us. I grabbed her hand, and she flinched back into her seat; it was like I was gripping an icicle.

"Just wait a minute, Grace. I need a minute."

"Are you okay, Mama? Two seconds ago you were about to bust right through the door." I started scanning the car for something to catch her puke. She looked as white as my polyester jumpsuit, even after a few deep breaths, which signaled to me that I'd just have to use my hands.

Instead, she exhaled, then spoke softly. "What if it's not anything special?"

I was confused.

"I've been waiting to see this my whole life. What if it's just...a house?" Where was the upbeat, positive Mama, who always saw the glass half full, even if it was half full of crap? After everything we had been through, I couldn't believe we were finally sitting in the parking lot and she was getting cold platform-wearing feet.

I decided to take the honest approach. "It *is* just a house, Mama."

"No. You know what I mean." She stopped stroking her skirt, and the sounds of the cars zipping by filled the emptiness.

I guess I did. "It's like climbing Mount Everest and you're not sure how the view from the top will be?"

"Or how I'll get down."

"Well, that one's easy. We are flying home." She gave me a look. "I don't know, Mama. Maybe you'll finally get to close a chapter. Finish the book. If I've learned anything from you, it's going to be what you make of it. You can't even walk into a room without making it feel like you're walking on stage. So that house over there?" I pointed across the street to the gates guarding the entrance to Graceland. "It's whatever you want it to be."

She squeezed my hand, her own palms back to a reasonable body temperature.

"I'm glad you're here with me, Grace. I didn't think this would actually happen. Not just finally seeing Graceland, but the whole thing, from the time we got in this old purple boat to pulling into this parking spot. It sorta feels like a dream."

"I can't believe I'm actually saying this, but that's kind of what makes life so exciting. You don't really know what's coming at you next."

That's when I again remembered the notes from the psychic. I rifled through the glove box, and in my ever-growing tote bag full of a weird combination of beauty products and snacks. Nothing. Nada.

"What are you looking for, darling?" Oh, just the paper that would tell *me* how to get down from this mountain.

"Eh, nothing. Honestly, everything I need is right here." I touched her cheek, a little more gaunt than I'd seen it, flush with a cream blush about twenty times too bright.

Watching her dormant in a hospital bed for a week without a computer to work on, a spouse to worry about, even a cat to mentally care for, gave me a lot of time to just think. I'd always been a thinker, but it never quite felt productive. More like a series of terrible scenarios and how I'd find my way out of them. Useful things like if my car would end up in a flooded river. Or if I was caught in a tsunami. I suppose I would have compared a road trip with my mother to some sort of natural disaster that would require some emergency preparation. But no matter how much you think about things, you're never going to be prepared for what's thrown at you.

Life's imperfections used to frighten me. The pain and disappointment were too messy. So it was either all or nothing for me, with little room for any sort of gray area, where people can hurt you and still love you. Where they can disappoint you and still care deeply for you. And while we are all flawed, that's what makes us amazing. These tender and fragile intricacies of our relationships, the ones where we could, at any moment, be lifted up or drowned by them, are what makes this life worth living.

"We are not going to be late for Graceland, Mama." I pointed to her door handle, and we both hopped out of the car. For a moment, I forgot I was in full Elvis regalia, until I caught a hint of myself in the car mirror and smiled at my utter ridiculousness. No wonder people were staring at me.

Mama and I walked toward what looked a bit like Main Street, Disney World, with huge signs and shops on either side, all seemingly different in name and style, but selling what looked to be the same exact items inside. It was one big Instagram photo op.

"Happy birthday, Mama!" I pulled her arm through mine as we walked past souvenir central and into the main building, hooked together, hoping to contain the inevitable celebratory jigs and whoops that were her trademark. "SEV-EN-TY!" I will never be able to say that number the same again.

But for as long as Mama had been waiting to see it, she wasn't her usual excitable self that some would describe as "childlike" or, as I would call it, "age-inappropriate." Instead, she walked up to the small VIP kiosk as if she owned the place, then onto the bus that took us over to the actual property, which dropped us right next to the front door of what really was just a house. Sure, it was a big, beautiful white house on a lovely property. But this was not the Bellagio, and it didn't matter. It never mattered.

For the first time, not one person whispered about the crazy Asian lady and her ridiculous wig, wearing go-go boots and a minidress. Instead, people shouted compliments and even asked to take a photo with her. With me too.

"Could you get one of both of us?" I asked the couple standing in line behind us, nervously taking selfies while trying to avoid unknowing photo-bombers.

"Hey, Priscilla!" someone called out. Mama looked around for where the voice was coming from, then waved and blew a kiss. The people behind us snapped the pic and cheered, handing my phone back to me.

I texted it to Asha, who replied that she was making it her new Facebook profile photo.

And I sent it to Wyatt too, which elicited an impressive number of emojis that he immediately regretted. *Oh god. That was embarrassing. Would you believe me if I told you hackers! Hackers!?*

I replied with a *Haha.* And a heart emoji.

As we waited to be let into the mansion, I couldn't help but overhear the conversations around me. People spontaneously singing Elvis tunes with strangers. Others asking questions about stuff the accountant in me might have wondered, like Elvis's net worth, and how much they thought "this place" made every year. Good friends, family members, even random people brought together by a love of a guy with Jell-O hips, an ever-trembling lip, and a voice that could soothe and inspire at exactly the same time.

And we were right in the middle of it all.

"We made it, Grace!" Mama shook her arms out, like a puppy coming in from the rain.

"Well, technically we've just got a kind of crappy view of a big glass door." I pointed to the entrance in front of us.

She grabbed my face. "The view's just magical from where I'm standing," she whispered, kissing my cheek and staring into my eyes. This time I didn't look away. And neither did she.

"I've been waiting to see this my whole life!" the woman in front of us told her friend. "Isn't it just everything you imagined it would be?"

Yes. Yes, it really is. I squeezed Mama's hand as the door opened and we walked in. Together.

Epilogue

One year later

Mama, I could drop this entire box and it would all be over." I shoved it into the last open spot in the crawl space, then dusted off my hands, wishing I had worn the gloves Asha had offered to bring.

"Just remember that's your inheritance, Grace," Mama yelled from the bottom of the ladder. "I hope you wrapped them well."

"How do you define 'well'?" I asked, hopping off the bottom rung, then pushing the ladder back up into the ceiling until it disappeared. "Besides, they're not going to be up there that long. Aren't the museum curators coming to look at them soon?"

"Yes, but they won't be looking at anything if they're all broken into a million pieces. I still can't believe they're coming all the way up here to Boston to look at them."

Well, I could. After Mama blabbed about her collection to the docent at Graceland during our VIP tour, who blabbed to her director, it turned out, after lots of Skype calls and emailed photos later, that Mama had several extremely rare and quite valuable Elvis collectibles that the foundation was interested in purchasing. I always knew there was a reason I liked Jailhouse Rock Elvis.

And so I figured that if I could get her to part with a few pieces from her collection, I could also convince her to move up to Boston with me to get her cancer treatments at the Dana-Farber Cancer Institute. Thankfully, good old Dr. Mac was more than happy to back me up.

Mama's prognosis has gotten a little better, with an extra couple years added to her timeline, maybe more. We both agreed that we wouldn't talk about it too much and instead fill our time catching up on all the things we had missed out on, living so far apart from each other all those years.

The thought of her not being here, clanging around in my kitchen washing dishes instead of using the dishwasher or talking loudly with her Texas friends on FaceTime, doesn't seem possible, so I only give myself a few minutes a day to think about it, as per my therapist's recommendation. While my panic attacks are mostly gone, the anxiety lingers in various other ways—like worrying about Mama's health, for one—so we've been working together on strategies I can use to help me cope.

Mama's been enjoying living in a city with an actual Chinatown. And even though people still give her funny looks when they hear her southern accent, they're more fascinated by it than anything else.

"How was mah-jongg today, Mama?" She still tells everyone I forced her to go because I thought she was a bad Asian mother for not knowing how to play. But she kicks everyone's butt, and it keeps her from rearranging my bookshelves over and over again.

"A blowout, as usual." She blew on her nails and rubbed them on her sleeve, but one got caught in her sweater, and she struggled to pull it out. "I still will never get used to wearing these things." The cold weather was the only thing Mama was having trouble adjusting to. Wearing hats over her wigs was almost more than she could bear. I reminded her that she was never one to shy away from a challenge.

"And you? How's the new CEO of her own accounting firm today?"

"That's a bit of an exaggeration, Mama, considering I'm the only one in the firm. But it feels good to be helping out the little guy, or rather, girl, I should say." After I got back from our trip, I decided I didn't want to spend my days in an office helping the yacht owners figure out how to write off their boat as a work expense, so I went out on my own, helping out female small business owners, and suddenly I liked crunching numbers again.

"Speaking of guys, how is that sweet Wyatt doing on that long drive up here?"

"Well, based on his last text, he's in North Carolina. He told me he was bummed that there were no graveyards or hospitals on his route."

"Don't forget haunted houses."

"That would be kind of weird in the middle of January."

After a year of never-ending text threads, late-night FaceTime calls, and monthly meet-ups in New Orleans, I decided to ask Wyatt to move up to Boston. He figured he could work on his second book from anywhere, "preferably in bed next to you," he told me. We even talked about kids, which made both of our mamas happier than two old friends cry-laughing over a bunch of old photos. I guess I just needed the right person in my life to make me believe I could be a good parent, and the right doctor to tell me that I wasn't too old.

"I hope he packed a lot of sweaters." Mama tugged at the waistband of hers, then scratched at the neckline.

"Thankfully, we have stores here in Boston, so I think he'll be just fine." Mama rolled her eyes at me. "Let's go out tonight, Mama. You pick. I'm going to change into something that doesn't look like I slept in it."

I walked into my bedroom, flopping down on the

bed, the brass Elvis statue I purchased in Tupelo staring straight at me. And just above it on the wall, the papers from the psychic, framed.

Don't wait, they both said, identically written by the all-knowing Madame Arabella.

Mama was rather disappointed with the two-word phrase, feeling as though somehow her fifty dollars should have at least gotten her a full sentence.

"It is a full sentence, Mama."

"Oh god, smartypants. You know what I mean," she replied, crushing it into a ball.

But for me, I knew what she was saying, to both of us. And after I explained it to Mama, she pulled hers out of the trash and secretly had them both framed for me. Since then, they've been our mantra. It's why I left my job to start my own firm, with my first big client, the Homestead Hotel, along with a few other small women-run businesses.

I even got a tattoo...of Elvis's lightning bolt on the inside of my wrist, which might have been the first time Mama was ever horrified by anything associated with Elvis.

After we got back from the trip, a few people asked me what it was like to see someone live their dream. They also asked me how I survived a thousand-mile drive with my mama. But mostly, they wanted to know what happened in that two-week period that basically changed my life.

Honestly, I don't quite know how to answer that, at least in words anyway. I figure the smile on my face is more meaningful than any explanation I could conjure up. Asha keeps telling me I'm a whole new person, and while I see her point, I like to think this version of Grace was always inside of me, just too afraid to come out.

But I do say this: I went on the trip to escape my life, and in the process, I actually found it.

"Okay, Grace, let's go for some chow-DAHHH!" Mama yelled from the living room.

I saw Asha had been coaching Mama.

"Sounds good. I'll be right there!" I grabbed my coat off the bed, and pulled open my nightstand drawer, sliding a blue rock into my pocket. That blue rock.

I heard Mama singing an Elvis song, but this time I started to sing along, then laughed as the door slammed behind us. The sequins on Mama's coat caught the light, almost as brightly as my shiny mermaid clogs.

Loralynn and Grace's Road Trip to Graceland

A few summers ago, I hopped on a plane, rented a convertible (sadly, only black was available), and drove the road trip I had written for Loralynn and Grace. Most of the places they stopped at do exist, in some form or another, and are certainly worth a visit. If you want to limit your trip to Elvis-related stops, I'd suggest starting in Dallas, which is also an easier airport to get to than El Paso.

El Paso to Odessa (283 miles)
Odessa to Dallas (352 miles)
Dallas to Shreveport (188 miles)

- Elvis Presley statue outside the Shreveport Auditorium
- Thrillvania Haunted House Park (only open during Halloween season)

Shreveport to Jackson (220 miles)

- The Coliseum at the Mississippi State Fairgrounds

Jackson to Tupelo (191 miles)

- Elvis's birthplace
- Johnnie's Bar-B-Q Drive-In
- Tupelo Hardware Store, where Elvis's mother bought him his first guitar

Tupelo to Memphis (115 miles)

- Graceland
- The Guest House at Graceland
- Mr. Lincoln's Costume Shoppe

Acknowledgments

Seeing this book come to life is a dream come true, which is to say, **never stop dreaming**.

I'm so grateful to my agent, Annie Bomke, for loving Loralynn and Grace as much as I did, and helping me find such a wonderful home for them. Your thoughtful edits and guidance throughout this process remind me that there are still good people in this world.

Before this book ever got to Annie's in-box, it saw many revisions thanks to Diane Glazman, a developmental editor I found in a Facebook group a long time ago. Your frankness was just what I needed to make this story come to life.

How lucky I am to be a part of the Forever family! My editor Leah Hultenschmidt's excitement about the book from the first time she read it is why it's in your hands right now. Thank you for seeing the beauty and joy in this story, Leah, and for getting my jokes.

I have so much appreciation for my work family, Liz Gumbinner and Lisa Barnes, who have become dear friends after all these years. Thanks for your support, and for picking up the balls I couldn't keep in the air by myself.

The only people I ever let read this book were my sister-friend, Tina Montagna-Tate, and my partner, Lucian Read, both of whom were kind, loving, and very honest with their feedback.

Tina, you are my Asha. I wouldn't be here without you. And, Lucian, you are my Wyatt, except we would have totally dated in high school. Thanks for believing in this book, in me, and in us, from day one.

And finally, my kids—Quinlan, Drew, Margot, and Bridget—who have heard me talk about this book for more than ten years now. Thankfully, they were so young when I started writing it, they probably don't remember most of what I said, only that I was sitting in front of my computer an awful lot. Don't ever forget this: the joy I get from parenting you four is indescribable.

Reading Group Guide

Discussion Questions

1. How would you characterize Grace's relationship with Loralynn? How does it evolve through the book? What similarities and differences are there to your relationship with your mother?

2. Do you have a bucket-list dream trip like Loralynn's? What would it be? Who would you go with?

3. Being with Loralynn brings back a lot of hard memories for Grace. Do you think Loralynn did the right thing in staying with her husband as long as she did? In kicking him out when he was sick?

4. Grace has several panic attacks in the book and talks openly about her anxiety. How did you feel reading about her struggles?

5. Wyatt and Grace clearly had such a strong connection. Why do you think they never dated? Never stayed in touch?

6. How does watching Loralynn connect with Cal change Grace's view of her mother? Have you

ever had an experience where you saw someone you thought you knew well in a different element and it changed how you saw them?

7. How did you feel when Loralynn was hospitalized? Why do you think she kept her cancer diagnosis to herself? What would you do in that situation?

8. The costume shop was a big turning point for Grace. What do you feel finally made her decide to "join" Loralynn?

9. How has being Chinese American shaped Grace's life? What stereotypes did she face? What stereotypes did she have about others?

10. Do you have a favorite Elvis song? If so, which one and why? Is there a time when music has helped you through challenge and adversity? What music do you have fond memories of?

A Behind-the-Scenes Look at Writing *A Thousand Miles to Graceland*

By Kristen Mei Chase

I can't quite remember exactly how I got the idea for an Elvis-obsessed seventy-year-old woman, but when I first started writing this story, Loralynn was the star.

Sorry, Grace.

But I soon realized that if I was writing a book focused on healing the relationship between a mother and a daughter, the biggest change needed to happen in Grace (named for Graceland, and also what the word actually means: "goodwill"). And with that realization, a big change happened in me.

I truly believe that every writer brings a part of themselves to their stories, but pretty much all of me is in *A Thousand Miles to Graceland*. Writing this book has been the emotional road trip of a lifetime, and a lesson in putting myself out there and making the change I want to see in my life.

I didn't intend to use my debut novel to work out my difficult childhood and love relationships, but the gift of writing fiction is that you can create resolutions and endings that you never got in your actual life. That's especially pertinent when you spend much of your early forties thinking it's too late—for change, for reconciliation, for love.

Sometimes, though, the writing takes over, and the only thing we writers can do is just let it happen.

Bringing Grace and Loralynn's journey to life gave me the opportunity to explore the difficult stories of my past—alcoholism, abuse, and death—and close a lot of open wounds. I didn't get the same kind of ending that Grace and Loralynn got with my own mother because I'm not the author of my mom's story. But my mother and I did come to a better place in our relationship, and like Grace, I'm able to love my mom for the choices she made and the person she is, even if I don't completely agree with them. And I can thank this book for that.

I was also able to share a story of two Asian American women, and their struggles in a country that consistently misjudges us with negative stereotypes and stigmas. I can't stress enough how important it was for me to bring those issues to light, especially in the current post-pandemic climate. That type of representation matters, which is why most of my cast are BIPOC.

There are some of the best parts of the important people in my life represented in my supporting cast, like Asha's humor from my sister-friend Tina, and Wyatt's calming presence, one of the many things I love about my partner, Lucian.

Unfortunately, there are parts of some of the worst people in my life too. But without them, there wouldn't be such a triumph, for Grace, and for me.

Society seems to think that once you turn forty, it's all downhill. And forget about being seventy. You're pretty much invisible. But what I learned is that you can find yourself no matter what age you are. A new adventure always awaits, so long as you're brave enough to take it.

May the words of Madame Arabella be scribbled on your soul (or in my case, tattooed on my arm): **Don't wait.**

About the Author

Kristen Mei Chase is an author, web entrepreneur, and media personality. She is the co-founder of Cool Mom Picks, one of the most influential parenting networks on the web, reaching millions of parents each month with the best gear, gifts, advice, and tips. Her essays and articles have appeared in *The Washington Post*, NBCNews.com, The Daily Beast, and others. As a bi-racial Asian American, Kristen writes to share the little stories of bi- and multi-racial Americans in a big way. She lives in the Philly suburbs with her four kids and an extensive collection of vintage Elvis t-shirts.

To find out more, visit:
 KristenMeiChase.com
 Twitter @ThatKristen
 Instagram @ThatKristenAgain

YOUR
BOOK
CLUB
RESOURCE

VISIT
GCPClubCar.com

to sign up for the **GCP Club Car** newsletter, featuring exclusive promotions, info on other **Club Car** titles, and more.

 @grandcentralpub

 @grandcentralpub

 @grandcentralpub